ORPHAN BRIGADE

Also by Henry V. O'Neil

The Sim War series
Glory Main

ORPHAN BRIGADE

The Sim War: Book Two

HENRY V. O'NEIL

HARPER
VOYAGER
IMPULSE

An Imprint of HarperCollinsPublishers

EPub Edition JANUARY 2015 ISBN: 9780062359209

Print Edition ISBN: 9780062359216

10 9 8 7 6 5 4 3 2 1

This book is dedicated to the soldiers and families of the
Second Battalion of the Twenty-Second Infantry Regiment
Tenth Mountain Division, US Army
Past, present, and future
But especially the outstanding people I knew
1986–1989
And the two platoons I was privileged to lead,
The Battalion 81mm Mortar Platoon 1986–1988
and
First Platoon, Charlie Company 1988–1989
Lead With Courage

The British soldier can stand up to
anything except the British War Office.

—George Bernard Shaw

CHAPTER ONE

From the Final Interrogation of Lieutenant Jander Mortas, Infantry, Human Defense Force:

INTERROGATOR: You keep referring to the others as your platoon. There were only three of them. A platoon has more than three members.

MORTAS: We were marooned together. We found water together. We stole food together, and we fought for our lives together. I was their lieutenant, and they were my platoon.

INTERROGATOR: Except for one of them.

MORTAS: No matter how many times you ask, I can only tell the truth one way. I had no idea Trent [Pause] the thing that was pretending to be Captain Amelia Trent [Pause] was an alien.

INTERROGATOR: That's convenient, considering you brought it to a Corps headquarters.

MORTAS: You know, you talk pretty tough for a guy whose face I've never seen. How many times have you questioned me? How about sitting across from me just once?

INTERROGATOR: You brought a previously un-encountered alien entity to the Twelfth Corps main headquarters, an alien that had assumed the form of Captain Amelia Trent and was carrying a deadly plague virus. You had spent several days and nights in close proximity to the alien, and you still maintain you had no idea it wasn't human.

MORTAS: You people didn't know either. Not until the two of us were locked inside those decon tubes. It took whatever scan you put us through before you figured out she wasn't human, and you're surprised I didn't know she was a—what did you call her?—a pre-viously unencountered alien entity.

INTERROGATOR: There were no indications of any kind that a member of your party was an infiltra-tor working for the enemy?

MORTAS: She saved me from a giant water snake that tried to eat me and Corporal Cranther. She took care of Gorman when his blisters were giving him holy hell, and after Cranther was killed she was my right hand the rest of the way. We wouldn't have been able to steal the ship that got us off that planet without her, and she killed one of the Sim pilots herself. [Throat clearing] And when Gorman died, just after we took off, she convinced me it wasn't my fault. [Pause] Not exactly the acts of an enemy.

INTERROGATOR: You still don't seem to understand that this alien was deceiving you the entire way, Lieutenant.

MORTAS: She was more decent to me than anyone here has been. You kept me in that tube for hours even though I was injured and starving. Asking the same questions over and over and threatening to kill me. Maybe I should wonder if *you're* human. Any of you.

INTERROGATOR: We've given you food and medical attention. And we're still trying to understand how it was that you brought an enemy to the main headquarters of the Glory Corps, a corps headquarters that was a closely kept secret until your arrival.

MORTAS: I already answered that. Several times. Corporal Cranther knew where Glory Main was. [Pause] Except he just called it Main.

INTERROGATOR: No Spartacan Scout would have been given that location.

MORTAS: According to Cranther, Command loses track of the Spartacans all the time. He said you headquarters types basically forget you dropped them somewhere and that they have to find their own way back to safety. Knowing the location of the safe places helps, way out here.

INTERROGATOR: So the alien had nothing to do with finding the headquarters?

MORTAS: I already told you. Gorman was a mapmaker, a chartist. Cranther gave me the location of Glory Main, and I gave it to Gorman. He plugged the coordinates into the ship's system, we got off that awful planet, [Pause] then he died.

INTERROGATOR: Which left you and the alien.

MORTAS: Not for long. You incinerated her right in front of me.

INTERROGATOR: Am I detecting disapproval, Lieutenant?

MORTAS: There were four of us at the start, and I managed to get one of them to Glory Main alive. You have no idea what we went through, the hunger, the walking, the Sims hunting us, how four complete strangers became a unit. How they became my platoon. That means Trent was the last member of my platoon. And you killed her.

INTERROGATOR: She was an alien and an enemy.

MORTAS: I didn't know that. Don't you get it? I thought she was Captain Amelia Trent, a Force psychoanalyst. I promised her I'd get her off that planet, that I'd get her to safety. I did it, too. And then I watched you pussies kill her by remote control, trapped in that tube. You killed the only remaining member of my platoon. You murdered my platoon.

INTERROGATOR: You make no sense at all, Mortas.

MORTAS: You murdered my platoon.

End of transcription

Lieutenant Jander Mortas gave off a small, forced grunt of exertion as he pushed his chest away from the floor. Completing the last push-up in this particular set, he dropped to the cold surface with a long exhalation. He'd been alternating different kinds of push-ups with an assortment of abdominal exercises, a workout designed for confined spaces like the one he now occupied. The cadre at Officer Basic had referred to this as a prison camp workout, but Mortas doubted they'd expected him to be practicing it in a Human Defense Force lockup.

His current quarters were larger than his first cell had been, but that wasn't saying much. The bunk in the other lockup had been too short to accommodate his six-foot frame, a mattressless sheet of metal so hard that he might as well have been sleeping on the floor. That cell had been kept dark most of the time, but Mortas believed he'd spent only a couple of days there.

Mortas was uncertain of the time frame because he'd awakened in his current accommodations with no idea how he got there. The dryness of his mouth and the fuzziness of his vision suggested he'd been drugged, and he suspected he'd been transported off the giant space rock that concealed the main headquarters of the Twelfth ("Glory") Corps of the Human Defense Force. Glory Main was located a fantastic distance from Earth in a vast region of space known simply as the war zone, and he'd initially been carried there by mankind's greatest technological achievement. Knowing how far the Step had already brought him, Mortas feared it could have been used to transport him an even greater distance.

In other words, he could literally be anywhere.

Though concerned that his captors intended to make good on their threat never to reveal that he'd returned to Force control alive, he was mildly encouraged by the way his surroundings had improved. The bunk in the new cell was long enough to stretch out on, and it even had a thin foam mattress and a blanket. He could take five long strides from the back wall before reaching the door, which was outfitted with hatches for the delivery of food and commands. Mortas could also turn the lights on and off, although he was sure that his guards—a trio of military policemen who'd been his only human contact since his detention—could override his decision if they wished. So far they'd shown no desire to interact with him beyond the most basic requirements of their job, and he took their refusal to engage in conversation as a potentially ominous sign.

After all, they knew who Mortas was. Which meant they knew who his father was. And that meant they knew someone was going to pay a heavy penalty for this mistreatment if he was ever released. It was disconcerting to recognize that their behavior was exactly what Mortas would have expected from people who intended to claim never to have seen him.

Coming to a sitting position, Mortas rotated his left

shoulder as if trying to see if it still worked. He'd injured it while stealing the ship that had taken him and Trent—*the alien impersonating Trent*—to Glory Main, but it seemed fully healed. He grimaced slightly at the memory, the typhoon slap of wind that had tossed him through the air, the heat from the explosion, the pain when he'd landed on the joint. The terror and loss he'd felt upon rising, with flaming debris raining down around him in the darkness, seeing Trent and Gorman both felled by the blast that he'd set off as a distraction.

Even now, knowing that Trent had not been Trent, he cringed at the mental image of what his diversion had done to the two of them. Gorman had already been badly injured, but the blast had peppered him with shrapnel, and Mortas believed that was what had ultimately killed him.

The alien pretending to be Trent had been impaled by a flying splinter the size of a javelin, and if it had actually been Amelia Trent, she would have died on the spot. Instead it had pulled the spear from its side, claiming the wound was minor, and got them up and moving again, chasing the ship they were going to hijack.

No matter how hard Mortas tried, it was impossible not to think of Trent and Gorman and Cranther in the long hours he now spent by himself. All of the terrible things they'd been through, how hard they'd fought to survive, and that he alone had lived. Although it felt like an extreme betrayal, Mortas had good reason to limit the recollections. He'd been questioned several times by the mocking, disembodied voice, and it was absolutely vital to stick to the story as he'd first told it. He hadn't exactly lied yet, and even suspected that the voice didn't know the right questions, but still it would have been far too easy to slip up.

Mortas stood and began to jog in place, lightly because he was barefoot. He'd been given a pair of paper slippers that he wore when taken from the cell and when sleeping, but they were too slippery for the room's smooth floor. His feet were still heavily callused from the days and nights of walking on the planet where they'd been marooned, which suggested that his captivity could be measured in days.

He'd kept two crucial facts from his questioner so far, and was certain his fate would be sealed if either of them was uncovered. One secret would merely get him executed, while the other would probably get him scanned, examined, tortured, and then dissected.

Now he mentally reviewed the most important things to remember if he wanted to keep the voice from discovering his secrets. The first one was simple enough, the omission of the fact that he and the others had encountered Force personnel on the enemy-colonized planet. Those men had been the remnants of an assault battalion that had been defeated within minutes of arrival on the planet's surface, their armored vehicles bogged down by a new enemy weapon that turned solid ground into mud.

The only officer in that ragtag bunch had been an insane major named Shalley, a staff guy who'd wanted to use Mortas and his people as cannon fodder. They'd been saved from that fate by a sudden enemy attack on the ravine where Shalley and his people had been hiding, but Cranther had been mortally wounded during their escape. Mortas had altered the story so that the veteran scout had died in a chance encounter with the enemy. It had been hard to do that because Cranther had received his death wound after pulling Mortas out of the doomed fight in the choked ravine, when they had both been running away. He had carried the dying man a great distance after that, believing the two of them were alone.

Major Shalley had somehow survived, pursuing Mortas in the belief that he and the other maroons had brought the enemy to the unit's hiding place. Mortas could still see the maw of the Scorpion rifle pointed at his chest, enemy flares lighting up the night sky behind him, Shalley babbling his accusations. Cranther pouncing on the man, killing him with his fighting knife, but also ripping open his earlier wound and speeding his own demise. Mortas squeezed his eyes shut, blocking the tears that threatened to overflow, sure that he was under constant surveillance in the cell.

In that self-imposed darkness, Mortas remembered how Major Shalley had just started saying something about Trent when Cranther had killed him. It had been an accusation that Mortas now understood, that the female officer had spoken directly into the major's mind when they'd been arguing back in the ravine. Shalley had been wrong to suspect that Mortas had led the enemy to his position, but he'd turned out to be right about Trent's superhuman ability.

Mortas shuddered at the second secret, the one he was sure would get him killed with no word to his father that he'd been recovered alive. The thing masquerading as Trent had been identified as an alien while trapped in a decontamination tube at Glory Main. Mortas had been locked in a duplicate tube only a few feet away, confused by the flashing lights and blaring alarms. The alien had locked eyes with him, knowing it was doomed, and somehow communicated directly into his brain just as Major Shalley had said.

In only a few seconds, it had explained that the whole thing—the crash landing on the barren planet, the seemingly random set of skills possessed by each of the four maroons, even Mortas's status as a brand-new lieutenant—had been part of an elaborate ruse to get the alien inside a major headquarters.

Collapsing under the mental assault, Mortas had seen images that only the alien could have witnessed. His own face, unconscious inside a transit tube on the ship that had been transporting him to his first combat assignment. Sedated for the multi-Step journey and unaware that he'd been captured. Searing scenes of the torture the real Amelia Trent had undergone while the alien had penetrated her psyche in order to replace her. How the real Trent had fought the alien until it killed her. How the thing, trapped in the decontamination tube and knowing that its time was up, had asked Mortas to cry over it as he'd done for Cranther and Gorman.

Mortas stopped jogging, surprised to be so winded and not willing to acknowledge that his elevated heart rate came from the dreadful recollection. From reliving that experience and the sensation of having had his mind completely taken over. From the certainty that he would never be released if his captors ever even suspected the truth of what had passed between him and the alien.

As he'd done so many times before, when the images the thing had drilled into his mind jumped into his awareness, Mortas looked around the bare walls in search of something, anything, to occupy his attention.

As usual there was nothing new to see, but his eyes locked onto the one open corner of the small room, near the door. The ceiling and the lights were far overhead, but he now noted the texture of the wall under its coat of light green paint. Rough and grainy when he inspected it up close, Mortas was surprised he hadn't noticed that earlier.

For no reason other than to give his mind something to do, he backed into the corner with his knees bent. Mortas wore a flimsy set of black pajamas, and felt the cold of the wall on his shoulders when he pressed his palms against the surface on either side. A delicate vibration tickled, a distant thrumming that made him wonder if his new cell was inside a spacecraft of some kind. Mortas extended his arms and was pleased to discover he could raise himself off the floor this way. Twisting his bare feet outward, he planted them against the opposite sides of the corner and tried to take some of the weight off his hands.

Shinning up slowly now, enjoying the different view of the small room, Mortas was a yard or so off the ground when he abruptly slipped and dropped to the floor in a heap. It hurt just a bit, but Mortas experienced a thrill at finally having found something new to do, some kind of activity that was all his own. He imagined that Corporal Cranther could have gone straight up to the ceiling, a skill the dead man might have learned either as an orphan runaway on Celestia or as a Spartacan Scout. Cranther had been short and wiry, and the taller Mortas assumed the task would have been easier for him.

Pondering Cranther's size reminded Mortas of an ovular pile of smooth stones next to a gurgling river on a distant planet, and so he decided to think of something else.

He awoke in the darkness for no reason at all, something that seemed to happen often. Although his meals were identifiable as breakfast, lunch, and dinner, Mortas suspected they were provided at random intervals to keep him from establishing a day/night routine. He tried anyway, turning off the light after consuming the dinner meal, but sleep was usually a long time coming and there was no way of telling how long he'd been unconscious when he woke up.

This time Mortas had dreamt of the others, but

nothing in that unconscious hallucination should have awakened him. They'd been walking across level terrain in the dark of night, the four of them side by side in a way that they'd never traveled in real life. Cranther had taught them how to move tactically, using the ground to conceal their presence when possible, but in the dream they'd been walking along as if they had nothing to fear in the surrounding gloom.

Gorman, the pacifist, had been quietly telling a nice little story that Mortas had already forgotten, but it didn't seem to matter. The dead man's voice had been calm and comforting, just as Mortas remembered it, and he and Trent and Cranther had been enjoying whatever the chartist had been saying.

Lying there in the dark, Mortas pulled the blanket up tighter around his neck, his fingers digging into the fabric. He suspected he was being watched, but the memory of the dream was so vivid that he could almost feel the presence of the other three and couldn't keep from whispering the words aloud.

"I miss you."

Mortas awoke with the symptoms that indicated he'd been drugged again, and slowly sat up. His latest cell was round, with the bunk in the center. Squinting, he decided that his new quarters resembled the inside of a large, cream-colored drum. It was well lit and warm, and Mortas wondered if he was still dreaming.

The room was large enough that ten paces wouldn't

take him across it, and the bed was its only furniture. He now saw that it was indeed a bed, with white sheets and a gold-colored set of real covers, as opposed to the hard bunk and thin blankets of his previous accommodations.

The drum's curved walls were interrupted at regular intervals by unadorned columns that jutted out slightly. Those were gray, and he counted ten of them. The room's door was also white, but all of a piece with no hatches for food trays or guards' orders. His eyes coming into better focus, Mortas also detected a compression handle in one segment of the wall that he supposed led to a bathroom.

Try as he might, it was impossible to view his new surroundings without believing he'd somehow passed an important milestone.

Standing, Mortas noted that he now wore a sturdy set of green pajamas instead of the flimsy black ones that had been his uniform for so long. His feet were bare, but when he looked for the useless paper slippers he found something that made him catch his breath.

A new pair of rubber-soled exercise shoes had been placed at the foot of the bed, along with a set of athletic socks. Mortas grabbed one of the sneakers as if fearing it would somehow disappear, turning it over and over. Then, heedless of who might be observing him, he let his unadulterated joy spread across his face while pulling on the socks and the footwear. Mortas walked a few paces, enjoying the stretch and the bounce under his feet before striding quickly all the way around the cell.

The freedom to move in that fashion was simply delicious, and after so close a confinement it felt as if he were flying.

The athlete in him forced Mortas to warm up and even stretch, but he could hardly contain his excitement before he began to jog, then to run, actually *running*, around the perimeter of the room. It was intoxicating, the space and the light and the ability to enjoy it. He soon grew winded but didn't stop, turning easily so that he was moving backward, bouncing gently and throwing light punches at the air. Mortas was still smiling when he came to a halt, panting, staring down at the miraculous shoes. Remembering how hard it had been, trying to shin up the corner of the last cell using nothing but bare feet. That made him smile even more, and he spoke aloud.

"Well what do you know? All I had to do was start climbing the walls."

The ball was heavier than Mortas remembered, but he'd only played this particular game briefly, at Officer Basic. Stratactics Ball was a military invention, a constantly morphing competition that forced its players to develop game-winning strategies along with player-level tactics. That was how it had gotten its name, and he'd grown to enjoy it a lot.

Also referred to as Sim Ball, the game was a product of the decades-long war with an alien race that resembled humanity in so many ways that they'd been nicknamed the Sims. Battling for the habitable planets of distant solar systems, both sides had been forced to adjust their frames of reference to fit a war that spanned enormous regions of space, key locations that were constantly in motion, and enemy fleets that could appear almost out of nowhere.

Stratactics Ball was played on an enclosed rectangular court of no set size. That was intentional, as the game's limitless variations were designed to keep its players in a mode of uncertainty. The court where Mortas stood was probably forty yards long and twenty yards wide, with a ceiling ten yards over his head. He remembered that the side walls on the courts at Officer Basic had been transparent, with rows of seats rising away beyond the barriers. The walls on this one were all painted a dull gray that bore the smudges of past matches, and there was no audience that he could detect.

Three round holes set side by side in the walls at either end of the court served as goals, each of them only marginally larger than the ball and too high for any normal human to reach unaided. Even as Mortas watched, the panels on one set of goals rearranged themselves. The two outside apertures had been open while the middle hole was closed, but now the two openings to his right were available while the one on his left was blocked. The goals would open and shut at unspecified intervals and in no set order throughout a game.

Team size varied, but when there were more than

twenty players a standard restriction kept half of them from crossing midcourt. Throwing the ball to a team-mate was the only way to advance it, but the pass could include bounces off the walls, ceiling, and floor. Inter-cepting the ball or knocking down an enemy pass im-mediately switched the defenders over to offense, and vice versa. To keep the injuries to a minimum, a player was required to halt as soon as he or she had the ball.

That is, until the ball passed a dashed line just a few yards short of the goals. This was known as the Close Contact Space, and it was the only part of the Stratactics arena where it was permissible to run with the ball or to tackle an opposing player. Some imagina-tive scoring techniques had developed over the years, including scrum-like human pyramids over which the ballcarrier would charge in order to reach the requisite height to jam the sphere through an available opening.

Preventing a goal was quite difficult because the holes were located behind defensive players who could be expected to pay more attention to the bodies rush-ing toward them than to the shifting apertures at their backs. The attackers could see which goals were open, and so the defenders were forced to come up with their own schemes for learning what was going on behind them.

Regardless of their plans, both the defenders and the attackers could see successful strategies undone in an instant if the apertures rearranged themselves at the wrong moment. There was no time for celebra-tion after a score, as the ball was literally shot back into play almost at once—and from any one of the six goals. The projectile usually sailed the length of the court, rebounding wildly and causing a mad scramble.

Command touted Stratactics Ball as one of the reasons the badly outnumbered humans had stemmed the advance of the relentless Sims. They cited the game's complexity, unpredictability, and ferocity as being analogous to war in space. It was not lost on any of its players, officer or enlisted, that regardless of the strategy or tactics employed, gaining a victory usually hinged on a violent confrontation at close quarters with someone's back to the wall.

Remembering the spirited games in Officer Basic, Mortas walked a little closer to the two open goals and stopped. Even now, standing alone on a playing court as a prisoner of the armed force in which he served, he still obeyed the rules of the game. Faking a two-handed bounce pass, he shifted the ball into his right hand and then heaved it sideways over his head. He'd grown skilled at hitting the target this way, and had been recruited to play on different teams because of that talent.

The ball sailed through the stale air, seemingly on course, but its curved flight took it just far enough out of alignment that it whacked into the painted ring around the goal with a loud slap. It bounced twice before coming to a stop, and he had to walk over to retrieve it, feeling slightly disappointed that his skills could have eroded so quickly.

Quickly? Although his ordeal on the barren planet

had lasted several days and nights, Mortas had no idea how long he'd been in captivity. He looked around the empty court, still a little surprised to have been granted an unsupervised exercise period, and wondered who might be watching. The guard detail that had been with him for so long had disappeared in the last move, the one that had landed him in the round room with the real bed.

His new accommodations even had a bathroom with a shower, and Mortas had spent a long time looking in the mirror. The face that had stared back at him was thinner than he remembered, with almost a wolf-like cast to it, and he'd even detected the beginnings of a long, thin wrinkle across the skin of his young forehead. His dark hair had been cropped close during one of his transfers, and he'd remembered the bite of the burning embers that had landed on his scalp in the chaotic run across the enemy airstrip. Fortunately they'd left no scars.

"Still me," he'd remarked to the air before starting to wash his face.

Once he'd cleaned up, Mortas had been given a fresh T-shirt and athletic shorts to go with his new sneakers. Then a mildly friendly attendant had escorted him to a small mess hall where he'd eaten alone, after which he'd been offered the chance to exercise.

Which had brought him to the Sim Ball court. Mortas had been seen by several people in the corridors, and he was still trying to decide if that was good or bad. He already knew that large numbers of Force personnel had been searching for him at one point—befitting the missing son of Olech Mortas—and so being seen by random people was encouraging. That is, unless he was so far from Earth and the settled planets that it didn't matter who recognized him.

The air in the large room had changed while he stood there thinking, and he caught a whiff of something harsh in his nostrils. Mortas shut his eyes and sniffed hard, once, then a second time with his head turned to the side. A heavy, undeniable odor, filled with dire connotations. Having been through numerous shipboard emergency drills, he knew that fire was one of the greatest hazards of space travel. The scent contained more than a hint of smoke.

Mortas looked around quickly, trying to locate the source, his nose tipped upward and sniffing in loud, short inhalations. His eyes stopped abruptly when they detected the slightest shimmering movement from the two open goals facing him. He took a step forward, now identifying wispy gray tendrils wafting from the tops of both holes.

The ball fell out of his hands and he was running, straight across the court toward the low door that mated perfectly with one of the court's sidewalls. He was still two strides away when the noise came, making him jump because it was so loud, a mechanical slap that kept on coming. The alarm blasted at him from above, but he was still able to hear the emergency bolts shooting home on the only way out just as he reached the hatch.

He slammed into it anyway, hoping to spring it, and bounced off painfully. A robot voice boomed at him now, rebounding off the insulated walls, telling him that there was a fire and that all personnel were to secure all hatches and prepare to battle the blaze wherever they were. He found himself standing at the door, beating on the material with both palms, shouting for help even as the air grew thick with the aroma of smoke.

Mortas turned away from the unyielding exit to see that the open goals in the far wall were belching now, a cascading gray cloud that spewed forth and billowed toward the high ceiling. Tumbling, churning, thick with chemicals that were already poisoning the air.

Without thinking, he was prone on the hard floor and trying to remember what to do. Recalling a voice telling him to hold a damp rag over his mouth and nostrils, he dragged his T-shirt up over his nose. Not damp, but better than nothing. The alarm was still honking, so loud now that he couldn't make out the words that accompanied it. His vision darted across the flat expanse, knowing that there was no other exit.

His eyes began to smart, but Mortas hardly noticed because the floor beneath him was growing noticeably warmer. A grinding, machinelike rattling joined the booming siren, forcing him to bring his hands up over his ears. Crawling on his elbows, he dragged himself up against the wall near the door for no reason other than the desire to be close by if it miraculously opened.

Looking up through watering eyes, a stench far

fouler than ordinary smoke penetrating the shirt, he saw that a dark, roiling cloud had obscured the ceiling. A glance at the goals showed that all three were open, vomiting the noisome gas that was rapidly polluting an already-dwindling amount of oxygen. He saw the forgotten ball moving on its own, its material swelling with the heat and rolling, lopsided and silly, out of his sight.

The floor was actually hot now, and he sensed more than heard a long string of rippling burps that could only be the boiling of whatever was beneath him. His fingers pressed into his running, smarting eyes, and then a loud thud in the compartments below the court got him moving.

Up now, one hand clapping the fabric over his nose while the other tried to shield his eyes, bent over because the smoke had come down so low. Kicking madly at the door, feeling no give at all, several steps back, then running forward to jump with both soles only to rebound and land painfully on his kidneys. Back on his feet, coughing, eyes turned to slits, crouching, then running toward the exit again, knowing it wouldn't open, that the stinging in his feet wasn't the pain from striking the door but the heat of the fire on which he stood, the gas swirling around him, running shoulder first into the hatch and dropping like a stone.

The smoke was almost to the floor, the heat was everywhere, and Mortas realized with true terror that he had to abandon the room's only exit. Fearing he'd never be able to find it again in the cloud, eyes forcing themselves shut, the shirt back up over his nose, Mortas crawled blindly across the surface in the vain hope of finding a patch where the fire wasn't going to roast him.

Mortas was lying on a lukewarm patch of floor, curled in a ball with his entire head inside the sweat-soaked shirt, when a pair of hands roughly took hold of him. They pulled him to his feet, the shirt coming down to reveal that the room was being blown clear of the evil cloud and that the door stood wide open behind a tall figure holding him at arm's length. His eyes were refusing to open fully, and his lungs were fighting to expel whatever was roughening them, but Mortas recognized the coal-gray tunic of his father's security detail.

"Jan! Jan!" The hands, incredibly strong, had him by the upper arms and were shaking him even though he and the other man were the same height. Eyelids fluttering open just a crack as he recognized the voice but not believing it. "Jan, it's me! Hugh Leeger! Do you know me?"

Mortas shook his head to clear it, simultaneously relieved and angered by the dawning realization that the life-threatening event had been a setup. He contorted his body, trying to break loose, recognizing the man who was the chief of his father's security detail. The man who had practically raised him, from the day his mother died until the day he'd gone to boarding school. Big brother, surrogate father, coach, mentor, and friend.

Mortas's fists were flying without any instructions to do so, aiming for the face with the intent of doing real harm, but bouncing off Leeger's expert parries instead. Then the hands were on him again, his body twisting, his center of gravity gone, and he was face-down on the floor with one arm behind his back bearing Leeger's full weight.

The familiar voice in his ear, gentle but not kind. "Amazing. No matter how old we both get, I can still pin you in one fall."

"Lean your head back, please." The technician was short and pretty, with jet-black hair piled under a barrette. She was also very nervous, and managed to run most of the eye drops down Mortas's cheek. His eyes had been flushed out by a doctor who couldn't wait to pass him on to someone else, and now he saw an amused look on Leeger's face as the security man stepped closer.

"I'll do that." He took the drops from the tech, and the woman was gone a grateful moment later. Mortas scowled up at him as Leeger pried his eyelids open and carefully squeezed a few drops from the bottle, not wasting any. "Everybody gets so scared whenever your father is in the area. I've never understood that."

Mortas blinked rapidly, lowering his chin. He was sitting on a shiny metal stool in a small examination room, and although his breathing had returned to normal, his eyes still stung. The nervous doctor had said he'd been dosed with a harmless irritant similar to riot gas, but the insides of his nose retained the odor from the smoke.

"Where am I?"

"Home." Leeger returned to the small chair near the door and sat down smoothly. "Earth orbit. You might have had the shortest combat tour on record, Jan. This here is a Force research facility, for testing stress levels and physical readiness. That was a special Sim Ball court, in case you haven't guessed. It's rigged up to do all sorts of things to unsuspecting Force personnel."

"So why do it to me?"

"Oh, you already know the answer to that. You were exposed to an alien life-form we've never seen before, one that did things that none of our scientists can explain. Up until now everybody's been focusing on why the Sims can't reproduce and why they can't form our syllables, but the appearance of that alien put all that stuff on the back burner."

"You didn't answer me."

"Sure I did. Nobody knows what that thing was, how it could do the things it did, and what else it might have been able to do. We had to make sure you weren't carrying a passenger, in other words. So creating a situation where you believed you were about to die was the only way we could be certain there wasn't anything left of that thing hidden inside you."

"You didn't seriously believe that, right?"

Leeger leaned forward, his elbows on his knees.

"Jan, the entire Human Defense Force went on alert because of that alien. Almost every Forcemember in the war zone has been put through the same type of scan that caught that thing, the one that showed it wasn't human. That's how seriously they're treating this."

"What did they find?"

The older man straightened up. "Nothing. Not a single sighting of anything like what you encountered. And it's been weeks. To be honest, no one knows what to make of that."

"Weeks? I was locked up for weeks, and you knew about it?"

Leeger's lips parted in a disbelieving smile. "Son, you've been scanned in every way we know, several times, and they had one last look at your insides while you were enjoying the ambience of that Sim Ball court. It was the only way they were ever going to let your father come into contact with you, so I consider it a small price to pay."

"He's here?"

"His shuttle's docking even as we speak. Command wouldn't dare let the Chairman of the Emergency Senate on the same station with you until they were certain you were clean." Leeger stood. "So if you're done crying, let's get you into a uniform, Lieutenant. And then go see your dad."

The dress uniform's high collar seemed to bite into his throat as Mortas followed Leeger down the telescoping passage that joined the station to his father's shuttle. He remembered sealing the crisp new suit in a protective case and hanging it in a closet at the Mortas home not long before, in preparation for shipping out. As an infantry lieutenant headed for a platoon in the war zone he would have had little need for such finery, and his thoughts briefly went to the filthy, torn fatigues he'd been wearing when he'd finally reached Glory Main.

His left hand swung unnaturally, as if he were holding a small weight, and Mortas kept looking down at his university ring. That too had been placed in safekeeping before he shipped out, and he hadn't expected to see it again for several years. If ever.

The ship's hatch was open when they reached the end of the umbilical, and even though he'd traveled on his father's shuttle many times, he was still struck by its opulence. Perhaps it was the recent experience of being transported by standard military carriers, or maybe that he'd been locked up for several weeks, but the entire setup seemed grossly luxuriant.

Imitation wood decorated the edges of the craft's furnishings, and everything else appeared to be colored in rich cream. The crew contained no Human Defense Force personnel, instead consisting of carefully screened and highly trained members of Olech Mortas's considerable retinue. Even so, they all sported uniforms that were quasi-military, and Mortas found that it bothered him. Remembering now that he'd never felt fully at ease on this ship or with any of the more recent additions to his father's coterie, suspicious that the too-ready smiles were masks that these people probably practiced in mirrors.

And then he was at the hatch leading to his father's office, the traveling control room at the very top of humanity's governmental apparatus. Despite the disorganization and inefficiency he'd encountered in the war zone, Mortas knew from personal witness that the multidecade conflict was directed by the man who sat beyond this hatch. Leeger ushered him in and shut the entrance behind him, and Mortas felt a twinge of the same apprehension he'd experienced whenever his interrogations had recommenced.

A curtain hung before him now, intended to block prying eyes whenever the hatch was open, and Mortas took a deep breath before stepping through the drapes. It was exactly as he remembered it, a small room decorated with the same imitation wood, but festooned with electronic screens that currently displayed a variety of paintings depicting pastoral scenes of a bygone age. Many visitors to that office left without realizing that the screens had been arranged so that the Chairman of the Emergency Senate could view selected data or manage a crisis, all just by standing in the room's center.

The chairman sat facing the hatch with his back to the far bulkhead, behind a communications console that had always reminded Mortas of an old-style organ he'd once seen in a church. He'd found it funny, imagining his father's fingers dancing over the buttons and keyboards, directing the far-flung machinations of his latest schemes while a sonorous dirge blasted from pipes made of lead, copper, and tin.

A maestro more concerned with the activities of total strangers in distant solar systems than the two motherless children in his own home.

The man behind the desk looked up from one of its screens and gave Mortas the same smile he'd seen in the passageways leading there. Olech came to his feet, wearing a tunic and pressed trousers of a rich fabric colored something between dark green and dark gray. It was cut in a military style, but that was fitting in the Chairman's case because a single blood red bar was pinned to his chest, a decoration Mortas had known all his life.

Earned by an Olech Mortas he had never known, a volunteer in the early years of the long war, aged only fifteen because the fight had been going so badly. The award represented service in a special army formed by a temporary waiver that had dropped the volunteer age to twelve. They were still revered decades later, because most of them had perished in the desperate but ultimately successful bid to reverse the seemingly endless string of Sim victories. Olech Mortas had been severely wounded after several weeks of combat that he routinely referred to—humbly, of course—as total chaos that had consumed the lives of better men— better children—than he. They were collectively known as the Unwavering, and in a private moment Olech had once admitted to his son that their minimal training and panicked commanders had been the main reasons why so few of them had returned.

Olech was in his early fifties, but looked ten years younger. Matching Mortas's six-foot height and almost as lean as his twenty-two-year-old son, the Chairman still sported a full head of hair that was gracefully changing from blond to silver. His daughter Ayliss had inherited the golden hair and the blue eyes, while her younger brother Jander had come into the world with their mother's dark hair and eyes of the same color.

His father maintained the smile as he approached, and when Olech extended his hand Mortas took it. The Chairman's eyes bore straight into him, and when he spoke it was with mirth.

"Didn't expect to be seeing you so soon, Jan."

"—and they kept me in a cell, interrogated me, told me nothing, and finally brought me here." Mortas finished the long tale in the same even tone that his father always demanded. "Apparently someone thought I was possessed by a demon or something, so they put me through a fake shipboard fire where I thought I was going to die, just to see what would pop out of me."

"Station-board."

"Excuse me?"

"Station-board. You weren't on a ship, so it couldn't be a fake shipboard fire. And it was the only way I was ever going to get you back."

"Back?"

The chairman misunderstood the barb, and began to nod. He'd resumed his place behind the desk, and Mortas was seated before him in a straight-backed chair with no arms.

"Yes. Back. I have to admit something here, Jan. I knew you'd go out there and give it your best, but I had no idea you'd developed such talents at bringing people together. I've read all the reports, and the way you got the other three maroons to work with you was impressive." He paused, and Mortas prepared himself for a comment about his failure to spot the alien. "Especially Gorman."

Surprised by the words and unsure of where his father was going, Mortas decided to head him off. "Gorman was actually the easiest one to work with. He was a pacifist, Holy Whisper, and as long as we didn't violate his principles, he pretty much went along with whatever we were doing. He also figured out what planet we were on without being asked, and with no instruments."

"That's different from my experience. The representatives of the Holy Whisper that I've met seldom go along with anything. For some reason they don't seem to trust me much." He flashed the winning smile, and Mortas returned it in reflex. "But they sure like you."

"What?"

"I showed them the footage of when you had just reached Glory Main, as you emerged from that hijacked Wren. You looked like you'd been fed through a meat grinder, but when you asked that Banshee commander if there was a special rite for Gorman's remains, it really struck a chord with his people."

For an instant, Mortas was somewhere else. Listening to Ayliss, who had taught him early on to distrust their father completely. She'd been arguing against his decision to go to the war zone, and had warned him that whatever happened—whether he lived or died—Olech would use it to his advantage.

"I wasn't performing for an audience, Father. Gorman saved my life more than once. His religion was everything to him—"

"Exactly." The words came out almost as a hiss, and Mortas saw the fire in the blue eyes that usually meant his father was about to propose something. "That's what the Holy Whisper elders saw in that footage. I granted them access to a redacted copy of your report, and when they read how you'd accommodated Gorman's beliefs, I sensed this could be a turning point.

"I can't tell you how proud I am of what you did there, Jan. And that's why you're going to be my new ambassador to Pacifica."

Even coming so close on the heels of his recent experiences, this was a bombshell. Mortas looked at the office carpet in order to digest what his father had just proposed, noticing the seal of the Emergency Senate woven into the gold fabric. The university ring on his finger regained its weight, and he recognized the genuine urge to accept the appointment. Raised a child of privilege, he'd always been afforded a certain deference from people who feared his father or hoped to get something from him. The assumption that he would regain that status after serving in the war was not new to him.

Fresh memories of starvation, blisters, and far too many close brushes with death added weight to the argument to simply say yes. He'd come to like Gorman very much, and had cried unabashedly when the pacifist had died, so there would be nothing fraudulent about representing his father to Gorman's people. Mortas had gone to the war zone with every intention of leading an infantry platoon in combat, and it was hardly his fault that he'd been captured by the enemy while in transit.

Those thoughts brought up a different memory, Mortas's earlier expectations of what it would be like when he returned from the war. Hopefully not badly wounded, but not having emerged unscathed. Tempered by the experience, but also having gained true knowledge of who he was at his very core.

Mortas found his eyes on the red ribbon that adorned his father's chest, and not by accident. A question came to mind.

"You showed these Holy Whisper elders footage of me coming out of the Wren? With the alien right behind me?"

"Of course not. I applied a little judicious editing, in keeping with security protocol. The Force in the war zone has been informed of the new threat, but for the time being, news of the alien and its capabilities has been restricted to those units and the highest levels of Command."

"The word's going to get back, no matter what you do."

"I've got my people circulating a rumor to that effect already, but one so absurd that nobody's going to know what to make of the real story when it eventually comes out. You'll learn how to take proactive steps like that, once you've been a diplomat for a while."

"And what are people going to say when they find out that the son of the Chairman of the Emergency Senate brought this alien to a Corps headquarters in the war zone?"

"The same thing that the rest of the Force thinks: you identified the alien when you reached safety, and it was destroyed because of you."

Mortas shook his head, allowing a wry smile onto his lips. As usual in matters involving their father, Ayliss had been spot-on. No matter what happened to Mortas in the war, Olech would make a hero out of him.

"I imagine you think you don't like that story, Jan, but it beats the hell out of the truth. Maybe you don't know this, but the Twelfth Corps commander moved Glory Main from that rock within days of having it compromised. You have any idea how long it took to create that base, and how much it cost?"

"Yeah, Cranther said that the higher-ups go to crazy lengths to protect themselves in the zone." Remembering what happened when he and the alien had approached the dead space rock where Glory

Main was concealed. "Did you know they had a secret weapon there, one that took control of our Wren and was going to crash it into the ground just so they could stay hidden?"

"Of course. They even played me the transmission when you were about to crash, the one where you told them you're my son and that I'd do terrible things to them if they killed you."

A knowing smirk tickled the corners of Olech's mouth, and Mortas pretended not to notice. "They would have done it if I hadn't used your name. I hadn't mentioned it before. To anyone."

"Here's my point: the rest of the Force thinks you're a hero, but the Twelfth Corps leadership is mad as hell. They don't want you back . . . although technically you never reported to them in the first place."

"There are other units out there. Plenty of platoons that need a lieutenant."

"Too many, I'm thinking." The smirk was gone, and Mortas thought that he'd actually detected a look of fatherly concern. He couldn't be certain, however, having never seen it before. He was about to speak when Olech's face hardened.

"If you insist on going back out there, I'm not going to stand in your way. You should know that one of the most difficult parts of my job is keeping the coalition together, and that the Holy Whisper is never far away from banning their young people from service."

The words sounded genuine enough, but Mortas

had grown up with the other man's excuses for his absences and couldn't help wondering if this wasn't more of the same. He was of use to his father at the moment, and so had temporarily gained his attention.

"Gorman said they didn't have a problem with serving as long as they didn't participate in acts of violence. Seems like there'd be enough jobs they could hold without having grounds to quit the war."

"There are, but the elders are always looking for an excuse to sit out the whole conflict. Funny thing about the Whisper; in a lot of ways they're just like any other coalition member. Sometimes they need to have their hands held, or to get some kind of special recognition. You know that Hab planet where you were marooned? We're going to name it after Gorman. Calling it Roanum. That was his first name, right? Roan?"

"Yes."

"That would be a nice message for the new ambassador to carry to Gorman's people. Especially coming from the man who got him out of there."

Mortas's eyes blinked quickly, as if trying to remove the mental image of Gorman's bloody flight suit, punctured by shrapnel from the explosion that Mortas had set off. The picture disappeared, only to be replaced by the same man lying on the deck of the Wren after it had broken free of the hated planet's orbit. Mortas holding Gorman's hand, the alien holding the other one, both of them reciting the Holy Whisper prayer that the dying man had taught them much earlier.

Imagining himself emerging from a different shuttle, an ambassador's conveyance, to announce that the Chairman of the Emergency Senate had named the horrible planet of pain and loss after one of the men who had been killed there, in order to keep the dead man's people in the war. The obscenity of it almost made him gag.

"I'm sure your ambassador will do a good job delivering that message. Whoever he or she is."

Olech stared at him for a long moment, perhaps giving him the chance to reverse the decision, perhaps already calculating his next move. The blue eyes shifted away finally, and his father punched two or three buttons on the console with a look of weariness.

"All right. Looks like Command will have to find you a new assignment." Olech rose, but when Mortas started to do the same his father waved him back down. Coming around the desk, he took hold of a chair identical to Mortas's and brought it close.

"Jan, I've watched the video of you and the alien in the decontamination tubes. I've studied your reactions when the alien was identified, when it transposed into all those flying specks, all the way through to when it was incinerated.

"I know you've kept this from the interrogators, but I'm your father, and I know something more happened there. I think you'd agree that it is vitally important for me to understand the nature of this new opponent. Completely."

The face was grave until Olech replaced it with the winning smile. "Now. Tell me everything about the alien that impersonated Captain Trent. Especially what happened to you in that tube."

"**T**urned me down flat, Hugh." Olech turned his son's university ring over and over in his hands. "Why are my kids so fucking stubborn?"

Seated in front of the desk, Leeger answered him with raised eyebrows.

"All right, I suppose I shouldn't be all that surprised." With the slightest of sighs he put the ring down. "So. This is where you get to remind me that I shouldn't have sent him to the Glory Corps in the first place."

"It wasn't such a bad decision. They don't call them the Senate's Own for nothing."

"That's not why I sent him there—or tried to, anyway. Sure they're political as all get out, and they can't fight worth a damn, but at least they know it. One of the quietest sectors of the war . . . and look what was waiting."

"You had no way of knowing that was going to happen."

"I suppose it was a bizarre kind of blessing, that Jan was involved. I doubt I would have gotten the straight story from Command, no matter how much of a threat that thing was. Turns out it was telepathic, in addition to its other tricks. It spoke right into Jan's head even though it was sealed in a decon tube."

"You probably don't want that becoming common knowledge."

Olech raised his own eyebrows while sliding back into his seat. "Thanks for the tip. Good thing I thought of it in time to warn him to keep his mouth shut."

"You think he's all right? To go to a new unit, I mean?"

"It's what he wants. He's just like Ayliss; once he gets an idea in his head there's no getting it out." From his slumped position, the chairman exhaled loudly. "So you still think we should send him to the Orphans?"

"It's an excellent combat outfit, almost one hundred percent blooded veterans, with strong leadership and seasoned NCOs. You can't give him a better chance than that."

"A better chance . . . they're a fire brigade, for God's sake. One of these times they're gonna get thrown into something that's way too big for them, and that'll be the end of the Orphans."

"I believe the term is 'independent' brigade. And they've been tossed into a few scrapes they shouldn't have walked out of, but they survived anyway."

Olech's lower lip disappeared under his front teeth, but then he brightened somewhat. "Sounds like what happened to Jan out there. Talk about an impossible situation, and he came back from that."

"He's always been very tough."

"All right, then. Lieutenant Jander Mortas is now the newest Orphan." Olech kept the smile, but it was forced. "Fitting in a way, isn't it?"

Leeger's face darkened. "Don't do that to yourself. You made a very difficult decision when they were young, and the fact that they're still alive shows it paid off. And someday you'll be able to explain it to them."

"I don't know about that." Olech pointed to one of the largest screens on the office walls before hitting another button. Leeger turned to watch, yet again, the final moments for the alien that had accompanied Jander to Glory Main.

Lights strobed around the transparent tube, and a voice was broadcasting an emergency warning that the alien was transposing into something else. One instant it resembled Captain Amelia Trent, the human being it had impersonated, and the next it burst into thousands of dots with wings, storming around the tube in a cloud of chemical poisons. Fire exploded inside the cylinder, destroying the alien, the light so intense that it blinded the camera for an instant.

Although they'd watched it many times before, the two men sat in silence when it was over. Leeger sensed that his boss needed him to say something.

"We always knew there were things out there that we wouldn't be able to explain. Now we've seen one of them."

"Still not sure what we've seen." The chairman's voice was contemplative, and his eyes were distant. "Or why there was only one of them."

"Maybe it was a test, to see if they could get by our technology."

"Maybe." Olech changed the image on the screen. A kind-looking man with gray hair was waving at them now, an old picture of Interplanetary President Daniel

Larkin. Olech and a small circle of senators had come to power literally over his dead body. "You know, the longer I hold this job, the more I wonder if Dan Larkin wasn't right after all. Probably looking down on us all these years, laughing his ass off."

Mortas was back in the circular room, but no longer considered it a cell. He sat on the bed, reading a long string of messages that had accumulated during his ordeal. The screen of his handheld was loaded with outdated notes from classmates and other friends, wishing him safe travel and an even safer time in the war zone. Although it had been only a few weeks, Mortas felt a great deal of time had passed and that an enormous gulf separated him from those people.

The jacket of his dress uniform was on the bed next to him, and he would have changed completely except his father's minions hadn't managed to scrape together a set of fatigues for him yet. It was just as well; he'd been cleared to make one communication to Earth and needed the privacy.

Punching in the access codes he'd been provided, Mortas found his heart beating just a little faster when the device on the other end activated. A familiar face appeared, blond hair and a giant, excited smile.

"Jan! It's you! It's really you!" his sister Ayliss shouted at him, the image distorting as she shook the device at her end. A line of code at the bottom of the screen said she was in Buenos Aires, and from her outfit he guessed it was night. The golden hair had been fashioned into long curls that were then pinned up at the back of her head, and she was wearing a light blue dress that exposed one shoulder completely.

"Yeah, it's me." Mortas couldn't keep the smile from his features. "I suppose you heard I didn't get very far."

"That's not what I heard at all." The face grew older-sister grave. "I heard you did some great things out there."

The inexact wording brought him back to one of the more unpleasant realities of being a member of the Mortas family, the basic assumption that someone was always listening. Security personnel, friends of their father, enemies of their father, journalists, even out-and-out spies. It had always irked him, and with so much to tell his sister, it annoyed him even more.

"Oh, I didn't do all that much . . . it was the people I was with. They really pulled me through."

"From what I was told, you did a little pulling yourself."

He allowed the smile to return. "And who would have been telling you that?"

"Olech's got his sources, and I have mine." An impish grin, which usually meant she was about to do something that would rankle their father. "And sometimes they're the same people."

"He asked me to become one of those people, just a while ago."

"I know. You took it, right? You're going to be smart, this time?"

"Never done the smart thing before, why start now?"

The blue eyes lost their humor, and he thought some of the color left her cheeks. "No. You're not going back out there?"

"I have to."

"No you don't!" The words were soft, the voice angry. "How can I make you see that? I work with the veterans, they tell me all about what it's like out there, and now you've seen it—"

"Exactly."

An expression of pain, mixed with sadness. "You know, I only heard you were missing after they'd found you. And even then it was like the floor just fell away from me, as if somebody punched me right in the stomach. I thought I'd prepared myself, but now I know there's no getting ready for something like that. And you've got the chance to keep me from going through that again, and what are you doing? Throwing it away."

"You like the idea so much, you take the job. I'm sure he'd give it to you."

A minute shake of the head, the curls bouncing. "So not fair, Jan. I will *never* work for him."

"I'm sorry." The words came out as a frustrated whisper. Wishing he could speak freely, to explain it all, to tell her what it had been like and not sure he could actually do that if given the chance. "Listen—"

There was a buzzing sound at the hatch, and he realized he didn't know how to open it. Looking back at the screen. "Hey, someone's at the door, can you give me a moment to let them in?"

"That's all right, Jan." The finality of the words was matched by the leaden tone, and for a moment he was looking at his father again. "I gotta go too. I've got a function."

Her head cocked to one side reflexively, an Ayliss quirk that told him she'd just rolled a tear back into her eye before it got loose.

"You be careful out there, all right?"

"I will. Don't worry."

Ayliss's eyes were no longer focused on him, his sister's voice growing distant as if a shell were closing around her. "You come back. No matter what you have to do. Come back. That's all I ask."

"You can count on me."

"I love you, Jan. No matter how stupid you are."

"I love you, Ayliss. Don't worry."

The communication broke off, terminated from the other end.

The gray fatigues were stiff and new, and his boots were black and unscuffed. Shipping out for the first time, Mortas had been terribly conscious of the way his attire had screamed his status as a newbie. Now he found he didn't care.

Alone in the circular room, he experienced a strange feeling of suspension, a frozen disassociation with his surroundings. Thoughts cascaded over each other, tumbling from his survival experiences to his incarceration, rebounding off the interview with his father and Ayliss's anger. Why had it been so difficult to tell them what he'd discovered out there, the things he'd learned about himself and the bond he'd forged with the others?

The attendant who'd brought his latest uniform had also given him a small daypack, and Mortas reached for it now. It would probably contain the same food ration and toiletries that had been in the other bag, the one that had been stolen from him once he'd been sealed in the transit tube that was supposed to have taken him to his first unit.

All those things were in there, but his searching hand closed on something eerily familiar, as if it had been waiting for him. Long and black, it had felt clumsy in his hand the first time he'd hefted it. It once had a smaller partner, but that wasn't in the bag and Mortas presumed it was lost forever. Resting in its dark sheath, Cranther's fighting knife beckoned to him, asking him to draw it. Remembering the first time he'd used it, in a frenzy of fear as he stood face-to-face with a Sim militiaman whose only crime had been walking guard on a bridge Mortas and the others needed to cross. And the other time, right in the middle of the crisis at the enemy spacedrome, when he'd driven it into a Sim soldier who hadn't realized he was human and an enemy.

The evil blade came out pristine and black, making him wonder who might have cleaned it when a tiny piece of paper separated from the metal and fluttered to the floor. Mortas bent over and picked it up, mindful of the exposed blade. There was handwriting on the paper, a woman's script:

Paranoia is healthy, Lieutenant. Nurture yours.

The signature identified the author as a Captain Erica Varick, and Mortas was at a loss until he considered just who might have secured Cranther's knife for him. He'd last seen it being collected by strangers in biohazard suits, once he and the alien impersonating Amelia Trent had been safely secured in their decontamination tubes. Standing nearby, in the battle-scarred armor of the all-female Banshees, had been the commander of the armed escorts who had met them when they reached Glory Main.

Calm and confident, she'd contradicted the order telling Mortas to leave all weapons on the hijacked Wren. Next she'd told him to set aside anything he wanted to keep while he and Trent were stripping naked. She'd no doubt seen what Trent had turned into and, judging from the note, considered Mortas quite the rube. He'd never seen her face, and had assumed neither of Cranther's knives would be returned to him.

Mortas was sliding the weapon back into its scabbard when the screen of his handheld lit up and the device beeped at him. The new message was terse, orders assigning him to the First Brigade (Independent) of the Human Defense Force and instructing him to report immediately for embarkation. Mortas frowned, never having heard of the unit and wondering why it wasn't associated with a larger organization such as a division or a corps.

The handheld beeped again, with an addendum for the original message, and he opened it with interest. It was almost the same set of orders, except the unit's name had been changed to read:

First Independent Brigade, Human Defense Force—Orphans.

CHAPTER TWO

The party was in full swing by the time Ayliss got there. She'd spent most of the early evening at a tedious state function, where people hoping to eventually get close to her father had spent a lot of time trying to get close to her. Ayliss considered it funny that so many of the climbers hadn't bothered to learn how she felt about Olech, and she made no effort to educate them. After all, she was now in the information business and had already learned that knowledge can be a very pricey thing.

As a minor representative with the Veterans Auxiliary, Ayliss spent much of her time traveling, ostensibly to see how the returned veterans of the long war were being treated. She certainly did that, and with a vigor that had elicited the amazement of her Auxiliary superiors. They'd expected her to be spoiled and lazy, and their ignorance of her motives was another oddity that Ayliss Mortas found amusing.

But even her mirth had limits, so after the more senior officials had left the earlier function she'd decided it was time for some real fun. A few of the climbers had still been trying to make conversation with her, so Ayliss excused herself with the genuine explanation that she needed to speak with her security detail. As Olech Mortas's daughter, Ayliss had been surrounded by bodyguards—hers and those of her playmates—from a very early age. An informal protocol existed, designed to keep the protectors of the elite from getting in each other's way. At functions like this one the host was responsible for security, and so Ayliss's own modest bodyguard detachment had been required to wait outside the loud ballroom along with several other details.

Having found her team, she'd quietly whispered into the ear of its leader, a man not much older than her twenty-three years named Lee Selkirk. The security man stood an inch under six feet, which made him one inch taller than his charge. Selkirk's brown hair was cut short at the top of a frame that was toned and lean, and his eyes were in constant motion as he listened to Ayliss murmuring that it was time to seek entertainment elsewhere.

Elsewhere was a penthouse atop a skyscraper whose tenants were among Argentina's uppermost echelon. Ayliss had been raised and educated alongside the children of rich families from across the settled planets, and the penthouse party was being thrown by a friend from university days named Marco. Earth's overpopulation might have fueled the settlement of the nearest habitable planets many decades before, and the never-ending war had certainly taken its human toll, but even so, the streets were far too congested for people of her station to utilize surface travel most of the time. Their armored shuttle had been forced to circle twice before touching down on the penthouse's landing pad, waiting while other airborne partygoers were being dropped off. The enormous tower practically blazed with light, and dancing figures could be seen through a wall of rocket-proof glass. While they circled, Ayliss studied the darkly enormous expanse of the Rio de la Plata far below.

Her blue off-the-shoulder gown and fancy coif were only slightly out of place in the throng when she walked off the landing pad with her guards. Marco's jacketed attendants escorted Selkirk and the rest of the detail to an interior room where they would wait with the other security personnel, and Ayliss glided across the dance floor alone. The room was high-ceilinged with broad white walls and carpet the color of blood, and it contained at least two hundred people. A tray with champagne went by, and she took one of the long-stemmed glasses as her first drink of the evening.

Alcohol wasn't the only recreation available, and she detected the aroma of herbal intoxicants while sliding past the dancers. She was assaulted by wild greetings from university classmates, the driving beat of the music, and assorted dilations and gyrations, but she responded in good grace as she'd been taught. Normally Ayliss would have been all too happy to join in on the frivolity, especially after the dryness of the earlier function, but she wasn't there to mingle.

Several doorways punctured the unadorned back wall, and the rooms behind them were much smaller and considerably darker. Expensive couches and antique chairs took up most of the space, much of it having been moved from the main party area. Ayliss was pleased by the noise-dampening effect of the smaller chambers, and stopped for a moment to let her eyes adjust. Young figures writhed on the couches to one side, but she steered away from them toward a similar space where the attendees seemed to be taking a break from the action.

The seating in this room was individual, and she slipped past a circle of shadowy figures talking in spaced-out voices.

"Get it? The Sims are human. In fact they're *us*, but from the future. That's why they don't screw. They make new Sims in test tubes, which explains why there's so many of them."

"If they're just us from the future, how come their tech is so lousy?"

"It's not lousy, just spotty. Exactly what our tech would be like if we were on a spaceship that got caught up in somebody else's Step and tossed into the past. We'd have only what was on the ship, and we'd have to reinvent the rest."

"You think that was it? The Step? That was what caused this whole mess?"

"Of course. In all those decades of space exploration, we never bumped into anything sentient until we invented the Step. Moving faster than light opens all sorts of doors, like time travel. Don't you see? Nobody's creating the Sims at all. We just opened the door to the future . . . and out came our great-great-great-grandchildren."

Ayliss screwed up her face even though no one could see it. She'd never heard that theory before, and was pondering its value when she reached the far wall. Her eyes hadn't adjusted to the deeper gloom when a low male voice said hello from nearby. She made out a set of long legs that were attached to a large, lounging figure in a stuffed chair, and a hand moved in the shadows to indicate an open seat.

She only knew the man by his nickname of Python, but rumor had it that he'd served a full hitch in the war. Other stories spanned the gamut, saying he was European royalty, a minor music star, and even a fighter in underground death matches. Ayliss was only certain that he sold drugs, which meant he was connected to a wide range of illicit sources.

Once seated, Ayliss had a clear view of the open entranceway but was relatively sure the shadows concealed them. "Nice to see you again."

"I wasn't sure I was going to come out tonight, but Marco's parties are always so much fun. And I was bored."

The conversational style was a reflex among the upper class and the people who mixed with them, a response to the ever-present threat of surveillance. In an age of sophisticated circuitry the size of an eyelash, frank statements or pointed questions made in the wrong environment were greeted with suspicion, and repeated commission of such a faux pas could turn an insider into a pariah. As a result, public discussions among the upper crust were often so intentionally vapid that Ayliss feared the practice had turned one or two of her friends into morons.

Python's hand brushed against hers, and she took the expected delivery without being able to see it. A tiny capsule that she'd been anticipating all night. Ayliss tucked it into her bra, now able to discern the outline of Python's massive head. His long hair, which he usually kept tied in a ponytail, hung down over his shoulders tonight. The tiny cylinder sat heavy against her breast, urging Ayliss to violate the conversational protocol.

"What's in it?" she whispered.

"Truth." Python murmured before rising and passing into the light.

Ayliss waited, sitting there in the dark, until enough time had passed for Python to have left the party. It wasn't easy.

Rising, she passed into the bright room where the dancers were still going at it. One of the pleasant aspects of these gatherings was how much it reduced her status, making her just another face in a crowd of privilege. Though overdressed, she now attracted little attention while scanning the scene in front of her.

Marco had not been in evidence when she'd arrived, but Ayliss spotted him over near the bar. Black hair, green eyes, and dark skin, tremendously fit despite a bruising regimen of drugs and alcohol that had been his habit long before they'd met at university. One of many sons in a fantastically wealthy family, he would have been a hit with the ladies even if a pauper. At that moment a woman with cocoa-colored skin and red locks was standing close to him, her fingers toying with the mat of hair inside his open shirt.

The redhead glared at Ayliss when she approached, but Marco silenced her protest with a stern glance. The jovial face he turned toward Ayliss was one she knew well from the many times he'd attempted to bed her.

"Ayliss the Beautiful. Finally." The words were slurred, and his hand hung at the base of her neck when he gave her a two-cheek kiss. She didn't respond when the hand brushed her nipple while being withdrawn.

Leaning in closer, she whispered in his ear. "Would you mind if I used your safe room?"

Marco gave her an appraising look. "Ayliss the Beautiful becomes Ayliss the Enigma. How very interesting."

He waved a hand in the air, giving the redhead the opportunity to step under his raised arm and grab on tight. The glare returned, but Ayliss wasn't looking at her. One of Marco's security people, a tall man in a tuxedo whom she recognized from previous visits, slipped through the throng to receive quiet instructions. He then gave Ayliss a tiny, convulsive nod before indicating that she should follow him.

They were across the room in no time, through a door guarded by a jacketed security guard on the party side and a second one in full tactical gear on the other. Ayliss noted the attachments on the man's body armor: handcuffs, emergency radio, a can of spray immobilizer, and a short-barreled weapon designed for shoot-outs in confined spaces. Selkirk was waiting for her, and Ayliss had to assume that Marco's man had signaled ahead while they walked.

Another tactical escorted them down a side hallway to a room that was a fixture in the dwellings and offices of the powerful. The safe room was where the elite went to have frank discussions, or to view communications they did not wish to share with others. Yards of insulating material shielded the room's walls, ceiling, and floor, and the thick door made a scraping sound when it shut behind them. Selkirk opened his mouth to speak, but they'd been in front of people for a long time, and so Ayliss simply covered his lips with her own. The kiss was returned fully, and the iron bands of his arms crushed her to him.

The capsule in her bra shifted just then, and she broke the kiss but not the embrace. Her eyes were alight when her fingers reached into her dress. "Guess what I have?"

"I don't have to guess. I saw him leave."

"Then let's see what we've got."

The safe room was dimly lit, but Ayliss could see that Marco preferred his innermost sanctum well furnished. She moved a stuffed chair so that it faced one just like it, a few yards from the center of the room. Selkirk lowered the lights even more before returning and taking the capsule from her. He stopped, looked at the item, then at Ayliss.

"I still don't know why you take chances like this."

"Knowledge, Lee. Knowledge."

Selkirk shrugged at the answer, then produced a small metallic device from a jacket pocket. He inserted the capsule and stepped to the middle of the floor. Ayliss sat in one of the two chairs, and he looked in her direction.

"Ready?"

"Yes."

A tiny click broke the silence, and he lightly tossed the machine toward the ceiling. Paper-thin blades sprung open from its sides to disappear in a blur of motion, stopping its descent, then carrying it upward. Selkirk found his seat, and they waited until a dull glow materialized overhead. A narrow beam of blue light shot out of the floating platform, measuring the room's dimensions as it swung around in a circle.

With that completed, the glow blossomed until they were seated inside a shifting cloud of bright blue. The light abruptly dropped to almost nothing, and Ayliss felt the claustrophobic sensation that always seemed to accompany the experience. Just after that she was no longer in the room, and Selkirk had transformed into someone she had never met.

The floor was now hard-packed dirt, and in its center was a low fire inside a ring of round stones. Men sat to Ayliss's right and left, part of a circle that she quickly counted. Nine of them. It had been night when they'd made the prohibited recording, and so the figures were hazy at first. Fatigue uniforms, boots, and more than one bandage. A voice came from her right, and the recorder focused on the speaker by sharpening his features.

He was young, no more than twenty, and so thin that his face appeared to be painted directly onto his skull. His voice was soft, the words hesitant at first.

"I met Steve Wembley in Basic, and we were in the same squad once we got to the zone. Same team for four months, too, but after Locula they split us up to spread out the veterans. Same squad, though.

"He was the kind of guy who would share his last ration bar with you, without being asked. Just break it in half and hand you a piece. He always had some crazy story ready, to make you laugh when things were really shitty. Sometimes I'd wonder if he wasn't just making it all up."

The blurred figures responded with tight chuckles, bringing their shapes into resolution for the briefest of moments. All young, solemn, focused.

"I'm not saying anything happened to Steve and me that hasn't happened to everybody else, but we sure did end up in a lot of really bad spots. One time we were put outside the perimeter just a little too far. The lieutenant was worried the enemy would use this creek bed to sneak up on the platoon, so he had us hidden right next to it. Of course Sammy the Sim attacked in force that night.

"They came in standing up, running flat out, didn't even notice that creek bed, explosions all around and shit flying right over our heads. Incoming, outgoing, hugging the dirt, I swear some of them ran right over us at one point. Just after that I pulled out a grenade, but my hands were shaking so bad I couldn't arm it, so Steve reaches over and takes it from me.

"Didn't even look at the thing. He just tossed it away, shook his head like I was crazy, then crawled straight into the lieutenant's creek bed. It was maybe six inches deep, but that was six more inches under that shitstorm, and we were still there the next morning when a patrol came out looking for our bodies."

The other shades chuckled at that, their faces flickering in and out of existence. When the original speaker spoke again his voice was lower, muted, as if he'd remembered what they were doing.

"It's important to have a buddy like that. Somebody who'll stop you from doing that *really stupid* thing you were gonna do just because you couldn't think of anything better."

One of the other figures began speaking about the dead soldier, part of a group eulogy that had been a standard practice in the war zone for many years. Recordings of these tributes were prohibited by a Human Defense Force command structure that took full advantage of the enormous distance between the inhabited planets and the deployed troops to exercise a one-sided form of information discipline. Grieving families were receiving smuggled copies of the impromptu ceremonies more frequently now, and Command had labeled this trend a threat to the war effort. Possessing a copy of one of these rituals was punishable by a long term in prison, even for Olech Mortas's daughter.

Ayliss smiled when she pondered what the people running the war would do if they knew her true reason for watching the contraband recording. That she was actually looking for something that was a genuine threat to the war effort—and the apparatus that supported it. Viewing the ghostly figures surrounding her, she couldn't help thinking of Jan. Even then headed back to the zone when he could have avoided it. Once more an ignorant tool of their father.

She almost missed it, the reason Python had handed her this particular recording. Ayliss had given him some general guidelines, little things to look for that wouldn't tell him what she was trying to find. It made her feel like one of Command's intelligence officers, passing information requirements to the troops in the field without explaining why they were important.

A new face had taken up the collective story, a soldier so young that he looked like a child. He was smiling, reliving the memory.

"I hadn't even been assigned to a unit when I met

Steve. He was a corporal then, sent to pick me up from this crazy Force facility where I'd been sent when I got to the zone. Stupid headshrinkers—asking me all these questions about where I was from, did I get in a lot of fights, was I in a gang. I kept telling them I hadn't seen any combat yet, but they just kept saying that they were trying to establish a baseline for some bullshit study.

"Anyway, Steve had my orders when they finally let me go, and we were supposed to come right to the unit. Me, I didn't know *anything*, but here was this corporal who'd seen all this action so I just went with him. Next thing I know we'd stowed away on this supply ship headed to this tre-*men*dous base with clubs, hot chow, girls . . . boy did we have fun.

"We were both privates when we finally got to the outfit—"

Ayliss didn't hear the rest, her mind replaying the sentences that were most important to her.

Stupid headshrinkers—asking me all these questions about where I was from, did I get in a lot of fights, was I in a gang. I kept telling them I hadn't seen any combat yet, but they just kept saying that they were trying to establish a baseline for some bullshit study.

There. She felt pain in her palms, and forced her hands to release the arms of the chair. Finally, after all the long hours spent searching through the archives, all the mind-numbing inspections of the military hospitals and veterans-care facilities, all the interviews with returned soldiers whose distrust of Command—

and anyone associated with it—was so complete that their every answer was evasive. But there it was. The first indication that her suspicions weren't mere supposition, and that Command was actively digging into the psyches of the troops fighting the war.

If what they were doing with that knowledge was even half as extensive as she believed, it was going to generate a scandal that would remove her father from office and take away the only thing he truly cared about. Not his dead wife, his two children, his cronies, or his mistresses. Olech Mortas was going to lose his place in the game. And he was going to know who'd taken it from him.

The recording ended, even though she hadn't heard a word after the young soldier's revelation about a secret medical facility in the war zone where his personal aggression had been measured. The images and the fire evaporated, and she could see Selkirk again. Leaning forward in his seat, studying her with concern. Completely read in on her quest, and yet completely unable to understand why it was so important to her.

"Lee. We have to identify the unit this came from."

Approaching Unity, sir."

"Thank you, Jason." Olech smiled at the young staffer before the man walked off down the rolling office that was the chairman's personal underground train. Olech's immediate staff numbered more than one hundred men and women, and he prided himself on knowing all of them personally. Many more attendants were waiting at Unity Plaza, the sprawling complex that was both his headquarters and his home.

"You know what's strange? Every time I come back here, I feel completely detached." Olech spoke to Hugh Leeger, who was seated across from him studying a handheld.

"You were only gone for two days this trip, in constant communication the whole time. You've got an unusual idea of what 'detached' means."

The underground train sped along without a sound and almost without vibration, and Olech looked out at the olive-colored walls as they raced by. He briefly imagined himself as just a commuter on his way to work, but the sight of a security strongpoint studded with weaponry ruined the notion. He turned back to Leeger.

"I used to be gone for months on inspection tours. Those were multi-Threshold voyages, *really* deep space, and when I came back it was like I'd never left. Now that I'm not allowed to do anything even remotely like that, a two-day trip completely disorients me."

"There was a time when you weren't the Chairman of the Emergency Senate. And I'm not going to become the first security chief to lose a head of state in the Step." Leeger didn't make the obvious observation that he would probably share Olech's fate if anything ever happened to him. Leeger's predecessor had been killed protecting Olech during the chaotic gunplay that accompanied the murder of Interplanetary President Larkin.

"You thought you could lose one in his own private train tunnels. If I'd listened to your paranoia this thing would have no windows, and what would I look at then?"

"Plenty to look at right here in the car." It was no secret that young, attractive people constituted most of Olech's personal staff, and Leeger did his best to promote the mistaken assumption that the Chairman hired based on looks. Privately, he believed Olech had subconsciously replaced his own children when selecting the people who were his closest attendants. "And it was a mistake to put in the windows, no matter what kind of blast they can sustain."

"See? Paranoia. Utterly baseless concern. I'm directing mankind's first war in space, yet I'm in almost no danger at all."

"I wouldn't go that far."

Olech continued as if Leeger hadn't spoken. "I'm not sure if it's a good sign or a bad one, to be honest. I do my share of the whip-cracking in the alliance, and there are plenty of times when I have to say 'no' to people who are in a position to retaliate."

"You also hand out plenty of favors, and go out of your way to make the lesser members feel more important than they are. I'd say they balance pretty well."

"But I still have to call them out when they short the

war effort. That actually costs them, in real terms and prestige. You'd think they'd resent something like that."

"Maybe you've only caught them on the minor things, and they consider themselves lucky. Maybe they're getting away with murder, and you just don't know it."

Olech looked around the spacious compartment, glad to be away from the cramped office in the shuttle that had taken him to see Jan. Several of his private staffers sat on blue-padded seats, busy with various tasks, which made Olech smile. If security concerns were going to cut him off from much of the population, he was darn sure going to have real people around him at work.

One of those staffers, a pretty brunette seated on the blue cushions, abruptly set aside her handheld and donned a set of blacked-out goggles. She quietly acknowledged the incoming communication while slipping an electronic glove onto one hand. Shortly after that she became deeply involved in a whispered conversation, the gloved hand tapping away at a keyboard only her eyes could see.

Olech suppressed a laugh. "Remember the last full meeting of the Senate?"

Leeger turned in his seat, trying to identify whatever had lifted the Chairman's spirits. His eyes fell on the goggled staffer, and he almost laughed as well.

"You're thinking of Senator Bascom."

"Exactly. What an ass. Three times more assistants than anybody else in attendance, and he always had at least one them in the goggles. Even when they were walking."

The two men chuckled quietly, trying not to disrupt the work going on around them. "I remember that. Two attendants directing the poor guy's steps while he was supposedly handling vital messages for the very important Senator Bascom. I had one of my people chat that kid up later on; he was pretending the whole time and trying like hell not to trip. No messages coming or going. There never were."

"But that just makes sense. Who would want to communicate with Bascom if he wasn't standing right in front of them?"

They laughed again, but Olech's thoughts slowly returned to the disturbing topic of his own safety. No matter how distant the Sims might be, there was plenty of potential threat in close proximity. It was not lost on Olech that the tower he lived in had once been home to the murdered president of an earlier version of the same coalition he now led.

And while Earth was still seen as the predominant force in the alliance, Olech's power to influence the others was not absolute.

The short train slowed to a halt, and Olech saw one of the reasons why he wasn't considered a target by the government of at least one alliance member. Thick, rust-red hair fell to the shoulders of an attractive woman wearing a blue business suit that matched her eyes. Average height and weight, she showed a few minor wrinkles that came from an expressive face that wasn't afraid to laugh. The woman smiled warmly at the train, even though the glass was reflective and she couldn't be sure if Olech was watching.

But he always was, so she had no doubts.

The platform was bathed in a bright glow from above that suggested a skylight even though they were directly underneath the broad tower that was Olech's home and place of business. A tile mosaic made up of tiny lacquered squares covered the walls around the platform and the tunnel for many yards, a design conceived by the redheaded woman. Even the guard station had been subsumed into the tableau, which had the overall effect of transforming the tunnel and the platform into a dock on a subterranean river.

Olech was the first off the train, and the woman stood waiting until he covered the distance and took her in his arms. She stood immobile on purpose, so that the embrace would not occur in the path of the numerous staffers who would be detraining as well. The chairman's retinue was a busy group, and they passed the man and the woman in a long-standing longstanding tradition where they utterly ignored them.

In continuance of this homecoming custom, the members of Olech's immediate staff moved quickly to the waiting elevators and headed up into the complex. Alone now except for the guards, Olech broke the kiss but kept the embrace.

"Coming back to you is always so special. Even when I've only been gone for a while."

"You were gone?" Reena's eyes twinkled, and he pulled her in tight again.

Nuzzling her marvelous hair, Olech recalled how the woman in his arms had come into his life as a minister from Celestia, a rich planet where her brother ran the show. Her political genius and diplomatic acumen had attracted him right from the start, but they'd worked together for years before declaring their mutual affection. That had been long after his wife had died, when even the most libertine of his allies had begun to question the steady succession of women passing through his bed. Beautiful, every one of them, but none of them befitting a man of his station.

Reena Corlipso had put an end to all of that, and even if Olech suspected she'd been urged to do so by his partners—and especially her brother—it made no difference because it made so much sense. Earth and Celestia were the two biggest players in the alliance and, like an arranged marriage of old, the pairing of Olech and Reena had brought the governments of both worlds much closer together.

It didn't hurt that the two of them were also an excellent match and that the bond between them was genuine.

"How is Jan?" Her words brought him back to a less pleasant reality, and Olech gave her a slight headshake. Taking his hand, Reena turned toward the waiting elevator.

A short time later, Olech Mortas burst through the rippling surface of his private swimming pool. The pool doubled as his safe room, where he and Reena could discuss the topics they did not wish overheard—which meant they spent a lot of time there.

Reena had continued her tile-mosaic motif in the room's decoration, so that the chairman's seal stood out boldly on the pool's light blue floor. When the lights were turned down, as they were now, the arched ceiling resembled a medieval painting of the night sky. Brightly colored planets whirled in the dark background, the sun wore a happy expression, and comets dragged sparking tails behind them.

Reena was waiting for him when he swam up, her arms spread along the side of the pool while she bicycled her legs under the water. The red hair was braided behind her head, and the water lapped against her nipples as he swam over. Forty years old, born the year the war began, Reena Corlipso was what Olech considered a real woman. Her breasts were large and her hips curved away from her waist, but her muscles were toned and her blue eyes were alive with intelligence. They kissed for a long time before he pulled her away from the side, his long legs just reaching the bottom at that end of the pool. They slowly twirled in place, gently bouncing as he pushed them along, trying to take her into deeper water.

"No." She gave him a firm look. "We need to talk first."

He held on, still pulling Reena away from the shallow end, but her strong arms slipped from around his neck and easily pushed him off. Both of them routinely swam laps for exercise, and Reena gracefully glided off toward a small spillway where water flowed into the pool. A break in the wall allowed access to a round tub equipped with underwater jets, and Olech obediently followed her into it. A continuous stream of heated water flowed across them as they sat on a submerged bench, and she let him kiss her again before they began to speak, close in and quiet.

"I'm sorry Jan didn't take the offer."

"Maybe I should have followed your advice and made the announcement before seeing him. Left him nowhere to go."

"He still might have refused. And then where would you be?"

"Probably making a second announcement about my brave son asking to be sent back to the war zone instead of becoming an ambassador . . . which we should probably do anyway." A brief shake of the head. "Kid doesn't trust me at all. Neither of them do."

"I know you don't want to hear this, but maybe it's time to tell them."

"There's never going to be a time. I can give them the absolute truth about their mother and their upbringing, and they'll just assume it's one more lie. Look at Ayliss. She took a job she didn't want with an outfit she despises just so she can dig around for something that could embarrass me. She's getting better at slipping my surveillance, and she's got that fool Selkirk helping her do it."

"She'll get tired of playing revenge soon enough. And even if she does find something, we'll just muddy the waters. Not like we haven't done it before."

Another kiss, in gratitude. "Don't know what I'd do without you."

"Sure you do—you'd be miserable again. All those years, and I was right in front of you the whole time."

He nuzzled her ear, then spoke directly into it in a voice almost too low to hear. Olech described everything that Jander had told him about the alien, finishing with, "The thing communicated with him telepathically, through two decon chamber walls. Sound and images. Jan said at one point it was as if he was reliving the creature's injury, when they were hijacking the Wren."

"Do you think we've finally seen one of the Sims' creators?"

"Maybe. Everything we suspect about whatever made the Sims has been conjecture, so it's hard to know. It would have to be incredibly advanced, so a telepathic entity that can change its shape to replicate a living human certainly fits that description.

"But why only one of them? Was this some sort of probe?"

"Can we be sure there was only one? Command hasn't always been reliable about what's happening in the zone."

"They were pretty rattled by this. And they didn't

hesitate to pass the word to every unit out there. Every Forcemember in the war zone knows what happened, and yet there hasn't been a single report about anything like what Jan encountered."

"They said they detected a plague virus on the alien?"

"Yes." Olech's whisper was long for a single syllable. "That part makes no sense at all. Why would it be carrying something like that? Even if it infected the entire corps headquarters, even if it wiped them out, a virus wouldn't have gone far beyond that. Very low payoff, when you consider the delivery system."

"Think it was for deception, in case the thing was found out? Conceal its true purpose?"

"Exactly. According to Jan, the alien told him it was all a ruse right from the start. It said they included a Spartacan Scout among the maroons because a Spartacan would have to head for a high-level headquarters with the information that he'd found a new Sim colony. That's one reason they ended up at Glory Main."

"That Spartacan would have been passed even higher if his information was important enough."

"That's true, but once the group got back to Force control the alien probably wouldn't have continued up the chain with the scout." He shook his head. "None of this makes any sense."

Reena waited, comfortable in his embrace and enjoying the rush of warm water, but after a time Olech merely leaned his head against hers and went silent. She admired his ability to mentally dismantle the many complex machinations of their political rivals—and allies—but she'd also come to know when he'd simply shut down the machine. She let him rest for a time, then spoke.

"There is one thing we do know, and we're going to have to prepare a response. The heads of the coalition planets are never going to believe that the alien selected Jander by chance."

"Apparently it did. The thing told Jan that it believed his status as my missing son was what blew its cover."

"I don't doubt that, but none of the other heads, or even your fellow senators, are going to believe it. And it doesn't help that it took place in Glory Corps space."

"The Senate's Own."

"The most political corps in the war zone. Add in that this was Jan's first assignment, and it stinks of some kind of secret negotiation gone wrong."

His hands had tightened on her shoulders, making Reena understand that Olech had never even considered this possibility. The fingers relaxed almost immediately.

"What should we do about that?"

"Nothing." She shifted around to look into his eyes. "They won't believe any explanation we offer anyway. If they make an outright accusation, we ask them just why we told so many people about the alien if we were clandestinely communicating with it. And why, if we were trying to keep this quiet, we had Jan bring the thing to a corps headquarters where it was promptly incinerated."

"Keep going."

"Believe it or not, we got lucky when Jan turned you down. If you'd made him an ambassador after so short a time in the war zone, it would have proven all the suspicions. But he went back out, and as a new lieutenant looking for assignment to a combat platoon, so they'll at least have to wonder. About that, and about something else."

"Which is?"

"If this really was a secret meeting between your son and this incredible creature . . . what do you know now that they wish they knew too?"

The room was in the very core of the broad tower that stood in the dead center of the Unity Plaza complex. It was physically blocked off from the outside world and, although it wasn't as large as Olech's pool-cum–safe room, its ceiling was just as high. Its bare gray walls lacked Reena's artistic touch, and its only fixture was a high-backed chair with black cushioning. All hard angles and no legs, the seat looked like it had been carved out of a block of dark stone.

Olech Mortas sat down in it, alone, as the chamber's doors sealed him inside. His thoughts were scattered now, something he recognized as his mind's reaction to having focused on too many interconnected issues for too long. Using a complicated series of secure video communications, he'd personally briefed the alliance's senior leaders on the alien's appearance. Despite their loudly stated surprise, Olech suspected some of them had already learned of the creature's existence. It was impossible to keep the story hidden, and the disinformation campaign for the masses had already begun. As suggested by both Reena and Hugh Leeger, Olech had not disclosed the entity's telepathic communication with Jan.

No matter how the truth was shaded or bent, there was no denying that the alien represented an enormous change to the war. And even though he'd been waiting for such an event for a very long time, Olech Mortas now needed to view the entire conflict with fresh eyes. His palms rested on the wide, flat arms of the boxy chair, and the fingers of his right hand touched a control panel that he now activated. The room's dim light vanished, leaving him in darkness, and the voice of a trusted technician spoke through the void.

"Ready, sir?"

"Go ahead." Olech wondered if Jan's telepathic experience with the alien had been like that, a disembodied voice coming at his psyche from out of nowhere, but the room came alive and he refocused his thoughts. Light flickered across the blackness, and the chair began to move. A single lifting cylinder slowly slid upward, raising him to the very center of the space.

And that was exactly what the room was. Space. The chair itself vanished, giving Olech the illusion that he was free-floating. The light waves finished their work, and Earth blossomed out of the darkness as if he were viewing its creation. Blue water, brown terrain, and white cloud that blocked his vision as if he were orbiting the home planet in a space suit.

The projected imagery combined decades' worth of charting and outright simulation, but it was the only way that Olech Mortas could keep the vast array of vital information in perspective. Using the chair's control panel or, more commonly, directing the technicians by voice, he could figuratively travel anywhere in the mapped regions of the cosmos.

"Take me to the construction zone."

The Earth receded swiftly, giving the impression that he had turned away from it. The chair itself could rotate a full revolution, but usually the projected imagery performed the movements. Olech could have asked to start out at the construction zone, the belts of space stations cranking out the ships and weapons and engines of the war, but it was more fun to take the ride.

The construction zone was nowhere near the war zone, but it was a great distance away from any of the inhabited planets and so he flashed through an enormous amount of space in just a few moments. No rocket could travel that fast, and no one could get to either zone without the aid of the Step, but all the same Olech liked to imagine he was strapped to the nose of a racing ship spearing its way through the void. Boiling dust and bizarre arrays of light were the most common sights when he moved like this, and Olech was always struck by just how dirty it all seemed. Like diving into even the clearest ocean water and being surprised by the particles and the seaweed and the undifferentiated fragments that drifted in constant suspension.

A hair-thin line of white resolved itself into the construction zone a moment later, and he felt vertigo when the projection slowed, then stopped. The titanic rigs were everywhere, maximizing the advantage of zero gravity to create the machines of combat and send them forward without having to break free from the surfaces and atmospheres of the grasping planets. Shuttles and drone robots passed between and among the stations, and various ships of war stood perpetual guard.

Clicking on a button brought up a small arrow of light that he maneuvered using sensors in the chair's arm. Stopping the arrow on a station caused a status to appear next to it, reflecting its current productivity and supply levels. Large teams of technicians and analysts monitored these statistics for him, but Olech had his own reasons to review them personally in this format. The stations in the construction zone had been paid for by the alliance, but they were run by interplanetary corporations that often followed agendas tangential to his own.

Despite the army-sized staff that supported him, Olech was able to memorize and collate vast amounts of data in his head. More importantly, he knew what was significant and how it all came together, which was one of the primary purposes of this room. The war zone was confusing enough all by itself, starting with the very human tendency to see it as a front line when it was no such thing. If seen from far enough away, it certainly did appear as a barrier between the approaching Sims and the inhabited planets, but it was by no means a cohesive defensive belt.

Mankind might be fighting the Sims for the habitable planets in a vast but limited region of space, but that zone was constantly shifting because the planets themselves, and everything around them, never stopped moving. Sim fleets had appeared out of nowhere many times during the war, all without Step technology, and so Olech Mortas had trained himself to think in terms of threats that could come from any and every direction. Among its many benefits, the room helped him to maintain that orientation.

"Take me to Platinus," he ordered, and the void whirled in front of his eyes. Flashes of light that could have been comets or distant suns, the sensation of flying, long stretches of pure blackness hammering home the distances in humanity's war with the Sims. At one point the entire room flickered red, just for a moment, and a mechanical voice announced that he had crossed the CHOP line. The acronym was originally a nautical term indicating the boundaries between fleets at sea, but the CHOP line in this conflict was of even wider import. It marked the beginning of the military's jurisdiction in space, and the coalition government had established numerous laws with extraordinary penalties for crossing the boundary without authorization—both ways.

Once again Olech experienced the impossible deceleration, before a single habitable planet in one of the many solar systems of the war came into focus. Only a few years earlier it had been designated UP-2716. UP stood for Unoccupied Planet, and the four digits that followed were selected at random for reasons of information security. The Sim enemy might not be able to comprehend or even form the sounds of human speech, but they understood numbers, and so the four digits identifying a planet in the war zone followed no set order. When the Sims had landed on UP-2716 it had become EP-2716, Enemy Planet 2716, until the landing of human troops had changed it to CP-2716. Contested Planet 2716.

When the Force had triumphed there, CP-2716 had become Secured Planet 2716 or SP-2716. Only after a planet was secured did it receive a name, and this one had been called Platinus because of the vast deposits of minerals vital to the war effort that had been discovered there.

They'd also found other resources that would be highly valuable once the war was over, and so Platinus was one of the planets that received Olech's special attention. Force-supplied information suggested that nothing unexpected was happening there, but the Chairman relied on other indicators to provide a more accurate picture. Much of the status feeds he could call up were provided by agencies he didn't completely trust, and so the reports from his network of informants were added into the display as well.

As could be expected, Force efforts to extract and

exploit war-specific minerals were going full bore. However, data provided by Olech's supplementary sources showed that development of Platinus as a colony was far ahead of other planets in the war zone that had been conquered much earlier. Excessive numbers of troops were based there, and Olech's spies had already tipped him off that settlements were being mapped out by the army corps that owned that region of space.

It was an old-fashioned land grab that would have done justice to the worst of the colonial powers of Earth's rapacious history, and it was not easy to prevent. Despite Olech's best efforts, several alliance planets had managed to create corps-level units composed entirely of their own citizens. The commanders of those organizations frequently saw themselves less as Force officers and more as representatives of their home worlds, and their different power plays were a constant source of friction. Their greed knew no bounds, to the extent that Olech had put an end to an earlier practice by which the Force would claim an entire planet as a military base by giving it the designation MC, for Military-Controlled Planet.

Over the years Olech had become skilled at thwarting these land grabs, but he was never free of the nagging doubt that the war was simply too large to be managed.

Which was another reason for his special room. He knew that some of his critics referred to the boxy chair as Olech Mortas's throne, and that they mocked it as nothing more than a high-technology amusement park ride. In the privacy of his own thoughts, he sometimes agreed with that notion.

Somewhere out there, in this limitless battlefield with so many uncontrollable variables and so many ways to be fatally wrong, waited an opponent whose very existence was doubted by some of his alliance partners. An opponent so advanced that it was able to create the Sims and use them to wage a proxy war without ever showing itself. The appearance of the alien—whatever it had been—was additional proof that the void contained entities that were simply beyond human comprehension. Just thinking of the shape-shifting being that Jan had encountered was enough to drive him to distraction. As he always had in the past, Olech Mortas forced his mind from the things he could not control to the things he could.

"Okay, that's enough. Turn on the lights." He allowed himself a rueful chuckle. "Bring me down to Earth."

In the seconds before his command was obeyed, the chairman glanced around in the blankness and imagined a tiny dot of light, carrying his only son back to the war.

CHAPTER THREE

"**W**elcome to First Brigade, Lieutenant. Please have a seat." Colonel Jonah Watt returned Mortas's salute from behind a large metal desk. The brigade's head-quarters stood on a wooded hill, and Watt's office occupied one of its corners. Broad windows allowed him to observe the lower ground where the brigade's three battalions were situated. Military-Controlled Planet 1932, MC-1932, had been wrested from the Sims early in the war. The Orphan Brigade was not the first unit to have occupied this ground, nor was it the brigade's first home.

Mortas sat down on an old couch facing the desk. The long trip to the war zone had ended the day before, but he still felt a sense of private accomplishment. Sealed in his transit tube and awaiting the loss of consciousness that would allow him to make the multi-Step journey, he'd remembered a different tube and his first attempt to reach a fighting unit. Knowing how that other trip had ended, Mortas had been genuinely relieved when he awoke to find himself on the warship that would deliver him to the Orphan Brigade. He'd been even happier when his stiff gray uniform had been replaced by a set of weathered fatigues bearing the green, black, and brown of woodland camouflage. Every soldier he'd seen so far had been dressed the same way, and the slightly beat-up appearance of his new clothes helped him to fit in.

"I expect you've read the unit précis you were furnished." Watt was stocky and in his midforties, with dark hair cut very close to his dark skin. His voice was calm and instructive. "So you already know that this brigade has a lineage that dates almost to the beginning of the war. What you don't know, and what nobody knows, is exactly how this came to be an independent brigade.

"The records are quite spotty, not surprising given the chaos in the early years of this conflict, but I personally suspect we started out as the remnants of a decimated division or larger. It's my understanding that casualty figures were so extreme at war's start that Command was afraid to report them accurately. So instead of combining a few beat-up units into one, they kept them all on the books and fed them replacements." The eyes twinkled, and the corners of Watt's mouth turned up slightly. "I think the Orphans somehow got lost in that little shuffle, then somebody probably decided it wouldn't hurt to have an emergency brigade handy."

Mortas stirred uneasily, not sure if he was supposed to respond. Watt continued, with no indication of whether or not he'd expected a comment.

"So that's what we are. A fire brigade. We're used when and how we're needed, often on short notice. Which means we have to be ready for just about anything. We're currently in a period of rest and refitting, but you'll find that the tempo of our training is quite challenging. You'll be getting a platoon filled with top-notch NCOs and a lot of experienced non-NCO enlisted men, so you're in a position to learn from soldiers who really know their stuff."

Watt rose, signaling with a wave that Mortas was to remain seated. Unlike most of the soldiers Mortas had seen so far, Watt's fatigues were freshly pressed. The brigade commander looked out the window for a moment, hands clasped behind his back, before sitting at the other end of the couch.

"You have only one job here, Lieutenant. And that's being a platoon leader. Everybody knows who your father is and what you experienced with the alien. So here's how this is going to work:

"This brigade is made up of warfighters. Most of the men who volunteered to come here did so with the understanding that sometimes we get handed jobs that are too big for us. Many of them did that because they were sick of the second-guessing and other nonsense you find in far too many of the units out here. That was one of the worst effects of the Purge: it fast-tracked the careers of some extremely political officers who now hold high positions in the Force.

"Unfortunately, that means that some very important decisions are made based on factors that have nothing to do with winning the war or preserving the lives of our troops. You as an officer, no matter what rank you attain, must never forget that we're fighting to win the war, and to keep as many of our soldiers alive as possible.

"So from this point forward you're not the son of the Chairman of the Emergency Senate. You're Lieutenant Jander Mortas, platoon leader in the First Independent Brigade."

"Thank you, sir. I was hoping that would be the case."

A momentary smile. "I'm not surprised. I read the report of your experience with the alien infiltrator, and as far as I'm concerned you did a damn fine job in a tough situation."

"I wouldn't have made it without the others, sir." The words came out easily, and for the first time the memory of his dead friends didn't fill Mortas with regret.

"Well said. The Orphan Brigade is a team, and the team-building skills you demonstrated on Roanum got you into this unit. You relied on the talents and experience of the people who were with you, and I encourage you to do the same thing with your platoon.

"Which brings me to another issue. You'll be in First Battalion, but we have an excellent lieutenant in Second Battalion whom I understand is an acquaintance of yours. His name is Emile Dassa, and his father was executed for his connection to a general officer who died in the Purge. Do you know him?"

Mortas's feeling of calm evaporated. For a moment he wondered if the brigade commander had been lulling him into a false sense of security, but quickly decided the man must already know the full story.

"Yes, sir. I only met Dassa once, years ago in prep school. He made some accusations against my father, there was a fight, and he disappeared."

"Disappeared is right. He was abducted from your school's infirmary and forcibly enlisted in a colonial militia unit out here. He served with distinction, got transferred to the Force, and won a battlefield commission shortly after that. He's done a splendid job as one of our platoon leaders.

"He's been in the war for five years now, and his promotion to captain should be coming through shortly. He told me about your previous association when he heard you were coming to the brigade.

"The Emile Dassa you met at school is not the Lieutenant Dassa with whom you'll be serving now. He's internalized the values of this unit, and I can tell you from personal observation that he's left his previous life behind. I doubt you'll be seeing much of each other, but when you do I expect you to both to act as brothers in arms and part of this team. Can I expect that from you?"

"Certainly, sir."

"Good. The Purge was an awful thing, and it left some animosities that are nothing short of vendettas. Honestly, I've always been a little worried that somebody might decide to drop this brigade into a real meat grinder just to get rid of Emile." He nodded, as if confirming his own words. "Yes, Lieutenant. We have some weak, demented individuals out here who would do something like that just to curry favor with other weak, demented individuals further up the chain of command.

"And that's another reason why I accepted your application. You and Emile may just balance each other out for us. Anybody trying to harm this brigade to score points with one side or the other from the Purge would be taking the chance of killing both of you." Watt smiled. "The kind of people we're talking about don't like to take chances."

Mortas's head was simply swimming. The turmoil of his voluntary return to the war zone, combined with the arduous journey and the stress of reporting to his first duty assignment, was tough enough to handle but not unexpected. Now he was seeing that even here, in this reputedly apolitical unit, his father's deeds and misdeeds were still with him.

Watt took his silence as a signal to continue.

"I'm glad that's settled. Because there is one more thing that we need to discuss. The entire Force has been warned about the alien, but you're the only Forcemember who actually interacted with the thing.

As commander of this brigade, it is my duty to learn as much as I can about this new threat, but it's also my duty to make sure you get to focus on your new job.

"No doubt you'll have to answer the odd question here and there, from members of your platoon and other units, but I've already made it clear you are not to become our resident alien expert. So I'm going to have my intelligence officer join us now, and I'd like you to walk the two of us through your experience with whatever that thing was. After that, Intel will work up a briefing that will be promulgated throughout the brigade. After you've been here awhile, you should start to refer questions about the alien to that report."

The smile returned, and Mortas decided that it was genuine.

"We're not going to turn you into a celebrity, but we're not going to turn you into a freak, either." He extended his hand, and Mortas took it. "Welcome to the Orphans, Jan."

An enlisted man drove Mortas down the hill to First Battalion, and the man didn't say a thing the entire way. Mortas didn't mind the silence. Mulling Colonel Watt's words, he looked at the passing scenery through the side of the vehicle where the door should have been. Except for the windshield and a rubberized fabric stretched over its top, the conveyance was open to the elements. It was hot outside, and he enjoyed the breeze.

Everything around him was green, from the thick forest to the vast fields of trimmed grass, and he watched a family of small rodent-like animals sprint across the road when they came around a sharp turn. The sky was clear of clouds, and he'd already been told that the temperature never actually got cold on MC-1932.

The astonishing news about Emile Dassa had magnified the surrealism of his arrival in the war zone. Mortas knew that Dassa had disappeared from the prep-school infirmary the night of their confrontation, but he'd almost forgotten the incident during his years at university. Dassa had gone a completely different route, spending all of that time in the war zone and covering himself with glory.

Mortas calculated that Dassa would probably be only twenty, and it surprised him to realize that was the same age Corporal Cranther had been when he died on Roanum. Cranther had spent the previous five years in the war and, like Dassa, had been forced into service.

Mortas shook his head as the road left the cover of the trees. When the vehicle reached the base of the hill, rectangles of manicured grass appeared on both sides. The open areas continued in front of them, but widely separated groups of two-story buildings soon materialized. Beige in color, they were topped with rows of wavelike tiles bleached a dull orange by the sun.

Although he didn't recognize it right away, the three battalion areas of the First Brigade were all laid out in identical fashion. Fronting a long road, the head-quarters buildings faced the brigade headquarters hill with their backs to a lower, level stretch of ground. The long barracks housing each battalion's three infantry companies stood in a row to one side of that open area, perpendicular to the headquarters. Mortas was able to make out a tall tower on the other side of the First Battalion area, outfitted with a rock-climbing surface on one side and flat planking on the other, presumably for rappelling.

The driver stopped the vehicle behind the headquarters of First Battalion and was gone as soon as Mortas alighted. A ghost of a breeze brushed his cheeks, and Mortas realized he was alone for the first time since being awakened in his transit tube days earlier. He'd removed the cloth cap bearing his pin-on lieutenant's insignia after almost losing it to the wind on the ride down, so he took it out of a large cargo pocket and put it back on. When he'd been issued his fatigues, Mortas had learned that pin-on hat rank would be its only adornment. The supply sergeant giving him this nugget of wisdom had explained that the Orphans could be sent to so many different hot spots that one of the first indications of an approaching mission was the issue of fatigues in a different camouflage pattern. Lowering his voice, he'd also said that even the hat rank was removed in the field for fear of Sim snipers.

Looking out over the expanse below him, Mortas was able to identify the markings of two different kinds of athletic fields and another road just beyond.

Farther out, the woods started again and then climbed another hill that blocked his vision. Mortas was just beginning to wonder where everyone was when he heard a frustrated male voice from around the side of the building.

Walking over, he spotted two young soldiers fiddling with a military radio on a wooden table. Both men had their hair cut very short and were dressed in green T-shirts and black running shorts. One had a set of earphones on his head, and the other was working the dials on the radio set. It was one of the larger versions, usually vehicle-mounted but sometimes carried on someone's back, and a snaking black cable attached it to a three-legged antenna dish set up nearby.

"Station One, Station One, this is Station Two. Over." An impossibly young voice came from one of the soldiers, and the man waited a few moments before repeating the call. He did this one more time before sweeping the earphones from his head. "Fuck!"

"Fuck is right." The other soldier seemed amused by the difficulty, and Mortas, mindful of his status as an outsider, fought off a smile. "Just came back from maintenance. I told 'em it was in that mover that went off the bridge, but they wouldn't exchange it no matter how much water spilled out of it."

Muttering, the man who'd been wearing the headphones began disconnecting different leads on the radio and cleaning them with a rag. The other soldier's eyes passed over Mortas for just an instant, then he too became interested in fixing whatever was wrong.

Having spent his teen years in different prep schools, Mortas recognized the refusal to acknowledge the existence of a new guy. His face was just beginning to redden when a voice spoke behind him.

"Are you Lieutenant Mortas?"

He turned to see an older man approaching. Dressed in the same green T-shirt and black shorts, the stranger was soaked in sweat that beaded on a taut scalp shaved almost bald. Medium height, the man was deeply tanned and appeared to have no extra fat on him at all. Several lines creased his forehead, but his skin hugged his body so tightly that they were almost flat.

"Yes. Yes, that's me."

The man saluted while coming closer, and extended his hand before Mortas was able to return the military greeting. When he took the hand it was as if his fingers were in a vise, but the pressure dropped away immediately.

"Glad to meet you, Lieutenant. I'm Sergeant Major Zacker. Brigade said you were on the way." The man's dark eyes overtly scrutinized him, sliding from his head to his toes. An intrigued smile sprouted on his lips, and he spoke while walking toward the back door. "Colonel Alden's waiting inside, so we should get stepping."

Mortas followed him through the door and up a short flight of stairs, the battalion's most senior enlisted man talking the whole time.

"You're lucky to be assigned to First Battalion, sir, and in my opinion your platoon sergeant is the best in the brigade. You're going to B Company, which is funny because so many of the B Companies I've known have been such strange animals. Ya see, that whole A, B, and C designation carries a weird side effect that I've observed in a lot of different places.

"Your standard A Company is the power in most battalions even when they're not all that good, and your standard C Company is usually competing to knock them off the top of the mountain. That leaves your standard B Company in the unenviable position of either competing with C Company just for the honor of competing with A Company, or saying 'Fuck it' and doing their own thing."

Zacker stopped when they reached a large central room with big windows. Stairs led down to the building's front doors and up to its second story, and Mortas saw a group of offices through a door to his left.

"The thing is, our B Company is neither. They don't compete with the other two companies, but they don't say 'Fuck it' either. They're tough, they're tactically sound, and they don't much care what anybody else thinks. Me, I think ol' B Company . . . competes with B Company. And I think that's outstanding."

The sergeant major walked through the side door into what turned out to be the adjutant's office. Three other offices led off from there, and in time Mortas would learn one belonged to Zacker while the other two belonged to the battalion executive officer and the battalion's commander, Colonel Beekrek Alden. The adjutant, a captain in rumpled fatigues, exchanged greetings with Mortas so quickly that the new lieutenant didn't catch his name. He rose and entered the colonel's office to announce him, and Mortas was preparing to meet his boss's boss when Zacker spoke again.

"Your company commander's relatively new to the brigade, but he has an excellent war record. Your company first sergeant is very strong even though he's too banged up to deploy with us. Don't be afraid to go to either of them with questions, but I'd recommend talking to your platoon sergeant first. Good habit to get into."

The adjutant walked past them and returned to his desk, so the sergeant major took Mortas by the arm and steered him toward the colonel's office.

"Once you're settled into your job, come on by and shoot the shit with me. I'd like to hear about that bad ol' alien you met on Roanum."

Mortas was just turning to enter the battalion commander's office when the man appeared in front of him. Colonel Alden was stocky like Colonel Watt, and short hair was obviously standard among the Orphans.

Alden shook Mortas's hand and turned him in the opposite direction. "Welcome aboard, Lieutenant. I'm sorry to cut this short, but I was just called to brigade. Walk with me."

They headed for the back steps that Mortas had ascended only moments earlier. Alden spoke while donning a camouflaged soft cap.

"I read the report of your experience on Roanum, and I feel you performed quite well there. You still haven't had any actual combat experience, so your company commander will be putting you through a crash course on what you need to know to lead your platoon in the real thing—everything from casualty evacuation to resupply operations."

Alden stopped once they were outside, and Mortas did as well.

"The most important skill for you to master is supporting arms. This brigade is designed to be moved on a moment's notice, so we lack some of the organic firepower of a normal Force brigade. As a result, every now and then we end up outgunned. We make up that difference by maximizing all available assets, from orbital bombardment to drone fighters and gunships."

A wheeled vehicle rolled around the corner of the building and stopped in front of them, obviously the colonel's ride.

"Which brings me to something I believe very strongly. Every successful organization makes the most of its resources, and the resource with the greatest potential payoff is the human resource. You, me, and every man in this battalion has a brain and a desire to survive, and I want to get everything that combination can give us.

"In this outfit we let every man do his job, then we push him to do some things that *aren't* his job. Do that effectively, and you'll create a valuable asset. Someone who's always thinking, shows initiative in the absence of orders, and is ready to offer sound advice. Listen to that advice, Lieutenant."

Alden climbed into the front seat of the camouflaged vehicle.

"Remember that good units walk a thin line between indiscipline and ineffectiveness. Ignore the rules too often and you've got a mob, but enforce the rules too strictly and you've got a herd. Any questions?"

"No, sir."

"Okay then." He signaled the driver to go ahead, and Mortas took a step back. Just as the vehicle began to roll, Alden pointed a finger at him. "You need to learn to talk more."

He gave Mortas a wink, and then he was gone.

Looking around, Mortas noticed that he was in the exact same spot where he'd met the sergeant major minutes earlier. The two soldiers with the radio were there, still unable to communicate, and he decided to take a short walk. He probably should have reentered the headquarters to see the adjutant, but he needed time to digest the information and advice that had been thrown at him in the last hour.

Walking around the side of the building, he looked up the hill to see more lush greenery and a row of military-style housing that was probably reserved for the senior officers. There was a lot of it, too much for even a brigade's worth of majors and colonels, but it appeared well maintained and he wondered who lived there.

The road in front of the battalion headquarters was long and intermittently lined with a curious type of tall tree. It reminded him of palm trees on Earth, except the bare stalk rose up to a chaotic tangle of vine-like branches where he would have expected droopy fronds. A brightly colored bird was singing inside the tree nearest to him, and for a moment he was back on Roanum, walking with a column of exhausted Sim troops who didn't realize he and Trent and Gorman were human. The Sims, unable to form the vowels and consonants of human speech, communicated with sounds that resembled the chirping of birds.

A male voice sounded from down the street, and Mortas turned to see a squad of soldiers shuffling toward him. They were in a tight column, moving in a fashion that was somewhere between a fast walk and a trot. Bareheaded, they wore the green T-shirts and black shorts that he now believed was the brigade's PT uniform, but every man was also wearing the torso armor of the walking infantry.

Human Defense Force body protection was modular, and the armless torso armor was its most basic element. It could be augmented with a set of shoulder armor that had always reminded Mortas of his lacrosse pads, separate pieces for the upper and lower arms, and similar wraparounds for the shins, knees, and thighs. An armored groin protector was also available, but it was decidedly uncomfortable for anyone who had to march anywhere, so it was seldom seen in the walking infantry.

He briefly thought of the Banshee commander he'd met at Glory Main, the one who had saved Cranther's fighting knife for him. The Banshees were all-female fighting units who went into combat in powered suits of armor that were too expensive to be issued to the entire Force. The alien pretending to be Amelia Trent had told Mortas that the Banshees painted breasts and vaginas on their armor before going into battle, to let the all-male Sim fighting units know who they were up against. According to the alien, the Banshees refused to end the practice no matter how harshly Command punished them for it.

The torso armor for the walking infantry was flat black because it would be covered by camouflage fabric. Like the chest protection itself, the camouflage covers were two pieces, front and back. The rear section snapped onto the armor and was left bare to make room for a rucksack, except for a row of slots at the bottom where canteens were usually attached. The front half was likewise affixed to the armor, and the majority of a soldier's ammunition was carried there. The chest camouflage could be opened down the center so the wearer could lie prone or crawl across the ground, and a strap at its top went over the wearer's head to rest behind the neck. In a tough fight, the ammunition of the fallen could be removed with a good sharp tug on the strap and carried to the rest of the fighters, while still leaving a wounded man with body protection and water.

The male voice sounded again, closer now, and he saw an NCO who was shuffling along outside the rapidly approaching column. Despite his shorn head, the sergeant was clearly much older than the others. He was speaking to a thin soldier in the center of the hustling line who appeared to be having difficulty with the exercise.

"You think this is tough? Wait until you're loaded up with a weapon, ammo, water, rations, and whatever else they decide to make us carry." The voice wasn't a shout, but it didn't have to be. A quick look at the other faces showed that they ran the gamut from calm to queasy, and Mortas decided that the straining members of the squad were new men. "You're gonna be *dreaming* of the days when this was all you were hauling."

The squad went by, boots crunching on the pavement, but Mortas was suddenly struck by the number of scars on the exposed limbs. Some linear, some curled, some whitened with time while others were red or purple. Having grown up in the war he was no stranger to wounded veterans, but he'd never seen so much scar tissue in one place before.

As they passed, the sergeant gave him a knowing leer that blossomed into a grin that could have been mirth or malice. He was well up the road before Mortas was sure that the inch-wide red scar just above the man's left knee went all the way around his cruelly muscled leg.

"**Y**ou must have command philosophy coming out of your ears by now." The huge man walking next to

Mortas was Major Hatton, First Battalion's executive officer. He'd collected him from the front of the head-quarters just after the squad in torso armor had dis-appeared, suggesting that they go to the mess hall for lunch.

"Honestly, sir, I'm having a hard time just remem-bering all the names."

Hatton wore the same style fatigues as Mortas and had donned the brimmed soft cap as well. Three inches over Mortas's six feet, he moved like a bear as they went down the walkway toward the mess hall. The long buildings Mortas had seen earlier turned out to be four in number, one for each of the companies and another for the chow hall and the personnel from the battalion headquarters company.

"Don't sweat it. It's like that with every new unit. The first few days you can barely find your way around, and you can't tell whether the latest guy you're talking to is the village idiot or the corps com-mander. Although"—he gave Mortas a quick glance—"sometimes that's the same guy."

That last comment caught Mortas off guard, and he chuckled. They passed between two barracks, and when they rounded the corner a short line of soldiers was waiting to enter the mess hall. Hatton continued, once they'd joined the queue.

"The whole brigade's on a bit of a stand-down right now. They had us doing a major cleanup on this one Hab, a search-and-destroy in this really brutal terrain, and it went longer than it was supposed to. Lots of nickel-and-dime with the remnants of this Sim battalion that was hiding out in this mountain chain."

A soldier in line in front of them, also dressed in the woodland fatigues but wearing no rank, turned and smiled at Hatton. "What a motherfucker *that* was. How many of them did we finally bag, sir?"

"Confirmed, about a hundred. Counted 'em myself and reported the same. Somebody on high bumped it to two hundred."

The soldier shook his head, smiling ruefully, then turned away when the line began to move. Hatton lowered his voice.

"Believe it or not, that doctored report was what got us out of that hellhole. The intel estimate said there were only a hundred to a hundred fifty enemy in the area, so when we topped that it probably embarrassed somebody important. Besides, by then the boys were pretty worn-out from all that patrolling. Lots of sniper fire, shoot 'n' scoot, every now and then a full-blooded ambush, and the weather went to shit on us too.

"We got a bunch of replacements a couple of weeks ago, but we'll still be understrength even when the veterans all get back from the hospitals." He winked. "Some of them take the long way home, if you get my meaning."

They passed inside, and an unidentified NCO in fatigues approached the executive officer. They began discussing a logistical issue that had apparently come undone, but Mortas was unable to understand much of the terminology. The line kept moving, first along a windowed wall and then through the serving area, and Mortas took the opportunity to get a look at the soldiers of the command.

The mess hall was large enough to seat two hundred men, but most of it was empty. Clutches of troops were spaced out around the tables, dressed in fatigues or PT clothing. Once again Mortas was surprised to notice just how young many of them looked. Shuffling along in the line, he caught snatches of conversation, some boisterous and some not, but all indicative of long association.

"You can't be serious. I told you about her in confidence!"

"What can I say? They sent me to the same ward you were in, and she seemed to fit the description."

"And you used my line? The exact same words?"

"Yeah, and she didn't seem to notice. Honestly, she isn't all that bright . . ."

Mortas looked out the window to hide his smile, and the moving column soon took him toward another discussion.

"They were gonna fit him with a replacement leg, grown right there, just like new, but there was something missing."

"No shit there was something missing. His *leg*. I tied him off myself."

"No, no, something medical. Something only the doctors would understand. Cells in the replacement wouldn't match up with what was left of the old leg for some reason. So they're sending him back to a regeneration hospital."

"A regen? That takes *months*. Lying there with all those little DNA bots crawlin' over the stump."

"Yeah, but when it's done it'll be all him. Wonder if they'll send him back here."

A stack of trays appeared in front of Mortas, and he was through the line and following Hatton to a seat only moments later. They joined a small group, all in fatigues, one of them sporting pin-on rank and branch insignia on his collars. Mortas looked more closely as he sat down, recognizing the man as a captain and the branch as military intelligence.

"Hey, this is our newest officer, Lieutenant Mortas. I know you've all heard of him." Hatton spoke as if in an afterthought, sorting through the utensils on his tray. Mortas cringed at the introduction, but the others gave him an assortment of friendly waves. He recognized the adjutant from the battalion headquarters, and decided these were officers from the battalion staff. Their conversation confirmed this soon enough.

"Sir, we got another inquiry about Captain Pappas." The adjutant spoke across the table at Hatton. "His previous owners don't seem to understand he's not coming back."

"What did you tell them this time?" The captain with the military intelligence insignia asked in a wary voice. His short hair was blond, and even though he was seated, Mortas could tell he was tall and lean.

"I had to start recycling the older stories. You're quarantined again."

"What did I catch?"

"You got Thorn Worm from a prostitute."

"My wife's not gonna be happy if she hears this one."

"Aw, come on. She's bound to like it better than when we reported you were missing."

"But that one was true. I was actually missing at the time."

The adjutant gave him a look of surprise. "Really?"

Hatton stopped eating long enough to explain the discussion. "Captain Pappas here was sent with us on a mission a year or so ago. Technically he's still assigned to some high-level staff somewhere, but we lost our intelligence officer and decided to keep him. He's head and shoulders above most of the intel types at our level; he can read and write and speak in complete sentences. Every now and then his old outfit asks about him."

"Erlon Pappas." The captain extended his hand, and Mortas shook it. "I can get out of here anytime I want, but it's an interesting anthropological study, interacting with the infantry. I'm thinking of writing a paper on it . . . wait a minute." He turned to the adjutant. "You can't catch Thorn Worm from a prostitute."

"I know. Sometimes I include a screwy detail like that, just to see if they're seriously trying to get you back or only going through the motions."

Hatton leaned across the group and spoke to the

man next to Pappas. "Drew, you haven't touched your food. Bad sign from the guy who orders our chow."

Drew looked up with a dazed expression that he immediately replaced with a forced smile. Mortas noted the way his fatigue top hung, as if there was nothing but an empty rib cage holding it up. His own recent experience with radical weight loss came rushing back, but he and the other maroons had never looked as bad as this scarecrow figure. A set of watery eyes darted his way, then went back to Hatton.

"Oh, I'm all right, sir." The voice was soft. "Just remembered something I forgot to do back at the office. Excuse me."

He rose and carried his tray toward a refuse chute set in a nearby wall. Mortas watched as the slim man stopped, then turned in almost a complete circle while his eyes searched the nearest tables. Drew then set off, cutting through the rows until reaching a group of seated soldiers who greeted him in a friendly manner. Mortas couldn't make out the words, but one of the troops at the table accepted the full tray.

"Eat hearty, men," the scarecrow said, and headed for the door. The soldiers he'd addressed watched him go, some with pursed lips that Mortas mistook for bottled mirth. Once he was gone, eyebrow raises were exchanged and one man made a finger gesture that Mortas took to indicate a reluctant suspicion of insanity.

"That was Captain Follett, the battalion supply officer." Major Hatton sighed loudly. "He worries a lot."

"Yeah, but he always comes through. Remember when the Sims had us surrounded at Airhead Juno?" The adjutant was obviously trying to lighten the conversation, and turned his eyes to Mortas. "No normal resupply could come in, so Follett packs a company-sized personnel ring with everything you could think of and has them drop this narrow-beam cofferdam right in the center of the airhead."

Cofferdams were miles-long high-energy cylinders directed from orbiting ships straight to a planet's surface. They were used to deliver troops and equipment directly to the ground, and personnel coasted down the cofferdam in giant wheel-shaped carriers that hugged the sides of the vast tunnel. Because of their vulnerability, cofferdams were not generally used where they could be fired on.

Another of the staff officers joined in. "That was so crazy. The Sims shot the *shit* outta that thing. Directed every piece of ordnance they had at this giant doughnut as it slid down. That's what the men called it: the Doughnut Resupply."

Hatton was laughing out loud. "You don't know the half of it. I was waiting for the thing to land, so all the debris was raining down on me and the breakdown party. Giant chunks of metal, crates of rations, you name it, most of it on fire. Never knew I could run that fast while looking straight up at the sky."

The adjutant recovered some of his composure. "But here's the good part: the Sims saw that it was a company-sized ring and figured it was an emergency attempt to put reinforcements into the airhead. Now we'd been hookin' and jabbin' with them for days, but really hadn't taken major casualties. The Sims thought we must be really hurting for bodies, so they attacked all along the perimeter.

"It was incredible. We were mowing them down with direct fire, and the ASSLs brought in everything from orbital rockets to drone gunships." Mortas recognized the acronym for Aerial Support Systems Liaison, members of the Force air wing who traveled with the infantry and coordinated supporting fires. "We slaughtered them, then Colonel Watt comes up on the radio and just says, 'Stretch your legs, guys' and the whole perimeter jumps up and goes after the Sims. We chased them for miles, then new cofferdams came down with two mech brigades, and we got relieved."

Hatton shook his head at the memory. "Follett comes down with them, and I'm standing there wrapping a bandage around Martin's head—you guys remember Martin—because he got clocked by a can of peaches or something. And Follett's asking me how the resupply went."

Late in the afternoon, Mortas got to watch his platoon come back from the rifle range. His head spinning from all the people he'd met and the different advice and requirements they'd laid out for him, he'd gone back out onto the athletic fields behind the barracks. A row of chest-high wooden platforms dotted the far side of the open area, and he'd climbed up on one of them. Normally used by instructors directing physical training, the stands were a common fixture on Force bases and he'd found them comfortable places for thinking in the past.

The air was still warm, but life around the brigade area had picked up speed while he'd been in-processing at B Company. A long column of armored troops carrying various weapons had tramped into view a short time earlier. They were now spread out on the grass near A Company's barracks, cleaning their weapons. Ground mats had been laid out so that the men could sit together in loose groups, and various company leaders could be seen circulating among them.

In the distance, a flight of shuttles slid across the reddening sky. Here and there, pairs and trios of soldiers would come into sight from behind different buildings, headed for the barracks at what was presumably the end of their duty day.

Mortas folded his long legs and rested his wrists on his knees, palm up, in a relaxation pose he'd learned in a meditation course at university. He'd signed up for the class because it was reputed to have a high percentage of female attendees, and although that had been true, he'd been surprised to have learned something useful. Straightening his back and relaxing his shoulders, he looked out from under the bill of his soft cap, taking it all in.

He'd finally met his boss, Captain Noonan, after signing in at B Company's orderly room. Noonan had seemed distant in their meeting, and Mortas came away from the interview wondering if the man's coolness arose from concern over his lack of combat experience or his father's high position.

The company's most senior NCO, First Sergeant Ettleman, had been friendlier. Bald and heavyset, he had the air of a man without a care in the world. Following his in-briefing with Captain Noonan, Mortas had been treated to a cup of coffee in the first sergeant's office. Ettleman had gently explained that the commanding officer was still establishing himself with the Orphans and that Mortas shouldn't attach any significance to his demeanor. He'd then gone on to praise the platoon sergeant that Mortas would be inheriting, a senior sergeant named Berland who'd been in charge of B Company's First Platoon since the wounding of its last platoon leader.

Like most of the platoons in the brigade, First Platoon had been understrength when they'd deployed to their latest mission, the search-and-destroy Major Hatton had described. They'd suffered their share of casualties, and some of the veterans had yet to return from various hospitals. First Platoon had recently received six replacements, of whom four were brand-new to the war zone, and so Sergeant Berland had taken the platoon to the rifle range that morning.

Having been informed of the direction from which his troops would return, Mortas became aware of them when they were still far away. A double column of men, bent under the weight of heavy rucksacks, had appeared at a break in the far wood line and slowly moved closer. Soon he was able to distinguish the camouflage fatigues, helmets, head-and-shoulder armor, and all the weapons of a standard platoon. He observed the slight bounce of the walking infantry, the easy stride that chewed up the miles, and noted with approval that the troops were spread out with good spacing between them. The long Scorpion rifles were held at the ready, here and there he detected the larger silhouettes of the platoon's machine guns, and finally he saw the large-bored rocket launchers that the gunners carried across their shoulders.

Obviously his platoon sergeant was conditioning the unit to move on foot with all its equipment, even those items that hadn't been fired that day. Mortas couldn't determine which of the platoon NCOs was Berland, but he did identify the internal leadership as they moved up and down the truncated column, giving corrections or encouragement.

The platoon turned up the road that ran alongside the playing fields, allowing him to see them in profile. Some were hunched over under the loads and some stood tall. Some were hustling along at an almost feverish clip while others were sauntering as if they could go forever. Watching them, Mortas felt a twinge in his stomach, a feeling he didn't quite understand. For an instant he saw a different column, a long double file of the enemy, trudging along as they walked toward the Sim base where he and the others had stolen the spacecraft that had finally gotten them off of Roanum.

Roanum. How odd, to be thinking of the unnamed planet by its new name. The name of one of the people who'd been with him on that march, pretending to be Sims. The name of a dead man. That thought helped Mortas to identify the twinge, and he recognized it as doubt. Not doubt of his own abilities or his genuine desire to lead his troops well, but the ugly concern about events that were beyond his control. Events like the ones that had killed Cranther, Gorman, and even the alien pretending to be Trent. He'd been powerless to stop them, and he alone had been spared.

The platoon turned onto the grass in front of the row of barracks, and he wondered how his new troops felt about his having survived. He'd been marooned with three Forcemembers, yet he was the only one still living. Apparently his report (or, rather, the slightly doctored version where he was the hero) had been read by just about everyone in the brigade, and so hopefully these men would be able to see that he'd done his best. That he and the three strangers had become a solid unit and that they had all risked their lives for each other at different times.

Mortas saw the first sergeant's wide form emerging from B Company's barracks, and he watched the man approach the platoon. The troops were easing their burdens to the grass, and some had begun to shake out ground coverings like the ones being used by the nearby A Company men. First Sergeant Ettleman conferred with one of the soldiers, and Mortas decided this was his platoon sergeant. He'd just unfolded his legs and hopped down from the platform when Ettleman pointed in his direction, and the other man started walking toward him.

The NCO had already shed his armor and helmet, and now shook out a soft cap which he adjusted as he approached. Just under average height but barrel-chested, his fatigues were so faded that the greens, blacks, and browns of its camouflage pattern all seemed to blend together. Mortas walked toward him, and the NCO saluted when he was a few yards away.

"Good afternoon, sir. I'm Sergeant Berland. I'll be your platoon sergeant." Mortas had already returned the salute, and the older man shook his hand. He was indeed older; his black hair showed gray in front of his ears, and his forehead was creased with wrinkles. His eyes were green, but it was hard to tell because they seemed permanently set into slits.

"It's good to meet you." Like most new infantry lieutenants, Mortas had imagined this meeting many times. The first interaction with the seasoned NCO who was to be his mentor while also serving as his subordinate. Words failed him, and he lamely asked, "How'd it go at the range?"

Berland turned to look at the platoon, where the men had settled into cleaning the weapons. Most of them had positioned themselves to be able to see their new platoon leader, which brought back Mortas's concerns about how they'd judged his performance on Roanum.

"Aw, today was just marksmanship training. Nothing elaborate. We've got six new men, and only two of them are veterans, so I wanted to see if they could hit anything. They did all right, and it never hurts to get the experienced men out there either."

"I understand we're still waiting for a few men to come back?"

"Yes, sir. Five hospital cases, all expected to return." He gave his new officer an appraising look. "Some of the older guys have a little difficulty finding their way home."

"That's understandable."

His answer seemed to please the platoon sergeant, who gave him a slight smile. "To tell the truth, sir, I'm a little surprised you got out here as fast as you did. That was quite an experience you had."

Mortas sensed that this was a test, perhaps related to his status as Olech Mortas's son. "It wasn't easy, but it was only a few days. I learned a lot, I can say that."

"I bet you did." Berland nodded slightly, the narrow eyes unreadable. "Well don't worry about a thing, sir. I've been all over this war, and this brigade is the best I've seen. The platoon's loaded with guys who know what they're doing, and most of them have been together a long time."

"I'm looking forward to this." The words came out unplanned, and he was struck by how much he meant them. How long he had meant them. "So. Should I meet the men?"

Berland considered his response, seemed to change it, then went ahead anyway. "There is one question the troops wanted me to ask you, sir. I hope you don't mind."

And here it was. The question, and so many ways to ask it. How come you're alive, and the other three are dead? Are you a dumb-shit rich kid who's going to get us all killed? Why should we trust you with our lives?

"Go ahead."

Berland actually looked left and right, even though they were alone. Mortas glanced across the field, toward the platoon. Some seated, some standing, all of them appearing busy, but he imagined them trying to hear what was being said, even from that distance.

"There was this rumor . . . nothing official. Me, I don't care, but some of the men were curious." The platoon sergeant leaned in and lowered his voice. "Is it true you fucked the alien?"

Mortas felt his eyes blinking rapidly, and he made them stop. He felt a sensation akin to vertigo, something he normally associated with having narrowly missed major injury solely by chance.

Berland's eyes widened, waiting, and his mind raced. The answer was important; after all, this was the one question his troops had decided to ask their new lieutenant. For an instant he saw Trent as he had known her, annoying at first but unquestionably intelligent, then growing in his estimation until he would have gladly died for her. And yet he knew the right answer, from having spent so much of his life in the rough-and-tumble of prep school and university sports. A male world with its own expectations.

The right answer was a lie in this case, and it would have been a betrayal if that *thing* had actually been Amelia Trent.

But she—*it*—wasn't. In the end, the thing itself had been the ultimate betrayal. Mortas was surprised to realize he owed it nothing.

He cleared his throat, looked left and right in imitation of Berland, then spoke in a hiss. "Yes."

Berland's head jerked back in mock surprise. An instant later a grin spread across his face, and he nodded appreciatively.

"Aw-*right*. I've had a lot of lieutenants over the years, and all the good ones were sick, *sick* individuals." He wagged a playful finger at him. "You might be the best one yet."

He turned, and for the first time Mortas noted that many of the troops over by A Company were observing him and Berland closely. The platoon sergeant ignored them, taking a step away from Mortas and staring at First Platoon. A meaty arm came up, and he extended his thumb in the air.

The response was electric. The members of the platoon came to their feet, hooting and hollering like spectators at a sporting event. Then they were clapping loudly, drowning out shouted comments that were clearly approval. A moment later several of them were calling over to the A Company troops, words of pride and derision passed between soldiers in different units from time immemorial. Some of the A Company men waved dismissive hands at the B Company troops, but a few of them briefly joined in the applause and Mortas saw more than one thumbs-up.

Berland tilted his head in Mortas's direction, smiling broadly at the applauding First Platoon. "Welcome to the Orphans, sir."

CHAPTER FOUR

Ayliss's mind never seemed to completely shut down during the Step. Though heavily sedated for the voyage like any other passenger, she always emerged from the experience half-believing she'd been awake the whole way. Experts had assured her that those memories were only dreams—and that the dreams had been of brief duration—but she remembered them with great clarity and suspected they had gone on for a very long time.

Mankind's greatest achievement required her to be unconscious and sealed within a protective chamber inside the craft that would take her across the generated Threshold. As Olech Mortas's daughter and a representative of the Veterans Auxiliary, Ayliss always traveled in comfort, and so her sleep compartment was both spacious and luxurious. When strapped into its cushioned seat, she could just reach the chamber's low walls and the heavy bubble that was the cubicle's lid. The soldiers she'd interviewed had described the claustrophobia of the transit tubes in which they were forced to make the Step, saying they were so much like caskets that the transports were known as coffin ships.

The Step could reduce enormous space voyages from decades to days, and in this case—the trip from Earth to Broda—to mere hours. Even so, Ayliss routinely experienced a sensation akin to having been asleep for only minutes before shifting into semiconsciousness. As usual, she now became aware in some part of her brain that she was asleep in the bright compartment. The drugs kept her calm, but the constant activity of her intellect raced through thoughts and memories the same way her body was racing through the cosmos.

A picture formed around her, figures looming because she was only six. The ribbons from a black bonnet had been tied too tightly beneath her chin, but minders on either side held her hands and kept her from loosening it. Looking down, she saw the hated black dress that she'd torn to shreds many hours later and the black shoes that she'd thrown from her bedroom window.

It was a familiar dream, if a dream it was, and Ayliss could sometimes direct her actions in it. She usually made her little-girl self look over her shoulder, trying to see Jan, but she never accomplished it and often wondered why. He had been there, one year younger, and weeping not far behind her.

The minders shuffled forward slowly, mastodons in a black-draped herd, heads down and pulling her with them. Ayliss was unable to see anything except the dark trousers and skirts of the people in front of her, some of them in uniforms that she recognized from her father's office.

Father. Without her bidding, the girl in the bonnet began turning her head from side to side, becoming agitated, trying to see the only parent she had left. Astounded that he wasn't right there, where he should be, with her and Jan now that they no longer had a mother. Fighting the hands now, trying to break free and being told to stop it, that everything was going to be all right.

The legs in front of her finally gone, able to see now, and then not wanting to. The flower-encircled bier, a tripod with a photo of Father and Mother on their wedding day, and what looked like a short set of carpeted stairs. She'd stepped right up onto them, and been startled when she hardly recognized the face of Mother. Motionless, but not asleep. Heavy makeup, something Ayliss didn't recognize because Mother never wore any, the face so thin, much smaller than the last time Ayliss had seen her, only a few days before.

The hands again, telling her that we don't stand on the kneeler, asking her if she wanted to say a prayer for Mother, but Ayliss had looked around while she possessed the vantage point. Seeing Father at last, tall, strong, a few yards off to the side. Someone was talking to him—someone was always talking to him—but he sensed her attention and turned to look. The blue eyes that she loved so much, exactly like her own— Jan had Mother's eyes but she had Father's—looking directly at her, but different. So terribly different. She knew them as the indicators of affection and praise and mirth, and that day they held none of that. They held nothing at all.

Not even sadness that Mother was gone.

Father regarded her for several moments, blankly, as if not recognizing her, and when the hands pulled Ayliss away she started to scream. They misunderstood, picking her up, holding her, cooing words of comfort and the never-ending litany that everything was going to be all right, but they were too stupid, they were *all* too stupid, to know that she was screaming at Father to care about what had happened, to Mother, to her, to Jan, and then she'd been carried from the room and the hands were shaking her, trying to get her to calm down, shaking, shaking—

"Ma'am? Ma'am?" A male face appeared in front of Ayliss's, a uniformed technician, a familiar sight at the end of a space voyage. A hand was gently rocking her shoulder, still attempting to rouse her even though she was wide-awake. Sharp memories of the dream of that terrible day, when everything had changed. The dreams always stayed with her, which was why Ayliss doubted they were dreams at all. The technician released her and straightened up, standing respectfully outside the low compartment.

"It's quite all right, ma'am. You shouldn't feel embarrassed at all. The anesthetic often has that effect on people. You'll stop crying in a minute or so."

Broda was the smallest of the planets first settled by humans after Earth. It had been bypassed initially because, though habitable, it had lacked the natural riches that made other planets more attractive. The Brodans liked to joke that their home had none of the things politicians, corporations, and generals would want—which made it Paradise.

It also made Broda the destination of choice for people seeking that most fundamental aspect of freedom, the desire to be left alone. The planet's government reflected that desire, heavily codified in law, and over time a culture had developed on Broda that had morphed into its key industry.

The Brodans dealt in data. Clean, untainted data, accurately processed with a transparent history. Information that bore the stamp of the Brodan Data Guild was considered completely reliable, devoid of manipulation, and as free of bias as was humanly possible. The Guild's exacting methods for collecting, verifying, classifying, and analyzing information were open for all to see. Those methods were taught at universities on every settled world, not just for proper data analysis, but also as a rival to the scientific method and even a framework for philosophical thought.

Technology had made the corruption of information both simple and easy, to the extent that analysis and findings from non-Guild sources were automatically suspect. In a universe where every excuse, twist, and outright lie could be propagated instantly and endlessly, the genuine article was very hard to come by. The Brodans, devoted to clean data in a way that was almost worship, had become the lone trusted source—which of course earned them enemies in every corner of the inhabited planets.

None of those enemies hated them more than the Emergency Senate, which was an added reason for Ayliss to rely on them so heavily. She was a frequent visitor to Broda and, although her status as Olech Mortas's daughter had made gaining their trust difficult, she was now a welcome visitor.

Dev Harlec was as unlikely an ally as she could have imagined, which was why she'd set out to befriend him right from the start. As a professor of data analysis on Earth, he'd become famous for lectures and publications that skewered powerful entities for their twisted relationship with the truth. Those entities, tired of his assaults, had finally managed to have him removed from his teaching position and blocked from getting another. Much of his writing had then been banned under a blanket wartime-security act, and Dev Harlec had decided his days as a man of Earth had come to an end. On Broda he was regarded as a cross between a political refugee and a holy martyr, and he took special delight in tormenting the Emergency Senate and the leadership of the Human Defense Force from his new home.

"Naughty Ayliss Mortas! One of these days your dad's going to revoke your papers, and you're going to be stuck here," Harlec exclaimed when Ayliss stepped from the elevator. Sunlight streamed in from every direction because Harlec's floor—and it was all his—was perched atop a tall building, and most of its walls were transparent. The Brodans' obsession with openness was reflected in their architecture, and looking out over the capital city she saw miles and miles of translucent surfaces.

"I can think of worse fates." Ayliss crossed the shiny floor and deposited a kiss on Harlec's bald head. She would have been able to do this even if he'd been standing, but the researcher was seated in a chair with outsized casters which he enjoyed rolling from terminal to terminal. Freestanding electronic towers of astounding capacity reached for the bubble roof like pillars, a seeming throwback to an earlier age of technology. Ayliss, already immersed in Brodan technique, knew that many of their brightest minds preferred to perform their initial work unconnected to larger networks. Sharing and cross-checking of information might be mandatory, but continuous linkage to other systems was not.

"I would have expected your tan to be better, spending so much time under the sun." She reached for an identical chair and rolled it closer while Harlec smiled at her jab. The transparent material of the walls was a special polymer created to block dangerous rays and emissions, from within or without. Additionally,

Harlec's petite frame had never known exercise even though he favored athletic warm-up suits with hoods that hung down his back like a monk's cowl. What was left of his hair was all gray, and his slitted eyes looked across at her from behind thick glasses. Harlec was rumored to have already gone through several pairs of transplanted eyes because of the brutal hours he spent poring over data streams. Whenever he started wearing a set of glasses, the ocular anachronism indicated he was due for another surgery.

"Afraid I don't get around as much as you do."

"You know I only make the trip so I can see your smiling face."

"Of course. But it doesn't hurt to demonstrate you can pretty much go anywhere you please, while your outlandishly powerful father is basically stuck on Earth." One of the secret pleasures of visiting the different planets was the knowledge that Olech, despite his high position, couldn't risk being lost in the Step. With only a few exceptions, he was essentially Earthbound.

"Sometimes I think you dislike him as much as I do."

"Why would I have a reason to dislike him? He and his cronies wanted to put me in jail, and to this day they persist in their silly scheme of overloading Broda with data that's simply noise." Unable to combat the Guild's popularity, Olech and others like him had adopted the strategy of agreeing to every request for information, then providing oversized feeds loaded with garbage. "And we won't waste any time discussing their endless war."

"Oh, we would never do that." Ayliss winked. "Listen, I may have finally come across something juicy."

"I'm crushed. You only visit when you want something."

"If it's half as good as I think it is, we both might see my father headed into early retirement."

"Tell me."

"I've been digging through the Auxiliary's records for a long time, searching for something nasty, but I finally figured out I've been looking in the wrong place. Most of the returned vets don't trust anybody, and at any rate the database has been sanitized. Honestly, I suspect the good information never leaves the war zone.

"So I got hold of a smuggled eulogy, the ones the troops send back, and it mentioned a facility where a new soldier was questioned about his background. His history regarding violence, personal hostility, gang membership. When he protested, saying he hadn't seen action yet, he was told that they were establishing a baseline."

"That *is* interesting."

"So I began looking again, now that I knew what I was after. I didn't find much, but there were fragments. Tests of brain function on returned vets, for example."

"That could be easily explained, especially if the subjects had been concussed."

"Exactly. Which is why I screened out the ones who'd suffered trauma to the head. A surprising number hadn't even been wounded, and every one of those soldiers fell into one of two categories. Decorated for bravery, or punished for cowardice."

She let that hang in the air, watching Harlec's expression turn deeply contemplative.

"Sneaky Command. You think they might be looking into brain function as it relates to performance on the battlefield?"

"Fits, doesn't it? Get a baseline with the new guys, then compare that with the performance of the survivors at the other end. If there is a link, they should be able to find it that way."

"And if they can establish that link, they might be stupid enough to think they can alter the brain function through drugs or surgery. Take any normal human being and turn him into a hero." He shook his head. "It's been tried before, many times. All sorts of undesirable side effects, and the results were far from reliable."

"I found a couple of professional papers that came to that same conclusion. But that doesn't mean they wouldn't try it anyway. And here's where it gets really interesting: I couldn't find any record of this kind of testing on unwounded veterans that wasn't at least two years old. Prior to that it was pretty common."

"So either they gave up, or they found what they were looking for."

"If they found what they were looking for, they'd

need to do a lot more research and then move on to experimentation. Human experimentation. And they sure couldn't do that anywhere near the settled words. Probably not even this side of the CHOP line."

"Now *that's* nasty. But I've seen them do nastier things, and for dumber reasons. If they thought they could find the switch that takes flight and turns it into fight . . . Command would certainly consider that worth the risk."

"The risk gets a lot lower if they keep the experimentation in the war zone. So where would they conduct something like that, and how could we find it?"

"You're doing very well on your own. Where would you look?"

"There are a lot of possibilities. Space stations. Uninhabitable planets we control. Ships in space. Military-controlled planets. I ran some rough numbers and they're enormous. Besides, if they really are doing something like this, the location's not in any database."

"So stop looking at the data that's there and look for the data that's not."

"What do you mean?"

"Sometimes it's not what you see, but what you don't. The puzzle pieces that should be there but aren't. Large amounts of money that suddenly disappeared from someone's budget. Logistical support that got rerouted with no explanation. Even people who vanished, for asking the wrong questions.

"You mentioned reading some professional papers on this subject, which of course would have been authored by the people working in this field. What about the papers that aren't there, and the people who should have been writing them?"

"I don't follow."

"Sure you do. Command drafts people all the time, and so does your father, even if he never puts a uniform on the ones he selects. All sorts of noted scientists have dropped their civilian work and become part of the war effort over the decades. Some of them did it publicly while others simply packed up and shipped out.

"We need to identify the top experts in this field. Then we need to see who's still on the settled worlds and who's not. Should be easy to do, just by finding out who's no longer publishing. And if we find somebody who quietly disappeared in the last couple of years, we'll have a good prospect."

"What would that do for us, though? How would we track a brain expert in the war zone if Command and my father didn't want anyone to know they were there in the first place?"

"Ayliss, Ayliss, Ayliss." He gave her a smile. "Have you ever met a scientist who followed security protocol?"

After finally passing the latest in a long series of proficiency exams, Mortas shut off the monitor and rubbed his eyes. He was seated in the adjutant's office in the battalion headquarters, and it was late at night. Through the open door he could see the NCO and young private from C Company who'd been assigned staff duty with him, seated near a bank of radios. Although the building was empty for the night, an emergency order could come in at any time, and so it was always manned by at least one officer, an NCO, and a runner.

It had been a long day, the latest in a succession of them running back to his arrival. As a new lieutenant with no combat experience, his every waking moment was taken up with a crash course in the lessons that the veterans had all learned on the battlefield. Grueling physical training with his platoon, followed by live-fire ranges that were slowly increasing in complexity now that the new men were progressing past the more basic tasks. At the end of each day Mortas received further education from Captain Noonan, who was proving to be a bit of an enigma. The company commander alternated between a taciturn coldness and an impassioned energy that manifested itself whenever the combat scenarios in the training simulator became particularly intense. Mortas hadn't noticed this behavioral change at first, because it usually coincided with the point in the simulation where he was being overwhelmed by the many tasks he had to perform as a platoon leader.

Though equipped with a detailed understanding of the weapon systems available to an infantry platoon fighting the Sims, Mortas's knowledge came from his precommissioning training at university and the few months he'd spent in Officer Basic. Out in the war zone, however, he was discovering just how much of his schoolroom learning was incomplete or actually outdated.

He'd trained in the Force's excellent simulators many times, but the experience with a unit like the Orphans was a rude shock. Standing in a darkened room, wearing or holding exact replicas of his gear and weapons, he would be thrust into alarmingly realistic depictions of actual combat through a set of goggles almost identical to the ones he would wear in the field. Different scenarios would burst into existence before his eyes, and he could physically move around in that world by turning his head, jumping, or throwing himself prone.

Sometimes he was the only trainee, in which case the program would provide the voices and images of notional platoon members as well as important characters such as the company commander. Explosions would boom in his ears while Mortas was trying to hear what other players were saying, figures would be running, shooting, and sometimes collapsing nearby, and of course the enemy was present as well. The software had been modified to reflect the procedures that the Orphans used in the field, and so he was faced with a steep learning curve.

The most important skill Mortas had to gain was related to the Orphans' spartan firepower. Lacking the heavier weapons systems that were standard in Force infantry units, the Orphans worked hard at incorporating the extra muscle offered by drone gunships, higher-echelon artillery, and missiles delivered from orbit. Although most of that was managed by the ASSLs who accompanied the infantry, every Orphan was expected to become an expert at requesting and directing those lifesaving assets.

As the platoon leader, Mortas already knew he would be expected to assume the ASSL's duties if the man was incapacitated, but he hadn't anticipated the complexity of coordinating his troops' movements with the overlapping delivery systems available to him. Despite Noonan's personal coaching, he was finding it difficult to juggle all of the available support while also directing the actions of the troops he commanded.

"Up late studying?" He recognized the voice of Captain Pappas, the battalion intelligence officer. Mortas stopped rubbing his eyes and saw the blond-haired man standing in the doorway, smiling.

"I'm on staff duty, sir." That sounded a little self-important, so he added wryly. "You know, in case anything big happens."

"Yeah, big like having to go rescue some poor MPs from the boys." Pappas entered the room and pulled up a chair. Mortas already knew that the Orphans had a hostile relationship with most of the units near the brigade's area, and with the military police just about anywhere. "I'd like to ask you a few questions about the Sims you encountered on Roanum, if you don't mind. The ones you walked with."

"I don't mind at all." At first Mortas had been skittish about discussing his experiences on the barren planet that now bore Roan Gorman's name, but the brigade commander's edict had held and not many people had asked him much about it. "Although we really weren't with them for very long, so I probably didn't learn anything important."

"Now that's where you're wrong. The best information comes from the people on the ground, the ones who are right there. Always has. When you're out there with your troops, you need to keep your eyes and ears open—and theirs too—because everything is potentially important. Footprints, trash, the way the enemy operates, all of it means something. And don't just pass the information up the chain. Give it some thought yourself, and talk to your men about it. If the Sims change something they're doing, why did they change? What does that mean for us, and for your platoon?"

The words were soft and inoffensive, so Mortas merely nodded.

"You walked with that Sim column for hours, then hitched a ride with them right through the colony defenses. What was their reaction when you joined them?"

"They never figured out we were human, but that whole gang was pretty exhausted. Numerous walking wounded, their equipment and uniforms all beat-up; I'd say they'd been in combat for days. I did notice one thing: lots of human gestures that I found surprising. They smiled, nodded, even shook their heads, and they got plenty pissed off when they realized they had to walk all the way home."

"Yeah, that fits. I've watched a lot of the available footage of Sims in action, a little hobby of mine, trying to identify their most basic commands. It's not easy, with them all chirping and trilling away at each other, but I think I might have figured out how they say, "Come on" or "Attack" based on their hand signals." He raised an arm and waved it. "Very much what we do when we're trying to encourage people to follow us."

"Trying to decode the bird talk, sir?"

"Maybe. I know there are plenty of linguistic experts working on that, but so far there doesn't seem to have been much success. Did any of them seem to get sick while you were near them?"

"As I said, they were on the ragged edge when we slipped in with them. That was probably the only reason we were able to get away with what we were pulling. And we weren't with them long." A memory, a bizarre nonverbal exchange he'd had with an anonymous Sim soldier. "I touched one of them. We were going up a steep grade, and I almost overbalanced. This Sim walking in front of me had turned to give me a hand, and he pulled me up the incline. I was so surprised I almost thanked him."

"Very interesting. You see, in a unit like this, I don't get to observe the Sims even though I'm in their vicinity quite a bit—sometimes too close." They exchanged smiles. "There are all sorts of theories about why they resemble us so much, but a lot of it gets quashed by Command and . . ."

"People like my father."

"Yes. Back when I was on special staff assignment, before I got shanghaied by this gang of cutthroats, I got to hear all sorts of high-level stuff. But even that was censored in a way. The discussion only went so far, then it just sorta died." He pursed his lips, looking into a distance that wasn't there. "They say there's this circle of civilian scientists and linguists who are trying to answer these questions, maybe even work up a translation device, and that Command and the Emergency Senate don't want that to happen."

"Honestly, I'd never heard that one."

"The story goes that there's been a lot of duplicate effort because Command won't share the information from the war zones. Funny thing about our war, even with the Step and all our technology, we're more cut off from the folks at home than troops in many of the past wars on Earth. Really makes it easy for Command to keep a lid on things."

Pappas yawned, prompting a similar response from Mortas. "I gotta shove off to bed. Thanks for the chat, Jan."

The intelligence man was almost out the door when he stopped. "A word of advice for you. I get the impression you felt a connection with the Sims you encountered. Once you've fought them, and seen what they do to prisoners and the dead, you'll lose that. It gets pretty gruesome. Sam knows how we reproduce and that his equipment doesn't work, so he likes to mutilate our genitalia. If I were you, I wouldn't say anything too positive about the Sims in front of any of the veterans."

"Because they might think I'm soft?"

"No. Because they'll think you're an idiot."

Just after midnight, Mortas walked outside when he heard a burst of shouting. The NCO from C Company blandly told him it was just a bunch of rowdies headed back to the barracks and that it was best to leave them alone, but he went anyway because he was bored. He had no intention of interfering with the group if they were indeed merely headed to their bunks, and the volume of the yelling suggested they were over a hundred yards away.

Floodlights shone down from the roof of the headquarters and the barracks buildings, and he quickly detected the movement of several figures well in the distance. The shouts had simmered down to loud, drunken laughter, and he smiled as he watched the group cross the field. He already knew the Orphans were infamous for enjoying periods of stand-down to the fullest, but it didn't seem to rankle any of the commanders and so far there'd been no incidents involving members of his platoon.

The revelers disappeared beyond the side of the most distant barracks, making Mortas wonder if they'd seen him. Good tactics, if they had; by going the long way around, they made sure he couldn't tell which barracks they eventually entered. Having nothing better to do, he went down the short steps and walked out to the spot where the hill's decline resumed. It was a cool night, and Mortas looked up at the stars.

He jumped in fright when the silence was broken by the sound of someone vomiting explosively just around the corner. For some reason this surprise reminded him of Captain Noonan's latest lecture, about not focusing too intently on any one thing on the battlefield. In that simulation Mortas had been maneuvering a single squad around a knocked-out Sim assault vehicle, utterly intent on not being surprised by what it might contain, when he and his notional troops had been shot up by an enemy team concealed in a nearby stand of tall grass. Noonan hadn't been terribly exercised about the mistake.

"Security, Lieutenant. Security. All-around at all times. You focus on one thing too closely, and you'll walk right into something else."

The words were with him as he went around the corner, and Mortas was just beginning to wonder if he shouldn't get some help when he saw a thin figure slumped over the wooden table where the two troops had been working on the radio his first day. The table was in shadow, but there was enough light from the stars to make out the features of Captain Follett, the battalion's anxious supply officer. He wore a set of fatigues but no hat, and Mortas suspected he'd come outside the headquarters when he'd felt sick.

"You all right there, sir?"

The slight figure jerked into an upright position, Follett's head turning side to side in confusion.

"It's okay, sir. It's just Lieutenant Mortas."

"Oh." Follett's voice was choked, and he cleared it noisily while pulling a dark rag out of one pocket. "Hello, Mortas. Thank you for checking on me. Feeling much better."

An acidic scent reached his nostrils once Mortas was standing opposite Follett, but with no aroma of alcohol. Of course there were odorless intoxicants available, and their use was nothing new in the war zone, but he was still baffled. Follett abruptly came to his feet and began kicking dirt all over the spot that Mortas now knew was emitting the smell.

"Seriously, sir, are you all right? Want to come inside for a few minutes?"

The kicking became almost furious, and the thin man leaned heavily on the table while his boots rearranged the soil. It had little effect on the aroma, but after a minute he finally stopped.

"Actually, I think I'll just go for a little walk. Get some air. Been spending too much time inside."

"All right." His tone caused Follett to stop. Mortas almost expected some kind of arch comment about the way lieutenants were supposed to address captains, but he was mistaken.

"You haven't been out there yet, have you? With the unit, I mean." The words were far from arch. Pleading, almost.

"No, sir. Not with the unit."

Follett stepped closer, the edge of the floodlight giving his taut skin a silvery glow.

"Food, Mortas. Food. They all talk about water, but every Hab's got water. You can always find water. Food's the killer." His head tilted upward, his eyes on the stars. "Can't seem to convince them. The clock starts as soon as the troops are on the ground. You wouldn't believe how fast they consume what they're carrying, and then . . . if I don't get them more, if I don't *find* them more . . . they die."

"Yes, sir. I know. I was marooned my first time out."

Follett's eyes came back to him, blinking rapidly. The words appeared to have some kind of calming effect.

"That's right. You already know. You actually understand." He turned and walked off, weaving slightly. "Make your men understand, Lieutenant. As much chow as they can carry, and eat it slow. Make them understand."

Mortas watched the figure until the darkness swallowed it.

The sun was just beyond the horizon when Mortas felt its presence the next morning. The headquarters windows had shifted from black to gray with the end of night, and a stirring came with it. Motion. Activity. Direction.

He walked out onto the back steps and looked over the open field in front of the barracks. Most mornings at this time he would have been getting ready for physical training, which was why he'd never experienced this sensation before. The rising sun's rays reached up from the distant hills, and the growing light allowed him to see the battalion coming to life.

Individuals already dotted the grass close to the long buildings, some dressed in T-shirts and black shorts while others wore fatigues. The barracks let out a steadily increasing stream of men as the time for morning formation approached, and Mortas was able to hear the voices as they came together. Old hands joking easily, new men standing uncertainly by themselves, early risers already stretching while others— among them, probably, the carousers from the previous night—tried to move as little as possible. Light skin, dark skin, olive skin, almond skin, scarred skin.

As more men arrived, the rectangular formations began to assemble, squads in rows forming the brick-shaped platoons. Three companies side by side, facing the open field, with a smaller block representing the headquarters sections. Lone individuals, the company first sergeants, striding out in front to take charge. A definite straightening up now, a few of the platoon sergeants ordering their men to "square away!" in preparation for the first sergeants calling them to attention. Behind the blocks of men, several figures stood in a row or leaned on crutches, the returned wounded from the battalion's battles.

The shifting bodies finally locked into place like statues, personnel reports rendered and received, then the units released to their NCOs for training. Entire platoons headed toward the mess hall for early chow before moving out for a day at the range or some other kind of training. The wounded men limped or crutched away, looking to Mortas like the dejected playmates of his childhood who'd been too young for the game the older kids had chosen. The remaining troops extended their ranks to provide room for stretching and setting-up exercises before starting PT.

Mortas smiled, recognizing Sergeant Berland at the head of First Platoon. Pleased that he was now able to identify most of his NCOs and many of his troops, but reminding himself that they were still badly understrength. The stretching period ended shortly, and the battalion formation fragmented completely as platoons and squads moved out onto different portions of the field.

The movement was accompanied by shouted commands and answering cries of varying enthusiasm, and in short order the entire field was in motion. Physical training among the Orphans took many different forms, and the NCOs were given great latitude in designing their workouts. Here one group alternated push-ups and sit-ups while over there another section jogged in a circle to warm up before going on a run. One squad practiced combat rolls while an entire platoon duckwalked across the ground.

Shouting filled the air as the sun rose, repetitions and cadences that Mortas felt in his chest. First Platoon, in fatigues and boots but no hats, finished its preparations and began a drill that was one of Berland's favorites. He'd paced off a distance of fifteen yards on the field, and the men formed three files facing the markers he'd emplaced. On command, the first three dropped to their stomachs and began worming their way across the grass.

This was an infantry movement technique known as the high crawl, different from the low crawl in that the soldier's head was raised off the deck. It was much faster than the low crawl, but also more dangerous under fire. The Orphans were fanatics about these uncomfortable modes of travel, insisting that the high and low crawls were the only protection against the vaunted marksmanship of the individual Sim soldier and that they had to be practiced often. At a designated interval the next three men dropped to the ground and turned themselves into jerky starfish, arms and legs twisting and pushing as they followed the troops in front of them.

Watching, Mortas remembered how the dirt on Roanum would work its way into his trousers and boots when he and the others had been forced to crawl in order to avoid detection.

When the first three soldiers reached the finish line they hopped up and jogged in place, ready to repeat the exercise once the entire platoon was behind them again. Berland liked to alternate the drill with different techniques for casualty evacuation, from the buddy-carry to dragging the stricken man across the ground. Above the din of the other units exercising, Mortas was able to hear shouted words of both ridicule and encouragement from the First Platoon men waiting their turns.

Knowing the intense effort required to high crawl even a dozen yards, Mortas remembered a promise he'd made to himself just after meeting the platoon. Heavily identified as the son of Olech Mortas, he knew he'd be criticized for any failure to participate in unpleasant activities. Rich kid. Daddy's protected pet. Fucking officers.

He wasn't required to be out there after having been on duty all night, but all the same, Mortas called back into the building to tell the NCO from C Company that he was joining his platoon for PT. He jogged around the field's perimeter, dodging squads that were heading off to do a little roadwork, and was startled when the sweating face of Colonel Alden appeared in front of him.

"Going for a little extra credit there, Jan?" the battalion commander shouted happily, jogging past with Major Hatton and the other headquarters officers in tow. Mortas reflexively saluted, but the file was already gone before he realized that Alden had given him a thumbs-up as he went by.

Just as he jogged up to the rear of First Platoon, Mortas heard a familiar voice shouting to the soldiers in one line. The speaker was a veteran private, enormously popular in the platoon, a tall individual named Ladaglia.

"Come on, guys! We do this right, we can win the

war right here!" It was his signature phrase, and the first time Mortas had heard it, Ladaglia and some of the new men had been scrubbing the latrine.

Sergeant Dak, one of the squad leaders, noted Mortas's arrival. Everything about Dak was dark, from his hair to his skin to his humor, but Berland considered him the best NCO in the platoon after himself. Though only medium-sized, Dak emitted a formidable aura. The NCO stepped to the front of the line, stopping the soldier who was next.

"Lieutenant's here. He's a little late, so let's give him a chance to catch up." He swung an inviting arm toward the grass, and Mortas obligingly threw himself on his stomach and began to crawl.

Only a few hours later, Mortas was panting hard and trying not to get shot. The sun was high overhead, he was loaded down with full torso-and-shoulder armor, and his new helmet kept sliding down onto his goggles every time he hit the dirt. The platoon's three machine guns were chattering away on a low ridge several hundred yards to his left, firing real rounds at the fake enemy positions Mortas was assaulting with the rest of the platoon. All around him were the sounds of rifles and grenade launchers, and yet he could see none of it.

Mortas was surrounded by thick grass that was almost as tall as he was and seemingly without end. He couldn't stand at his full height to look around because, while the grass might keep him out of sight, it would do nothing to shield him from incoming Sim slugs. As a result he was either moving ahead in a crouch or pressed flat on his stomach. Though familiar with the piece of ground from earlier practice runs where they'd rehearsed with no ammunition, Mortas had lost contact with the assault squads almost as soon as they'd hit the grass.

The hill they were attempting to capture had been set up with fake enemy bunkers long ago, but the Orphans' absence during their last mission had allowed the vegetation to reassert itself. Berland was with the machine gun teams on a distant ridgeline, directing suppressive fire meant to keep their opponents' heads down while Mortas and the rest of the platoon physically assaulted the position. Their practice runthroughs had finally been deemed sufficient for live fire, and so now real rounds and explosives were being discharged very close by.

Dak's squad had been on his left with Mecklinger's on his right—as assault leader, Mortas's spot was in the dead center—and they'd maneuvered to the base of the hill before signaling to Berland to start the show. As soon as the platoon's machine guns opened up, reactive systems on the hilltop target had responded. Training mechanisms inside the enemy's low bunkers were now roaring the ripping sound of Sim machine guns, launching grenade simulators at likely avenues of approach, and firing actual projectiles at any indication of movement. The fake slugs were water-filled, gelatin-encased bullets fired by robot air guns, and although they could cause little harm, they imitated the real thing in an alarming fashion. Just then, a burst chopped through the grass over Mortas's head, spraying him with little droplets of moisture. He rolled several times to his right, and the searching gun turned its attentions elsewhere.

The assault element had approached the grass in an exaggerated crouch, the armored men duckwalking until they'd come under fire. At that instant the line had adopted a movement technique that appeared to follow the rule of every man for himself. Individual soldiers would roll left or right from wherever they had thrown themselves prone—to confuse any Sim marksman who might have spotted them—then hop up and rush forward for a few seconds before hitting the deck again. Almost immediately after that, the troops who had been stationary would roll, rise, and rush in the same fashion. It was the most basic of infantry skills, some men moving while others were shooting, and it presented the enemy with an unpredictable series of targets that were exposed for very short periods.

Unfortunately, Mortas had become separated from the men on either side of him and couldn't see anything but a wall of green. Struggling to his feet, he rushed forward with helmet bouncing, Scorpion rifle across his chest to part the grass, and hoping he wasn't going to end up in front of the advancing troops.

Two rubberized doughnuts abruptly pressed down around his ears, one of the reasons that the infantry helmet was referred to as a "grip" by the veterans.

Dak's voice came over the radio inside the twin mufflers, telling Berland to shift the machine guns' fire to the far side of the position. Although every member of the platoon could communicate using the helmet radios, the veterans had explained to Mortas that they attempted to stay off the net as much as possible. If everyone began talking, important messages and commands could be lost. Mortas had decided this was a gentle way of telling him that the squad leaders and team leaders could maneuver their men without excessive direction from their new lieutenant.

Dak's message to Berland indicated that at least one squad had reached the closest enemy fighting positions, and so Mortas leapt up and bulled forward. He knew the grass stopped short of the hilltop, and was telling himself to just get to where he could see something when the blades parted abruptly and he spilled out into the open.

It was as if he'd been thrust into a completely different world. Tan-colored ground rising in front of him for another hundred yards, mostly open with patches of low weeds. Machine gun noise that seemed far off because the dampers in his helmet had snugged down again to protect his ears from the explosions and rifle fire. Twenty yards to his front a dark, ugly slit in a hump of rock, the firing ports of the first Sim emplacement. Light blinking from inside, continuous ripping sounds, a line of small eruptions in the dirt to his right and more water drops on his face. Bracing the Scorpion against the dirt, firing into the slit, ridiculously exposed, but then smoke was blossoming right in front of the bunker.

Snug against his cheeks, his goggles automatically adjusted so Mortas could see through the cloud. Mechanical movement, the enemy gun traversing, then the image was gone, replaced by a flash of light that would have blinded him if the goggles hadn't reacted. An instant later he registered the blast of a rocket launcher ("boomers" in troop parlance) and knew where the searing light had come from. Turning to his left to see troops from Dak's squad, prone at the edge of the grass, functioning smoothly. The smoke had been provided by one of the grenade launcher men, known as "chonks" because of the sound their weapons made. The rocket team, needing to reload, rolled back deeper into the bush while Dak and several others began the alternating rush toward the disabled enemy position.

Dirt leapt up and slapped his cheek, and Mortas jerked his head to the right in wonder. More of the simulated rounds were being directed at him, and he finally made out the very edge of another bunker, farther up the hill. Rolling, jumping to his feet, boots kicking up more dirt as he ran, looking for something to hide behind and only seeing the edge of a rock the size of a human head, then he was down behind it, firing uphill at the new threat.

More movement to his left, Dak's men. Body armor, helmets, the dark goggles hugging their faces, impossible to tell them apart. They seemed to hop and skip as they rushed, then Mortas remembered that he was actually supposed to be in charge here and where the heck was Mecklinger's squad?

"East Team, East Team, get up here! Knock out that bunker on your side!" His voice rasped from the effort and the heat and the smoke that now drifted over him. The designation of the two assault teams was a First Platoon convention utilizing the points of the compass. Dak's squad, to his left, was on the western side of the objective while Mecklinger was on the east. The labeling was a good reminder of areas of responsibility and zones of fire, particularly important after they'd captured the position.

As if by magic, a salvo of chonks coughed from his right. More smoke rounds to blind the enemy gunners, but then a remarkable shot, low angle, that skipped an explosive round straight through the firing port. Again the goggles protected him, but Mortas saw a momentary snort of flame burst forth.

Up again, more rifle sounds, seeing that half of Dak's people were already past the first emplacement while the other half provided covering fire. Regardless of the rocket strike's effects, an unidentified soldier armed a grenade and tossed it into the position that they were now using for protection. Mortas, running toward it, heard the shouted warning of "Grenade!" and threw himself facedown in the dirt just as the explosive detonated. He imagined a gust of wind passing over him, an invisible wave of air carrying lethal shrapnel at titanic speeds.

Figures to his right now, camouflage fatigues, helmets and armor, the thick tube of a rocket launcher, and then he was at the base of the first bunker. Watching Mecklinger's people heaving grenades into the position farther up the hill, some prone while others fired over the canted sides of the low emplacement. Coming to a crouch, spitting dirt off his tongue, just peering around the side of the captured fighting position when Dak's voice came over the radio.

"All clear! All clear!"

Realizing that the machine guns had all stopped firing, Mortas looked up and over the enemy position to see that the third and last bunker had been captured by Dak's people. Facing in the opposite direction, it had been the easiest one because it had been attacked from the rear. More voices on the radio, team leaders reporting casualties—none in this case—and squad leaders already shifting the assault force into a defensive perimeter. The Sims were famous for counterattacking lost positions almost immediately, and with heavy forces.

Berland's voice came over the net, breathing heavily, rushing to bring up the machine guns.

"Support team comin' in! Support team comin' in!"

"—all things considered, that was not a bad iteration." Sergeant Berland was finishing his assessment of the platoon's performance in the live-fire assault. The troops were seated in front of him in a dirty cluster, some of the men swigging from canteens. They'd all removed their helmets, and some had taken off the goggles as well. The flat eyepieces could be slid upward on the face-hugging frames to allow normal vision, and Mortas and many of the others had done just that.

"Of course, this objective was a simple one because we've got some new men, and because our last assignment took us away from practicing this kind of mission."

The veterans in the group laughed or whistled at this. Mortas, seated in the rear with his rifle across his knees, smiled when he heard a few of the comments.

"Fuckin' rat hunt."

"Hump over all those hills, get in a shoot-'em-up for thirty seconds, then hump some more."

"Never thought I'd be so happy to see a fake Sim bunker."

Berland quieted them with a patient stare. "As I was saying, this one was easy. No mines, no obstacles, no defensive patrols. In other words, nothing like the real thing. Yes?"

One of the green troops had raised his hand. "Sergeant, is it true that their barbed wire will reach out and grab you, then tighten up until it cuts you in half?"

The question brought out some scattered laughter, but not as much as Mortas would have expected. Watching, he saw some of the veterans shaking their heads just a bit, and one exhaling through puckered lips as if trying to blow away a bad smell.

"I see some of the older men have been telling you new guys a few stories." Berland smiled paternally.

"That's close, but not quite right. You already know that the Sims have a reactive form of obstacle wire, attracted by the electrical field put out by humans. If it's not nailed down, or was blown into pieces, it will actually snake across the ground at you, and the barbs will latch on. The stuff emits a bright light when it comes into contact with us, and in low visibility the Sims are trained to shoot at that light.

"We do have some countermeasures, but we won't be training with any of that for a while. Let's focus on what we did today, and get the hang of that first." Berland cleared his throat. "Sergeant Dak, what happened with the abandoned Sim machine gun?"

Mortas had no idea what Berland was talking about, so he straightened up a bit. His torso armor shifted, and loose dirt tickled as it went between his fatigue top and his back.

"When we were assaulting the third bunker, half my squad provided a base of fire while I took the other half with me. We passed a dropped Sim machine gun in a shallow ditch, but we were so focused on the next target that we didn't take it with us."

Mortas suspected that one of the new additions to Dak's squad had missed the enemy weapon, but Berland addressed the correction to the group.

"This is important, men: never miss an opportunity to add firepower—ours or the enemy's—to the platoon. Machine guns, boomers, chonks, bags of grenades. Especially when we're assaulting a position like this one. When the Sims lose important terrain, they counterattack as fast as they can with as much as they can. The veterans will tell you that we've ended more than one fight firing mostly enemy weapons because we were out of ammunition for our own. So keep your eyes open, and grab it as you go by."

The barrel-chested NCO raised his narrow eyes to Mortas. "Anything you'd like to add, sir?"

Caught off guard and still embarrassed from having fallen behind in the grass, Mortas simply responded, "No, Sergeant Berland. I think you covered everything."

"Okay, squad leaders go ahead and take a few minutes to talk with your people about what you saw." The platoon broke up into smaller groups, and they moved off in different directions while Berland approached Mortas.

"How'd you like it, sir?"

"Honestly? I felt like a spare part."

Berland gave him a gentle smile. "I know. I put up a couple of dragonflies during the assault. Wanna have a look?"

Cringing inwardly, Mortas reached up and slid the goggle lenses down over his eyes. They made a slight clicking sound upon mating with the frames that pressed against his cheeks, and he watched Berland do the same.

The platoon sergeant triggered a video of the assault that had been shot from overhead by tiny flying robots called dragonflies. Every man carried several of them, each in a straw-like tube from which the aerobot was launched by blowing into one end. The dragon-flies flew for only a few minutes, but their miniscule cameras provided overhead footage that went directly into the goggles. Every dragonfly in the air synched up with every other dragonfly, so it didn't take many of them to cover a wide area.

Inside the advanced vision devices, Mortas saw dirt erupting around the three enemy positions when Berland's machine gun position had started firing. The view widened, presumably when another dragon-fly had added its feed, and he watched in chagrin as Dak's and Mecklinger's squads easily pushed their way through the grass. In the middle of the undulating row of men, Mortas saw himself fighting his way through the vegetation with increasingly frenzied movements.

The soldiers to either side of him reached the edge of the clearing and began firing rifles and chonks at will, but his armored figure kept struggling forward for several more seconds. It was only after his frantic form fell out of the grass into the open that Mortas noticed he'd had a much greater distance to travel than the others. The vegetation in the center bulged out-ward into the clearing for several more yards, and he now remembered feeling hemmed in by bodies when the assault team had been arranging itself at the lower edge of the grass. He stopped the transmission and slid the goggles up to see Berland's waiting eyes.

"They did that on purpose. They worked it out so I'd go through the worst part of that shit."

Berland was obviously trying not to laugh. "I'd

take it as a sign that they accept you, sir. They usually ignore the lieutenants they don't like."

Mortas shook his head, but soon saw the humor in the prank. "I guess I have a lot to learn, don't I?"

"That's all right, sir. You're not the only one. Like I said, this objective was really basic. Gotta get the newbies comfortable with the bang and the boom before they can start focusing on their jobs. Just wait 'til we do this in darkness; with the goggles on, you can see the rounds going by, and it's pretty scary the first few times . . ."

Berland's voice trailed off, and he looked past Mortas. Turning, the lieutenant was surprised to see several big-wheeled military movers rolling toward the hill.

"What's that about?"

"I think we might not be able to continue training today, sir." Berland slid his goggles back down. All across the hilltop, the troops were noticing the transports. Mortas fumbled with his goggles, but the message was there when he got them in place.

A tiny red dot was blinking in the corner of one lens, and the text of a prep order began scrolling in front of his eyes:

All B Company units are ordered to return to the battalion area. Draw jungle camouflage fatigues and accessories. Prepare to receive mission orders.

The words appeared on the squad leaders' goggles as well, and the effect of the message on the platoon was immediate.

"Jungle camouflage. Fuck."

"This shit *again*?"

"Oh, you greenies are gonna *love* this one!"

Mortas gave Berland a quizzical look, but the platoon sergeant was already calling out orders for the men to collect all their gear and move to the transports. When he was done, the veteran quietly explained.

"There's a planet not far from here, one of the Habs that isn't really a Hab. We took it from the Sims a long time ago, but it's covered in jungle and the water's basically muck, so there aren't many humans posted there. It's mostly a few retransmission sites and a couple of planetary-study stations, but there's a bunch of Sammies left over from the fighting who keep screwing with them.

"Because we're close by, whenever the Sims get out of hand one of our companies gets sent to chase 'em through the bush for a while. The whole place is really hot, the terrain's a killer, and the Sims there have gotten really good at planting booby traps." Berland gave him a shrug. "I guess break time's over."

The next hours were a blur of activity, and Mortas was relieved to see that everybody else seemed to know what to do. Issue points manned by troops from the other companies had already been set up back in the battalion area when they rolled in, and in no time at all he'd received two sets of jungle fatigues as well as covers for his body armor in the same pattern. The fabric was lighter than the woodland camouflage he'd been wearing, and its color was a dark green, striped horizontally with black and brown.

A host of details had to be sorted out before their departure, but the Orphans were familiar with this particular job. The rocket teams exchanged the bulky boomers for rifles because there would be little use for them on this mission, and the understrength squads needed the extra bodies. For the first time, Mortas realized that the entire brigade was well below its authorized strength and would remain so even with the eventual return of the hospital cases. He was also surprised to see the length of the line when he went to receive a full complement of immunizations along with the other new men.

The sun was setting as he strode along the walkway toward the battalion headquarters with Captain Noonan and a veteran lieutenant he'd never met before. All of B Company's platoon leaders had been hit during the brigade's last mission, and only one of them was still on MC-1932. The platoon leader of Third Platoon, Wyn Kitrick, walked with a limp. His troops had sprung him from the nearby hospital when the prep order had come in, and Noonan had been visibly pleased to see him.

As they walked, Mortas noticed a group of soldiers packing up B Company's rocket launchers for transport. He was about to ask the obvious question when Kitrick answered it without looking.

"If the rest of the brigade gets alerted while we're

gone, we'll have to meet them en route. So anything we leave behind has to be ready to go—especially the boomers."

There was a brisk air of purpose when they entered the building, and Mortas was surprised to see so much woodland camouflage among the hurrying bodies. Every deployable member of B Company had been wearing tiger stripes for the last few hours, and the sudden discrepancy hit him like a physical blow. He was actually going in harm's way.

Seeming not to notice the heightened activity, Noonan led them up the stairs and through the operations section. Home of the battalion's chief planners, Operations was a buzz of voices talking on radios and conferring over lit map screens as they finalized the mission order. The three officers passed into a large conference room, and Mortas was relieved to see several tiger-striped uniforms amid the throng. Most of B Company's senior NCOs were already present, and Berland gave him a reassuring nod from the back of the room.

The wall at the opposite end of the conference table was taken up with a lit display screen. It showed an overhead photo of what Mortas could only assume was one of the threatened stations on the jungle planet Verdur. Standing atop a tall, almost cylindrical mountain, it consisted of several heavily reinforced buildings surrounded by a double wall of antipersonnel fencing. On all sides the ground dropped away like a brilliant green waterfall into dense foliage.

Captain Noonan and Lieutenant Kitrick had already taken seats at the table, and Mortas was about to join them when a hand took his arm. He half expected it to be Berland, and so was surprised to see it was the battalion intelligence officer. The smiling face from the previous night was gone, and Mortas only had a second to wonder what could be wrong. Pappas spoke in a low voice.

"Jan, did you see Captain Follett last night?"

"Yes, sir. He was outside throwing up, but he said he was all right and walked away." Remembering the supply officer's bizarre advice. "Is something wrong?"

"I'm afraid so. He's dead."

Noonan, overhearing the quiet conversation, rose and joined them. "Drew's *dead*? What happened?"

"I should have been paying closer attention, but you know how he was. Always going on about how we were all gonna starve if the resupply got messed up, asking why couldn't we figure out a way to make captured Sim rations edible . . . it seems he was conducting an experiment."

"Experiment? With Sim chow? It's *poison*."

"Yeah. We found a case of it in his room. It looks like he'd been slowly adding it to some of our rations . . . and eating it." Pappas's face was pale, and he licked his lips rapidly. "Poor stupid son of a bitch. I guess he thought we could bulk up our food with theirs, something like that. He was always so worried about everything, but I should have noticed. He was so . . . thin."

Colonel Alden walked in just then, not smiling, and

Sergeant Major Zacker called the assembled men to attention. For those moments before Alden reached his chair and told everyone to relax, the room was silent. Standing there, separated from much of the group by his uniform and now touched by the real presence of death, Mortas felt his heart thumping heavily.

CHAPTER FIVE

"**H**ow many times do I have to say this? There is no Sim home world!"

Olech Mortas sat in one of Unity's largest safe rooms, listening to brilliant men and women argue around a doughnut-shaped conference table. Stretching away from him on either side were a collection of doctors, scientists, and historians who collectively formed the Select Committee on the Sims. As was his habit, he sat back and let the great minds talk in an overlapping free-for-all.

"No Sim home world? They just burst into being in the middle of space?"

"Everyone here already agrees that the Sims were—and are—a manufactured opponent. A designer enemy. So no, they didn't just appear in the middle of space. But they didn't evolve, either. They were created someplace—perhaps in many places—which means it is a pointless exercise to keep looking for this mythical home world."

"Didn't evolve? You're telling me they mastered spaceflight within forty to one hundred years of their creation?"

"Hold on there. Just because we're only now seeing Sims with gray hair in the war zone doesn't mean they're the oldest Sims in existence. It only means that we haven't seen any elderly Sims, which could be easily explained as a cultural unwillingness to send their elders out to fight."

"Are you even listening to yourself? For the first twenty years of the conflict our troops never encountered a Sim who was even middle-aged. It's only in the last two decades that we've been seeing older Sims. Which is pretty strong evidence that the Sims don't predate the war by very long."

"Not necessarily. What if they changed their terms of military service? What if they're getting desperate, and have turned to sending out the older males?"

"Getting desperate? We're seeing larger and larger numbers of them, despite having gotten quite efficient at *killing them* in large numbers. They've got an inexhaustible supply of soldiers, most of whom are estimated to be twenty years of age. They don't *need* to be sending the elder males out, assuming they've actually got any."

"Wait a moment, let's back up the conversation. I think we all agree a humanlike opponent that can't form any of our words, can't consume our food, and dies within days of captivity is probably a good bet to be a 'designer enemy' as you said. Which of course means they're being manufactured by some other entity. An entity so superior to mankind that I have to ask yet again: why didn't this entity just wipe us out?"

"I'll answer you yet again: whatever is making the Sims is doing so because it *has to*. If it didn't have to, why go to all that trouble? So this entity probably lacks most of the capabilities we see in the Sims. I'd wager they're not physically large or strong—if they have any material existence at all—and so they needed a material, physical agent to combat us once we began to spread across the solar systems."

"If this entity has no material form, why would it care if we got closer, or even if we moved in next door? And why is it fighting us for the Hab planets if it can survive anywhere?"

"The Sims are fighting us for the Habs, not this *alleged* creator entity."

"I cannot believe you still think the Sims came into existence on their own. They can't reproduce, and we keep seeing more and more of them from the young end of the scale. There is only one explanation for that: somebody is making them."

Olech cleared his throat, and the room fell silent. Folding his hands, the Chairman of the Emergency Senate rested his forearms on the table as if getting ready to pray. "I enjoy the spirited debate as much as anyone, but your latest comments reminded me of something I've told this group before.

"In the early years of the war we thought the Hab planets were the key to victory, when in fact they're only the prize that will ultimately go to the winner in this conflict. Don't confuse the prize with the key. The key gets you the prize. So let's all remember we're trying to answer the question, 'What is the key that wins us the prize?'"

A cold silence followed his words, and Olech sat back to indicate that he was done for the moment. It didn't take long for the debate to resume.

"The Chairman's right. The Sims may see the Habs as key to their survival, but how does that fit the goals of whatever is making the Sims? Is their plan to create a bulwark of Sim-occupied Habs, to keep us away from them? And if so, why?"

"The Sims are far too aggressive for that to be the case. They aren't seeking to contain us. They're meant to replace us."

"Replace us? More like exterminate us. I think whatever is making the Sims views us as an infestation, and they're responding exactly the way we would. If we couldn't get rid of an infestation any other way, we'd find or breed an organism that could enter the infestation's environment and destroy it. And we wouldn't use an organism that was going to end up being worse than the infestation. We'd pick something that we could easily eradicate once the infestation was destroyed."

"Oh, not the Kill Switch Theory again."

"I really wish you wouldn't call it that. But it makes sense that whatever is creating all these Sims would want some way to get rid of them once they've gotten rid of us." Cold, clinical eyes directed at Olech. "And if we can figure out what that 'Kill Switch' is, we might just have your key, Mr. Chairman."

"Let's not get ahead of ourselves here, making promises to the Chairman when we're dealing almost completely in hypotheses. And let's not forget that the Sims, even if completely victorious, will die out in one generation because they can't reproduce. In other words, whatever is making the Sims has no need for a 'Kill Switch' at all. They just have to turn off the machines making the new Sims and wait a few decades."

"That's not necessarily the case. The Sims can't communicate with us, eat our food, or come into close contact with us for prolonged periods. I say they were designed that way because their creators were concerned they might *join up* with us. And if that is the case, the creators would want a means of turning their creations *off* if they turned against them."

"Just how would that work? A chemical? A biological agent? The Sims are spread across numerous solar systems. It would be impossible to deliver such a thing to all of them. They're not stupid, you know. They've faced diseases just like we have, and they'd figure it out pretty quickly if something was trying to finish them off that way."

"They're not stupid, but they don't possess the ingenuity of humans. Their technology moves forward in fits and starts, and there's no explaining how it developed."

"Our technological history is not a smooth upward line, and even if it were, remember that some human cultures never invented the wheel."

"Just a moment. How does the evolution of their technology bear on the theory that their creators could turn them off at will?"

"Their tech keeps improving, but in weird, spotty leaps. They jump from Point A to Point D without any indication they passed through the developmental stages of Point B and Point C. Some of that could be explained by their exposure to us and captured human devices, but not all of it. Personally, I believe that whatever is making the Sims periodically provides them with the knowledge they need to stay in this fight."

Olech's face tightened, despite his years in politics and a fine ability to hide his emotions. Fortunately, the discussion was so electric that no one seemed to notice.

"I have to agree with my colleague on that. At different times when the war was going badly for them, the enemy suddenly demonstrated new tools and techniques that put them back in the game. And there is absolutely *no way* that the opponent we've been facing for forty years could have developed this new 'mud' munition, the one our troops encountered on Roanum. It turned solid ground into mud so thick that it almost swallowed armored vehicles, and shortly after that the dirt returned to its former state. The Sims aren't smart enough to come up with something like that, and I know that for a fact because *we* aren't smart enough."

The silence returned, with brooding expressions and eyes directed at the table. Olech was just about to prod them when one of the scientists spoke up.

"Mr. Chairman, a few of us have heard a disquieting rumor about something else allegedly encountered on Roanum. Everyone here recognizes the heroism of your son, and the contribution your family has already made to this war. But if this committee is to be of any help at all, we need the latest and most complete information possible.

"Mr. Chairman, is there any truth to the rumor about a shape-shifting alien?"

Olech wasn't surprised by the question, and ready with an answer.

"I can neither confirm, nor deny, those rumors."

Eyes widened, and meaningful glances swept across the table. The phrasing of the response had significance for this group, and was always taken as an unqualified yes. The ramifications for such a being's existence were hard to fathom, but at a minimum it confirmed there was intelligent life in the universe that was not human and not Sim.

A series of hollow thumps emanated from the sealed entrance behind Olech, and the room went silent when the door opened. A staff member whispered in his ear, and the Chairman rose.

"A matter has arisen that requires my personal attention, but please continue the session without me. I'm sure you have a lot to discuss."

"Thanks for getting me out of there, Burke." Olech smiled at the young staffer, who beamed with the compliment. Although Olech had found the session highly interesting, he'd arranged to be called away because of an important event he wanted to witness personally. Despite that, he seldom missed a chance to praise his subordinates, and it didn't hurt that the scuttlebutt among the youngsters would suggest he found the SCOTS meetings tedious. The cover story about the alien was not the only disinformation campaign Olech Mortas had in progress.

They walked briskly, following the curve of the circular hallway in that particular part of the Unity complex. Young people in the uniform of the chairman's staff passed them coming and going, and Olech greeted most of them by name. Artificial light brightened the cream-colored corridor, flowing down from tall screens projecting images from outside the building. Every common area in the fortified complex boasted these screens, to the extent that most of the people who worked there at least subconsciously believed they were surrounded by windows.

The walk didn't take long, and Olech gently dismissed Burke before stepping past a sentry guarding a door set into the corridor wall. Not far from that entrance, a large set of wooden doors led into one of Unity's main briefing rooms. The side entrance gave him admittance to a much smaller space with a two-way mirror that would allow him to watch the proceedings without interrupting them.

A row of comfortable chairs faced the wide window, and Hugh Leeger already occupied one of them. Sitting down, Olech heard Reena's voice on the speakers. He nodded at Hugh, then leaned forward to look down into the room.

Two long tables faced each other from a distance of ten yards, and microphones stood up in front of the people taking part in the proceedings. Reena sat at the center of the main table, her red hair done up in a bun and wearing a blue business suit with a high collar. Two other ministers sat to her right and left, but they were mostly for show, to give the impression that this was simply a fact-finding interview.

Across from them sat a uniformed officer of the Human Defense Force, a general named Merkit. Heavyset with a florid face, his tunic displayed a surprising lack of combat decorations for a man of his station. Merkit was the officer in charge of Force personnel, and he was surrounded by members of his staff.

The rear of the room, behind the general, was taken up with several rows of seats. Sessions in this room were always recorded and usually broadcast over the Bounce, and so the chairs were filled with an assortment of Olech's staff people and several reporters who'd been alerted that this particular interview might be worth watching.

"—so thank you, General Merkit, for taking us

through the latest numbers related to discharged Force personnel currently taking advantage of the educational opportunities they earned while serving our race in its hour of need.

"I'd like to change the subject slightly, and divert from our prepared agenda to ask a question about a different category of Force personnel. The troops I'm interested in are approaching discharge or already past that date, but still in the war zone."

Olech grinned when Merkit's face turned a shade redder. The officers seated closest to him immediately snatched up their handhelds and begun punching or thumbing through their prepared numbers, but Reena wasn't willing to wait for them.

"Specifically, I've been reviewing the number and disposition of the troops currently residing on Platinus."

"Stationed, Minister."

"Excuse me?"

"The term is 'stationed,' Minister, not 'residing.' Those soldiers are an important part of the work that begins on every Hab planet as soon as it is secured. This is for the benefit of—"

"Oh, I'm sorry. I thought it was inaccurate to say they were stationed there when such a large percentage of them had already passed their discharge dates. I assumed they had elected to stay on as colonists, as is their prerogative—Force demands permitting, of course."

Conditions on many of the home planets were far from ideal for returning soldiers who'd completed terms of enlistment that were a minimum of seven years in duration. Many of the veterans elected to settle on the captured Hab planets in or near the war zone. Those colonization efforts had proceeded on some of the earliest conquests to the extent that loved ones and families had joined the veterans as well. It was an effective and equitable way of developing the new worlds, but the excessive number of troops on Platinus was not an example of that policy.

"I'm glad you mentioned Force requirements, Minister. As you know, Platinus was declared secure only two years ago and it is well within the range of Sim fleets. As such—"

"Oh. So these soldiers who are past their discharge dates are not there voluntarily?"

Merkit's eyes had narrowed, and he seemed on the verge of an accusation of some kind when one of his aides leaned in and whispered to him. He nodded, paused for a moment, and then spoke into the microphone.

"My apologies, Minister. I wasn't familiar with the exact disposition of the troops on Platinus. Apparently local commanders identified Platinus as a good location for quarantined soldiers, troops who had been exposed to some of the many unusual diseases we've encountered on the planets in the war zone. These soldiers are currently showing no symptoms, but because these diseases are new to our medical personnel, the quarantine period is of an indeterminate duration."

"That certainly makes sense, General. Thank you

for clearing that up." Reena tilted her handheld, and let her eyebrows rise. "One other thing, though: according to my figures, almost all of the troops on Platinus—discharged or not—are citizens of Tratia. How did the Tratian leadership respond when they were informed of the large number of their soldiers who'd been quarantined?"

Merkit folded his hands on the table, staring at Reena with a half smile of realization. When one of his officers tried to feed him an excuse, he shook his head minutely, and the assistant subsided.

"The Tratian leadership, as would be expected, is quite concerned about the welfare of their troops—on Platinus or anywhere else. There are many Force concentrations across the war zone that would appear to reflect an imbalance such as this one, but closer examination usually reveals that it is mere coincidence. For example, there is a very large concentration of troops from your native Celestia on—"

"Thank you, General, your answer is already sufficient."

Merkit allowed the smile to broaden. "Are you sure, Minister? I could go on."

Reena returned the smile, and Merkit's face lost some of its humor. "Are you certain that would be the best use of our time, General? Because I'll let you continue . . . if you think it's wise."

Merkit's smile vanished. "No, Minister. On second thought I believe I've said enough."

In the observation room, Olech turned to see Leeger smirking. He grabbed the security man's forearm and squeezed it tightly. "*God* I love that woman."

"Kletterman."

"Who?" Ayliss sat down in the chair held by Selkirk, her eyes on Dev Harlec. The data genius had been waiting for them at a table in a restaurant frequented by the Brodan elite. Selkirk took a long look around the crowded floor before seating himself across from Harlec, who was wearing a suit that was only slightly more formal than his normal warm-up clothes. The contrast reminded Ayliss that Lee looked especially good tonight; a jacket of a dark green fabric outlined his muscular torso to great advantage. Security uniforms were frowned upon in Brodan society, and the rest of her detail was likewise dressed in mufti as they circulated in the cavernous dining room.

"Dr. Yost Kletterman. I've spent the last two days looking for behavioral specialists who disappeared in the last couple of years, and he's a prominent name in the field. His last published work was eighteen months ago, and he's listed as being on sabbatical."

A string quartet was playing somewhere in the wide balcony that circled the room. The restaurant's color scheme was bright gold and rich red, and the cream of the capital city had turned out in all their finery. Data was a lucrative business, and Brodan openness lent itself to displays of wealth. Ayliss herself had chosen a backless silver gown that hugged her curves and looked good next to Selkirk's green.

"This Dr. Kletterman sounds like someone who might just be involved in something he shouldn't be. Any luck finding him?"

"Of course not. If he's doing what we think he's doing, someone's buried him under many layers of cover stories and security classifications."

"I thought you said scientists don't follow security protocols."

"They don't. Which is why people like your father send them to the war zone and have their communications completely severed. Very thorough people, the folks who work for your father." Harlec gave a dark look at Selkirk.

"Don't I know it." Ayliss smiled broadly before taking Lee's hand. His head jerked toward her just a hair, and she was surprised to have startled him.

"Sorry." He raised the hand to his lips, briefly, before returning his eyes to the rest of the room. "Not used to sitting down with you."

"No reason to be nervous, young man. This is Broda. No one's planning an attack." Harlec waved his arm, and a jacketed waiter moved toward them. "Anyone watching is most likely wondering why Olech Mortas's daughter is sitting with me."

Selkirk gave Harlec a smile that Ayliss recognized as something he practiced in the mirror, a look of idiotic acceptance Lee reserved for very senior people with whom he completely disagreed. She quickly spoke up.

"So, Dev. Where does this leave us?"

"Having dinner." Harlec briefly conferred with the waiter, ordered for the three of them without asking permission, then continued. "I'm not stumped, in case you were wondering."

"I wasn't wondering at all. I have faith in you."

"As you should. One of the big advantages of living here is that when I've determined that the answer is not in the existing data, I can often turn to others to find that data, sometimes even to create it. I'm not the only denizen of this planet who came here because of an ideological disagreement with the authorities elsewhere."

"And who are these other criminals?"

"Oh, they're not so much criminals as persons of intellect who, unlike me, would rather not come into direct contact with you. But they did share some of their thoughts, based on their own research."

"Someone else was looking for this Kletterman?"

"Don't be silly. I wouldn't take them down the same dead end I'd already investigated. No, I asked if they'd encountered anything that might sound similar to your theory about Command dabbling in behavioral modification."

"And they had."

"In a manner of speaking. I was intentionally vague, to avoid biasing the results, and it had a serendipitous effect in that they haven't seen anything involving *human* behavior."

"I do hope you're not going to tell me you're surprised that Command is studying the enemy."

"Nothing Command does surprises me. But this is important: there is a small group of linguistic experts who have been trying to decode the Sim language for many years. They're not the first, and I understand this has been an ongoing project in the Force since the start of the war, but this is a private collaboration. Their hope is to open a dialogue with the Sims, with the intention of negotiating a peace. As you can imagine, people like your father probably wouldn't like that at all.

"So they're staying very much in the shadows. It's been enormously harmful to their research, but they've assembled a surprising amount of knowledge from casual interviews with returned veterans and nonmilitary contractors. Funny thing about the war zone—Command's information monopoly ends as soon as somebody gets home."

"I'm not seeing how this connects to what we're doing." Selkirk spoke lightly, his eyes momentarily halted on Harlec's face.

"Oh, is it *we* now? Well, I suppose one does have to join in on the battles of one's romantic interest. Even if one probably doesn't understand a word of it."

Ayliss's hand tightened on Lee's, and Harlec gave an airy grin when the security man subsided.

"To continue. The Sim language—or languages, that's how little we understand of this—consists of birdlike sounds that we humans have difficulty discerning, much less imitating. However, the Sims do have a written form of communication. It may be nothing more complicated than a basic symbology, or it may be more complex than that.

"Captured Sim equipment was a good start, basically matching up a symbol to an item's function. For example, the symbols for an On and Off switch." Harlec turned to Selkirk. "Still with us?"

"Don't be like that, Dev."

"Sorry. I was a teacher for many years and sometimes went too fast for some of my students. To resume, the linguists' research recently revealed something interesting. A number of years ago, during a prolonged campaign for control of a particularly arid Hab planet, the Sims attempted to poison our troops by leaving caches of tainted water in the path of advancing Force units.

"In addition to the Sim symbol for water, these containers had a previously unknown marking that, based on the results, is believed to indicate poison. You see, the Sims leaving the contaminated water behind didn't want to take the chance of ignorant comrades finding and drinking it. It seems that the evil enemy has a heart after all.

"More recently, several small supply dumps captured by our troops yielded crates of Sim emergency rations bearing the same symbol, the one for poison."

"But that makes no sense. Humans can't eat Sim food. For us it *is* poison. So why contaminate their own rations?" Ayliss's blue eyes became unfocused as she tried to sort through the puzzle.

"Because they're not trying to poison humans." Selkirk's face had grown hard, and his eyes burned into Harlec's.

The scientist displayed amused wonderment. "Remarkable. I may have misjudged you. Or perhaps not . . . people in your line of work do develop a kind of low animal cunning, so I'm not surprised you understood this so readily."

"Finish the story."

"Your boyfriend is right. The only target for such a trick would have to be of Sim physiology."

"But that doesn't make sense. No Sim POW has lasted more than a few days in human captivity, even when they were fed with their own rations."

"It seems that the enemy believes someone, somewhere, has gotten around that."

"And are they right?"

"Yes." For the first time, Harlec looked at the people seated closest to them. Placing a hand on Ayliss's shoulder, he leaned forward and whispered directly into her ear. "And you'd be so very surprised to know where they are."

"**A**bsolutely not. You do not go anywhere without me and the detail. And you have to be out of your mind to trust that little bastard Harlec. Secret gang of linguists my ass."

Back in their rooms, Selkirk stood with his arms folded across his chest. Harlec had arranged for Ayliss to meet the people who believed they'd discovered an ongoing Sim prisoner-of-war camp, but the group was so fearful of her father that they'd agreed to meet Ayliss and Ayliss alone. She'd agreed before Selkirk could stop her, and an emissary was due to arrive at any moment.

"Don't you see this is the only way? I go by myself, or I don't go at all."

"So don't go at all. I don't trust that Harlec, never have, and even if *he* believes this fairy tale, what does that mean? Guy stares at a screen all day long."

"He's plugged in with all sorts of people who hate my father. He got chased off Earth—why would he be lying?"

"I already said it. Maybe Harlec's dumb enough to believe this story, but it doesn't mean we have to be. We don't even know who these supposed conspirators are, and you're wrong to think that your fight with your father puts you in both camps and keeps you safe. Powerful people get snatched all the time, and it usually happens when they ditch their security."

Her eyes were damp when Ayliss walked up and placed her palms flat against his chest. She'd already changed into a set of dark travel clothes and boots, but Selkirk still wore the suit from dinner. She tilted her head to one side, stopping the tear that had almost rolled out.

"I know there's a risk. But everything is falling into place. Don't you see that? The camp we're talking about is on *this* side of the CHOP line. *Well* on this side.

That breaks so many laws, and is so unacceptable, that there is no way anyone connected to this could escape punishment if it was made public. I've wanted this for so long, and you're going to deny it to me?"

"I'm trying to protect you." His arms unfolded, and he pulled her close. "This is what I do. No one in my position would let you do this."

"You don't understand. You don't know what it was like, being pushed aside the way Jan and I were. We were raised by strangers while Olech was partying on the Bounce. A lot of people said my father changed when my mother died, but I don't believe that. I think he finally showed who he actually was—a cold, selfish bastard only out for himself who never wanted us. He was my *father*, for God's sake, and he's going to pay for what he did."

"Look. If this POW cage really does exist, we can find it some other way. Why rush like this? Why take the chance?"

The door buzzer sounded, and she looked up at him in pained resolution. "I *have* to."

Ayliss broke away and activated the door. It was dark outside, and at first all she could see was the outline of a large man. He quickly stepped across the threshold, and the outline resolved into the form of Python, her longtime conduit to illicit information. Ayliss's face must have registered surprise, because Python glanced at Selkirk and then gave her a broad smile.

"Oh come on. You didn't think I was just a drug dealer, did you?"

The armored mover was a big vehicle on bulletproof tires, and it rolled up next to a shuttle when they reached the spacedrome. Python was ready for her consternation at seeing that her trip to meet the linguists would involve an interplanetary craft.

"It's up to you." He switched off the engine and sat back. Python's hair was tied up behind his head, and he'd recently clipped his beard. His normally rough attire had been elevated a notch, but he was still Python. "We aren't going to meet anyone here, because they weren't willing to meet with you at all. To be honest, this bunch is pretty chicken. We had a long talk, and they suggested that I just take you to see the camp itself."

"I'm not understanding this. You mean *you* know where it is?"

"Of course. I was there when they delivered the first batch."

"And just how did that happen?"

"Have you heard the rumor about me serving in the war? It's true. I got stuck on an island on this one Hab, right in the middle of a gigantic fight. It was me, what was left of my company, and a bunch of Sims. Both sides had wounded, no way off the island, and there was only one water source. So we declared a truce using made-up sign language. Didn't come near each other, the Sims were very clear about that, and we rotated using the water.

"After a week we realized we'd been forgotten. So

we kept up the truce, spent some time waving at each other every day, then Command caught up with us. They weren't happy with what was going on, so they killed all the Sims and locked me and the other guys up. We did a couple of years, then they released us when our enlistments ended. All sorts of vile threats to keep our mouths shut, but who would have believed us anyway? Saying it's actually possible to coexist with the evil aggressor.

"A few months later they called me in and offered me some money if I'd talk with this Dr. Kletterman— not a bad guy, by the way, I've gotten to know him pretty well—and some others. They were shocked that the Sims on that island hadn't died, with so many of us humans nearby. Apparently keeping our distance was the key.

"From talking to me, Kletterman figured it was possible to transport captured Sims if they kept them isolated before, during, and after the trip. They wanted to reproduce the island on a captured Hab, but stock it only with Sims and observe their behavior." He gave a short laugh. "They call it the Ant Farm. Long-range surveillance, the Doc and his people watch everything the ants do.

"I guess whatever kills the Sims in captivity is human-related, because these ones are thriving. Right now they're growing their own food, but at first the Doc had to drop captured rations on them every now and then. They know they're prisoners, but they've got no contact with anybody and can't even see the mainland. The Doc and his gang seem to think they're learning a lot about them."

"You've got access to this place?"

"They call me out there every now and then, to compare notes about what happened on that other island. The Doc likes me a lot, and because this is a hush-hush Force operation, they're not allowed normal communications with anybody. Everything goes through a series of buffers, so if I showed up there with Olech Mortas's daughter, they'd accept it without question. And it's not a long trip. They're on Echo."

Echo was a tiny Hab close to Broda. Completely missed during the early decades of mankind's expansion across the stars, it had been declared off-limits so that its ecology could be studied. Except for a few scientific stations, the planet was untouched by humans.

"They've got living Sims all the way back here?" Ayliss could hardly control her excitement. The only thing that truly frightened the populations of the settled worlds was the idea that the Sims would find them. The conflict could rage on for generations as long as it stayed in the war zone, but anything that might tip the enemy off—such as bringing prisoners anywhere near the human planets—would cause a firestorm.

"Yeah. And they don't seem to think it's a big deal, either. I guess that's what happens when you have all that power—anything goes."

"I know all about that." She pursed her lips. "Why would you want to show me this? Why help me?"

"I've been watching you dig around for a long

time now, Ayliss. I had to know you meant it, that you weren't a plant." Python looked at the shuttle. "What they did to me and my buddies was wrong. What they did to those Sims on that island was wrong. And what they're doing on Echo, that's wrong too. I've had enough of what's wrong."

He stopped talking, and didn't turn to look at her again. Ayliss regarded the waiting spacecraft, but had already made up her mind.

"Let's go."

CHAPTER SIX

"Come on, greenies, you gotta do it better than that!" Berland called out in a weary voice, the sound echoing in the metal chamber. The platoon had been granted the use of an empty storage bay on the huge transport, and was practicing battle drills.

"Listen: the Sims we're facing have been cut off for a long time. There aren't that many of them left, but they know the terrain, and they'd just love to get a bunch of newbies to chase them straight into an ambush.

"That's why we're practicing *not* chasing them into an ambush. I've done this mission enough times to know it's not going to make any difference if we kill a few of them or never see any of them at all. We want to avoid what happened to the last Orphan company that was out there—"

"An entire squad got blown to shit when they

chased the Sammies past a hollow tree that was filled with explosives and scrap metal."

"Thank you, Sergeant Dak. I was trying not to tell our new men that story."

"We already know that one, Sergeant Berland." Even with the body armor, goggles, helmet, and weapon, the new man volunteering the information looked like a child. "And the one where they poured fuel on the grass and burned up that entire platoon—"

"Stop. Just stop." Berland removed his helmet and goggles. "There is no way to set fire to *anything* in that jungle. Even if you poured fuel on it. And we've never lost a platoon on this mission.

"Here's how it's going to go: the Sims try to shoot down the resupply drones when they come in, which means they converge on whichever site is getting its monthly delivery. Our company will be inserted in the jungle while the drones are in the air, zipping all over the place to confuse the Sims about which ones are full and which ones are empty.

"Second and Third Platoons will circle around the site on its east and west sides, and if the plan works, Sir Samuel will try to escape by going south, where we'll be waiting. The veterans have been on this mission before, so we know that's not going to work. The bush is so thick, and the Sims know the terrain so well, that there is no way they're gonna do what we want.

"So after they slip by our block position, we're gonna have to pick up all our stuff, including all the water we're gonna need because the local goop is so nasty, and we're gonna take a few long walks through the jungle. If the Sammies don't feel like playing, we're not even going to see them, but if they do feel sporty we're gonna get ambushed. So let's go back to the start line and try this again. Remember: You see something, hear something, or get shot at by something, *drop to the ground*. Then move up just enough to create a base of fire and don't go anywhere until you're told to do so."

"Why are they making us hump all this water when they can resupply us anytime?" This came from one of the veterans, a dour man whose name Mortas had not yet mastered.

"Yeah, Sarge—why don't they give us some of that powdered water instead?" Ladaglia managed to keep a straight face until one of the other veterans provided the punch line.

"Yeah, that's what we need, Sarge! Dehydrated aych-two-oh. Just add water."

The three squads got a good laugh in as they headed back across the storage area. Berland had marked out their different start positions on the oil-stained metal floor, and Mortas stepped away from them to consult with the senior NCO. He was tugging at his fatigue shirt under the torso armor, and Berland didn't wait for him to speak.

"Problem with the rig, sir?" Much earlier, Berland had showed Mortas how to adjust his helmet so that it no longer slid down onto his goggles whenever he hit the deck.

"Sorta." Mortas half turned, rifle in one hand, while

raising the curved plate of the armor's rear piece to show the handle of Corporal Cranther's fighting knife. "I wore this thing for days on Roanum, but that was without armor. This is the way the Spartacan Scout carried it, but it's not working for me."

"The Spartacans don't believe in body armor, sir. Or heavy weapons, for that matter. Can I see that?"

Mortas drew the long knife from its sheath, the blackened blade long and sharp. Handing it over while remembering the two times he'd used it, the first in a frenzy and the second without conscious thought. Berland hefted the weapon as if testing its balance.

"Any idea where I should carry this?"

"Yeah. The bottom of your ruck for now, and when we get back, I'm thinking it should go in one of your desk drawers." He handed the knife back. "Or you could hang it on the wall in your room."

"Huh?"

"Sir, all you're gonna do with that thing is hurt yourself. Seen it before with those commando knives. Me, I try to keep the enemy as far away as possible. If I could, I'd engage them with orbital rockets every time."

Mortas was about to object when a loud voice echoed through the bay, "Platoon, atten-chun!"

He turned to see Captain Noonan striding toward him, accompanied by the still-limping Lieutenant Kitrick. The company commander breezily told the men to relax as he went by, but he was followed by expressions that combined curiosity with concern.

"Lieutenant Mortas, Sergeant Berland, our mission

has been scrubbed. The brigade has been ordered to ship out to Fractus, and we will be linking up with them on the way."

"Fractus? They've been stalemated there close to *forever*, sir." Berland's words came out slowly, and Mortas detected a hint of apprehension.

"Apparently the stalemate is over." Noonan nodded at Mortas. "Seems the bad guys found another place to use that new ordnance you encountered on Roanum, the one that turns solid ground into mud. So far they've used it to cut off and destroy most of an armored division.

"Platoon sergeants and platoon leaders assemble in the galley in thirty minutes for a briefing." Noonan stalked off, but Kitrick stayed behind for a moment.

"Looks like we'll be getting our boomers back." He swatted Mortas's arm lightly before limping after the commanding officer.

"**B**roadcast to begin in three, two —" The technician mouthed the word "one," then pointed his index finger directly at Olech. The Chairman of the Emergency Senate was seated behind an impressive wooden desk in a sound stage at Unity that was made up to look like his office. He wore a dark gray tunic with a high collar, and his award for being one of the Unwavering stood out prominently.

"Hello, and greetings from Earth. I apologize for the unscheduled nature of this address, but I have im-

portant news that I would like to share with all of you."
Olech had rehearsed the words several times, and experts on his staff had coached him on his facial expression. His graying hair complemented a businesslike demeanor that was intentionally tinged with subdued cheerfulness.

"Few experiences are happier than the moment when one of our many heroes returns from military service. With that said, it has recently come to my attention that a considerable number of enlistments are being extended in the war zone, owing to concerns about possible exposure to the vectors of dangerous illnesses. I personally assure you that the veterans in question are healthy and that they are receiving the attention of our top medical experts. With that said, I must side with the commanders in the field in their decision to err on the side of caution, and to keep those troops in the war zone until a definite conclusion can be reached regarding the potential for carrying foreign pathogens to the settled planets.

"Every day of this conflict our brave Forcemembers encounter environments that are utterly alien to human experience. Rather than risk transmitting a completely foreign virus, bug, or biological agent to the settled worlds, Force commanders have established camps on conquered habitable planets for the quarantined veterans.

"Wartime security measures prevent me from disclosing specific locations, but these camps are located on the most desirable of the Habs that have been won for humanity by the blood and sacrifice of your sons and daughters. That was by design, and I laud the cooperation of the planetary councils, the rest of the Emergency Senate, and the highest command levels of our Human Defense Force in providing these troops with such an excellent environment.

"Sadly, we have no idea how long it may take to clear these brave veterans to return home. Although this is highly unlikely, it is possible that they may never be able to return. And that is why it was vital to place them on resource-rich planets that will also serve as admirable locations for the founding of new colonies. Words cannot express my humble gratitude for the selfless fashion in which our planetary governments gave up their claims to the bountiful resources of those planets, all in order to give these potential colonies every chance of long-term success.

"As Chairman of the Emergency Senate and the commander in chief of all our forces, I feel it is my duty to assist in this noble enterprise. And so I have lifted the burden of administering these colonies from the shoulders of generals and admirals whose primary duty is fighting the continuing war.

"As most of the troops in question are either past the end of their enlistments or can be expected to be in quarantine past that date, I am placing the management of the new colonies under the Veterans Auxiliary. I promise that the veterans in the new colonies will continue to receive the highest levels of medical care. They will also receive every assistance necessary to guarantee their success should they be required—or should they choose—to remain as colonists and the first citizens of what will someday be brilliant, shining additions to our alliance.

"Needless to say, top priority will be given to establishing a time frame for families to join their loved ones in these new colonies. In the meantime, rest assured that I will be supervising this personally while we move forward as a people, as a race, as a family, toward that great day when we will have secured the safety of humanity and returned our worlds to peace. Thank you."

"Is this how it's supposed to go? I do all the work, and you get all the accolades?" Reena stepped up and wrapped her arms around his neck when Olech moved away from the desk. They kissed warmly, enjoying the culmination of yet another plan. The broadcast wouldn't reach the other planets for some time, but it was too important to be tampered with and so would go through unchanged. No doubt the leadership on certain planets would soon be beaming their own coded messages to the Force commanders they owned in the war zone, but the deed was done. Olech broke the kiss and spoke.

"You set 'em up, and I knock 'em down."

"I've knocked a few of them down myself, you know."

"I do indeed. I enjoyed the way you handled General Merkit. What do you say I send him to the war zone to get some combat experience?"

"What combat experience would an office politician like him get? You send him out there, and he'll find a way to take charge of those rich new colonies."

"Oh, I've got someone else in mind for that."

"You can't be serious. She's twenty-three, and she's been with the Auxiliary less than a year."

"Every story the Bounce has ever run on Ayliss has received high approval numbers, especially when she wears the Aux uniform. Besides, it would give her something to do other than taking shots at me."

Reena's face clouded. "You do know that some other people are going to want to take a shot at you because of what we did today."

"What can they do? They overplayed their hands by stuffing those planets with their own people, and they paid for it. They've got no alternatives other than to smile and go along. That's why I didn't bother consulting them."

"That was a nice touch, giving them credit for something they didn't know about—and wouldn't have agreed to, ever."

"They'll be smart enough to take the credit. And maybe next time they won't try to pull a stunt like this one."

"Probably, but there are plenty of other actors in this who don't care about public opinion, who are going to feel their good buddy Olech Mortas just did them in."

"At first, sure. But you know, you gotta shake people up every now and then. Otherwise they get complacent, or they take you for granted. I'll be hearing from some unhappy pals for a bit, but then they're going to remember who controls the Auxiliary. And then they'll come to me about the contracts for building these new colonies, and the mining rights, and the shipment of the goodies off-world, and they'll find out that we're still pals."

Reena laid her head against his chest. "You know I already warned my brother, right?"

"You always do. And that's one reason we never have to worry about Celestia. Your people weren't involved in this nonsense, so it was a smart play to give them a heads-up, to let them know we consider them grown-ups."

"I don't know about that."

"You don't think your brother and his cronies are grown-ups?"

"No. I don't know if we never have to worry about them."

The door opened, and Hugh Leeger appeared.

"I'm sorry to interrupt, Mr. Chairman, but we just received word from Command that the enemy has just used the mud-creating munition that Jan saw on Roanum. They've just launched a fresh offensive on Fractus, and it looks rough."

"**T**his is indeed an honor, to have the daughter of Olech Mortas visit our facility!" The man was enormous, with a thick head of gray hair and looming eyebrows. Lines crossed his forehead, and his cheeks showed a day's worth of dark beard, but his lab coat was immaculate and so was the rest of the site. "Dr. Yost Kletterman. Welcome, welcome."

Ayliss shook the proffered hand, trying to give Kletterman her full attention but too excited to keep her eyes from roving. Python had flown them to an unmanned satellite orbiting the planet, part of Command's effort to keep the site isolated. After docking, they had entered a spherical pod just large enough for the two of them. It was programmed to travel between the satellite and the research site, and that was all. It had shot toward Echo with little warning, tearing through the thick atmosphere in a ball of flame, then slowed itself to land on a flat platform that jutted out from the facility's lone structure.

The site was little more than a tall building, a white rectangle with enormous windows set into the side of a lushly forested hill. There were no other signs of civilization anywhere, and a chorus of birds trilled all around as they stood on the platform.

"We probably should get inside before the pod lifts off," Python intoned, and Kletterman turned bright eyes in his direction.

"Python, you rogue! Why didn't you inform me we were going to have such an august visitor?"

"She wouldn't let me."

Kletterman chuckled as he took Ayliss's arm and led her toward the building. The wall facing the platform was solid, and she guessed any windows on this level would be in danger when the pod landed or lifted off. The mechanical orb was steaming away behind them, emitting clicking noises that could be excess heat or preparation for departure. Kletterman talked as he guided her through the open blast doors.

"I see you and your father share a lot in common, including a love of secrecy." They passed inside, and the wall closed behind them. Ayliss imagined she heard the pod lifting off, but they were already going around a corner and heading down a flight of stairs. They soon entered a high-ceilinged, open floor where over a dozen people in lab jackets were hard at work. Some sat at various terminals while others were gathered around a hologram that seemed to float over a large table, and huge windows let in light from three sides. Kletterman continued.

"Please assure the chairman that we are gaining an impressive understanding of our subjects. As planned, we're almost completely cut off here—so he needn't worry about the information going anywhere it should not."

The staff ranged from young to middle-aged, and most of them were seated at consoles of differing sizes. Ayliss caught a glimpse of a graph that appeared to be comparing the chemical compositions of varying substances, and on another screen one of the techs was running a piece of video footage back and forth as if studying a minute gesture by one of the Sim subjects.

Several of the researchers greeted Python warmly as they passed.

Ayliss had just reached the center of the floor when she saw a giant screen many yards overhead. The display was a video feed in full color, shot from above a clearing bordered by heavy forest and the thatched roofs of numerous huts. People were moving around in the clearing, some carrying building materials while others were working with hand tools. A circular wall of indeterminate height took up the very center of the clearing, and a long, narrow projection ran from it and disappeared offscreen. Kletterman spoke from behind her.

"Yes, yes, there they are. Our charges. Remarkable people. It is simply amazing to see how well they work together, regardless of the difficulty."

"Like ants, huh, Doctor?" Python gave Ayliss a wink.

"Tsk tsk, Python, you heathen. This is a scientific effort, and we do not use such terms for our subjects." He pointed at the screen. "See that structure in the center? Of course they located the freshwater spring the first day, but the communal water tank and the aqueduct are both new. They still need to pour the water onto the aqueduct at its source, but it saves them the effort of hauling it all the way to their camp.

"The spring is not in a good location for dwellings, and they never even attempted to build near it. Amazingly practical people, and do you know that they come together every single day for what appear to be group planning sessions from which no member is excluded?"

Ayliss fought to keep the glee from her voice. "Are they aware that they're being watched?"

"Certainly. I was not consulted over the manner in which they were captured and transported, and of course whoever was in charge of that operation was trying not to expose the subjects to human influences of any kind. The subjects were part of a Sim colony that was scheduled for eradication by our forces, but our subjects were located a good distance from the main settlement. I am unclear as to how they were taken, but I was told it involved a gas that rendered them unconscious.

"Needless to say, when they awakened on the island they knew they'd been deposited in a different location under mysterious circumstances." Kletterman gave Ayliss a meaningful stare. "Our subjects are not stupid. Additionally, we had deposited an assortment of tools, emergency rations, temporary shelters, and a complete set of seeds captured from other colonies. They made use of all these items immediately, so they must know that some agent placed them here."

The words floated past as if uttered by a ghost. Already Ayliss was imagining the story breaking, the outrage, the scandal. Standing in front of her defeated father, informing him that it was all her doing. She forced her brain to form a pertinent question.

"Forgive my ignorance, Doctor, but I've heard speculation that the Sims might actually have a sort of hive mind. Have you observed anything that supports that?"

"No forgiveness is necessary; we only learn by asking such questions. I am aware of that theory, but thus far we have seen nothing to suggest they interact in such a way. I mentioned that they hold communal meetings, and it seems unlikely they would need to do that if they shared this 'hive mind' suggested by certain people. I personally believe the authors of that theory wish to portray the Sims as unthinking beings, and I can assure you from my own observation that they are highly intelligent and analytical.

"Every one of our subjects has demonstrated a willingness to serve in any capacity necessary, but we have observed that they are broken down into various teams. For example, certain individuals are clearly assigned to handle their water requirements while others are responsible for planting and tending their crops.

"The males and the females appear to be equal in social stature, and the few conflicts that we have observed were resolved in group consultations." The meaningful look again. "They are an eminently practical people and, if I may be so bold, we could learn much from them as a society."

Ayliss shot Python a bland look, which he returned the same way. "I agree, Doctor. I believe your work here is going to prove highly illuminating."

Ayliss walked through the silent complex later that night. Kletterman and his people didn't get many visitors, so they'd thrown a dinner in her honor. It had been a raucous affair, largely because the isolated station had been generously supplied with alcohol and its occupants were not shy about imbibing. Python had apparently formed a romantic relationship with more than one member of the female staff, and Ayliss had last seen him reeling down the dormitory corridor with his arms around two of the prettier scientists.

Her handheld could neither send nor receive, and so she'd decided to wait until everyone was asleep before inspecting the devices in the main control room. Python was convinced that the site had no means of communicating with anyone, but she wanted to check anyway.

Ayliss had to be circumspect about this, as she soon learned that not everyone had called it a night. She had already passed one laboratory where a researcher was poring over data on a screen. The display glowed in the reduced lighting, and for a giddy moment she imagined the pale scientist was trying to get a tan. The unfamiliar hallway was dim, but the complex was not terribly large and Ayliss soon found herself in the main room where she'd been briefed by Kletterman earlier.

Most of the consoles were dormant, but the large overhead display cast a gray wave of dull light across the workspace. Walking over, Ayliss recognized the projection as the Sim village on the distant island. The surveillance robots had switched to infrared with the setting of the sun, and she could make out the whitened outlines of slumbering Sims through the thatch of some of the roofs.

"It's early to bed and early to rise out there." The voice made her jump, but she recognized that it belonged to Python. Her eyes penetrated the gloom just outside the screen's luminescence, and she saw him leaning back in a padded chair. Python's hair hung loose over his shoulders, and he wore a dark robe that was open to expose large muscles and curly hair. When he sat up, the faint light caught the silver scar tissue of an old wound high on the left side of his chest. The whitened line reminded her of the Sim images overhead.

"Why do you still have that scar?"

"Oh, I could have had it erased. And believe me the Force pushes that pretty hard—don't want to upset the civilians when we send the brave troops home." He reached into the shadows, and his hand came back with a tumbler of dark liquid. "But this scar here, and another I can show you when we're better acquainted, they remind me of the buddies I lost."

As her vision improved, Ayliss began to suspect that Python wore nothing under the robe. She tried not to smile at the notion of getting "acquainted" with a double-dealing criminal who, to her knowledge, had just bedded two other women.

"That must have been a very difficult experience." Ayliss didn't give him a chance to reply. "Is there a place we can talk? Safely?"

"Sure. The landing platform. It'll be nice out there, too."

They went up the stairs, and Python led her through a small hatch near the blast doors. The night was clear and warm, and the light from the stars cast the landing space in a blue glow. They walked out to the far edge, where a waist-high railing was the only thing separating them from a long drop to the forest floor below.

"You should have seen this place when they were setting it up. Shuttles constantly coming and going from right where we're standing. Takes a lot to put something like this into action, even a small site like this one."

"Why isn't there a security force?"

"No need. The prisoners can't leave the island, and even if they did, there are some huge catlike things around that would get them long before they got here—assuming they found the place at all. Besides, I think your father wanted to keep the number of people involved to a minimum."

He let that hang in the warm air, and Ayliss walked closer to the edge to regard the fluffy green outlines of tall trees not far away. The forest was thick, and the birds that had been singing in it that afternoon had all gone silent. She rested her hands on the thick bar that topped the railing, enjoying the sensation of vertigo.

"Just imagine what's going on out there." Python came up next to her, bending to reach the low barrier. "The forest primeval. The true state of nature, unspoiled by man. All sorts of things creeping and climbing and jumping and slithering around. Foraging. Feeding. Fighting."

His hand brushed her arm. "Fucking."

"Sorry, Python. Spoken for." Ayliss stopped herself from taking a step away, the nearness of the wild telling her it would be mistaken for retreat—and followed up.

"He'd never know."

"You'd be a dead man if he ever found out. And he's probably trying to find me already." Ayliss let herself take one step back, gaining a little space, reminding herself that she still needed Python. And that she owed him a lot. "When can we get out of here?"

"Not for a couple of days. When I visit, it's for at least three days, usually longer."

"How many times have you visited with Olech Mortas's daughter?"

"Even more reason to stick to routine. The Doc likes me, but he knows better than to completely trust a guy who does the things I do. Lucky for us he's so grateful to your father that he hasn't stopped to wonder why you turned up with no prior warning. Let's not make him suspicious."

"So what if we do? You said there's no communication from here. Who's he going to call?"

"There's a Force cruiser that patrols this sector and prevents unauthorized landings. The Doc's got a kind of panic button direct to that ship, a burst transmission he can send if he needs help."

"He'd call up a cruiser if he got a little antsy about my visit?"

"The cruiser would send an armed party down here to see what was going on. If we left suddenly, and the Doc hit the panic button, in no time at all your father would know you'd been here. And before you could spring the news to anybody, this whole place would evaporate."

"You seem to know a lot about how my father does things."

"Not really. I just remember what happened to those Sims I was marooned with—especially the wounded ones—when Command found out we'd made ourselves a separate peace. I'm pretty sure that's another reason they've kept the staff here as small as possible: less to clean up if necessary."

"So two more days?"

"That's my recommendation. Nice and easy, cool and calm. And then we whistle for the pod, get out of here, head back to Broda, and let Harlec spread the word."

"No. Not Harlec. Me. It has to come from me."

Somewhere out and below, a stricken creature uttered a frantic cry that was suddenly cut short.

CHAPTER SEVEN

"—as you can see, this is going to be a fluid situation." The Orphan Brigade's commander stood at the front of a briefing room packed with officers and NCOs, many of them from First Battalion's B Company. They were on the flagship of a fleet headed to Fractus, and B Company had come aboard only a few hours earlier. There was an electric sense of haste to the whole thing, and accommodations reflected the rush to reach the fighting. The rest of the brigade was scattered across several other transports, and Watt's image was being projected to them.

"The enemy's use of the new 'mud munition' has ruptured a defensive zone that has been in place for almost a year. Our fellow soldiers on Fractus have taken heavy casualties, and been forced to give a great deal of ground."

Behind the stocky colonel, an enormous satellite

photograph was projected on the wall. It was covered in military graphics, but in such a fashion that the terrain was still distinguishable. Having been trained in this kind of symbology, Mortas could tell that a front line stretching for many miles had been broken by the revolutionary munition. Fired directly behind the zone defended by a human armored division, it had robbed the tanks and other fighting vehicles of their ability to maneuver. A massive Sim armored force had pinned them against the newly impassable acreage, and crushed them.

In his mind, Mortas saw the mired mastodons on Roanum again, the tanks with their guns pointed at crazy angles and the personnel carriers tilted like ships on a heavy sea, all trapped in the solid ground that had temporarily become mud. In the darkness of the room's tiered seating, Mortas shivered.

"There is reason for optimism, however. On Fractus, the enemy has employed this new weapon with dramatically mixed results. The first time we saw this munition on Roanum, it transformed solid ground into mud that bogged down an entire assault battalion, and then the ground hardened again. Clearly this ordnance is designed for temporary area denial, but on Fractus this has not turned out to be the case. Far from it."

The photograph display enlarged rapidly, as if the assembled soldiers were dropping out of the sky toward the ground. The big picture of the entire elongated front shrunk down to just the region where the enemy had broken through. Much of the battle area appeared to be open ground, rough terrain largely without cover, and its predominant shade was gray. Now that the picture's resolution had increased, a blob of dark brown appeared.

"The enemy was unable to exploit the hole it created in our lines because the ground hasn't firmed up as expected. In fact, aerial reconnaissance has not only confirmed that the ground remains impassable, but also that the morass is spreading. Two entire enemy armored divisions, presumably meant to cross this area once it hardened, have been held up by this enormous mud field of their own creation."

Colonel Watt cracked a brief smile. "Yes, even the Sims can get too clever for their own good."

Shaking off the memories of Roanum, Mortas exchanged a glance with Berland. The B Company soldiers could be easily identified in the audience by the tiger-striped fatigues from their aborted jungle mission while the rest of the assemblage, various higher-echelon attachments whose jobs Mortas did not yet know, wore a mottled gray camouflage.

"This giant obstacle has given our forces an opportunity." Watt turned to face the photograph. "To the north of the mud field, there is the beginning of a long mountain chain that was the anchor of our left flank in this defensive zone. The fighting is shifting far south of that high ground, now that the Sim advance is blocked by the mud field. The enemy's attention is focused on getting around the impassable territory they created, which may give our forces the chance for a major counterattack in the north.

"Beginning just a few miles inside those northern mountains, there are three passes that were so heavily mined by both sides in earlier fighting that they might just as well not even exist." Humans and Sims had been fighting over Fractus for years, and at one point it had been considered sufficiently secured for the Force to give the planet an actual name. The Sims had landed a new army soon after that, and the conflict had been stalemated for many months.

More military symbols popped up on the photo, thin lines that indicated movement lanes that twisted through the rugged terrain from west to east. For the first time, Mortas was able to make out the passes about which Watt was speaking. The southernmost lane was the shortest because it ran through a thumb-shaped ridge pointing south that tapered down to the plain. The two passes farther north twisted this way and that as the elevation increased, and as far as Mortas could tell, the indicated corridors were widely separated.

"As you all know, an obstacle that is not observed at all times and covered by fire is no obstacle at all. Anybody can come up and remove it or chop their way through it. Even now our engineers are preparing to clear these three gaps, and the Orphan Brigade is going to protect them while they work. Once cleared, these three passes will be used as counterattack lanes by our armored and mechanized forces to swing wide around the enemy's northern flank while his strongest effort is many miles to the south.

"Three passes, three battalions. We will secure the high ground on both sides of each of these lanes, preventing enemy scouts from discovering what our engineers are doing. It is vital that we not attract attention, so our use of air assets will be limited at first. Rest assured those assets will come into play the moment we need them, but if we do this right, the enemy won't know what we're up to until it's too late.

"When the passes are open, we will have set the stage for one of the greatest counterattacks in the history of the entire war."

When the briefing ended, most of the assembled officers and NCOs immediately began circulating about the room, coordinating the tasks that the mission required. Mortas almost rose as well, but Berland remained seated and so he followed his platoon sergeant's example. The older man was staring at the enlarged photo of their intended area of operations, and for the first time Mortas believed his platoon sergeant was worried about something.

"What is it?" The room was full of voices and the sound of movement, so he was able to speak normally.

"This isn't making any sense, sir." Berland caught himself and forced a smile. "Not that it ever does. Sitting here, I'd guess those lanes are between fifteen and twenty miles long, jam-packed with old mines and booby traps. It will take the sappers *forever* to clear them if they're trying to do it by stealth.

"All it's gonna take is one Sim aerobot to fly over and notice all this activity, and that'll be the end of this whole counterattack. They'll rain artillery and rockets down on us, and they may even be able to reseed those minefields the same way." Area denial was a mainstay of the war for the Habs, largely to preserve the planets for later colonization, and so both sides had evolved sophisticated methods for shooting minefields into place from great distances. "They'll plug those lanes back up, and while they're doing it they'll be shelling the shit out of us up on the high ground."

Memories of a different piece of elevation on Roanum, Sim munitions falling out the back end of high-altitude rockets, madly fleeing the explosions and the lethal rocks they sent hurtling through the air. Mortas stared at the photo, surprised to have not seen the plan's many flaws, while Berland continued.

"Colonel Watt's no dummy, and I can't be the only one who sees this. There's got to be a reason why they think this will work."

"He did say those passes haven't figured in either side's calculations for a long time. And the Sims are doing a mad scramble to shift their forces south of that mud field . . . You think maybe that has something to do with it? The mud still spreading like it is?"

"Maybe." Berland rubbed his thumb across the screen of his handheld, switching the aerial view. The overall situation had been loaded onto the handhelds when the briefing began, and he took a long look at the vast acreage of muck. It was surrounded by a set of military graphics, unit designations and boundary lines that shifted frequently. "Even if they think this swamp is going to get big enough to keep the Sims outta range, that wouldn't keep their air assets from finding us. If they come looking."

"Lieutenant Mortas!" He recognized Captain Noonan's voice, and peered through the throng of uniforms to see the company commander standing in front of the first row of seats. Lieutenant Kitrick was with him, but they were surrounded by faces Mortas didn't recognize in smudged gray fatigues.

"I'll ask the CO if anybody's mentioned this," he said to Berland, not sure the brooding NCO had heard his words. Mortas slid along the row of now-empty seats and went down the aisle quickly. A clutch of logistical officers held him up for a moment, but when he slid around them he came up short.

Emile Dassa, wearing the pin-on rank of a captain, stood in front of him with a look of blank appraisal. It had been five years since he'd seen the other man, who'd only been fifteen at the time. Dassa's dark hair was cut short Orphan-style, and he'd filled out a little, but he was still a lean individual just a little shorter than Mortas. An inch-long whitened scar ran parallel to his right eyebrow, and his dark eyes were unreadable.

"Hello, Jan. Last time I saw you, you were sitting on my chest, hitting me."

Dassa was a captain now, Mortas's superior though

two years younger. Insubordination was a serious crime in the Force, but Mortas decided to take up the gauntlet anyway.

"The last time I saw *you*, you were bouncing down a flight of stairs, out cold. Sir."

The face relaxed, and Dassa extended his hand. "Broke my fuckin' arm, asshole. I'd make you buy me a beer or something, but it turns out that was the best thing that ever happened to me."

Mortas shook the hand, searching for a response and finally choosing the truth. "Well I still shouldn't have done that, not after you were unconscious. Sir."

"It's Emile. I was a lieutenant until yesterday."

Mortas saw Noonan's impatient face from only yards away, but he needed to know. "So how was getting your arm broken a good thing?"

"The school officials figured out who my father was, so they shipped me off to the zone. I was in this crazy-ass colonial outfit for a while—you think Force discipline is rough, the colonials are completely out of control—but I survived. Got into a Force unit and met up with some guys who fought for my dad. I learned more about him from those vets than I'd ever found out from my mother."

"Mortas! Get over here!" Noonan bellowed. Dassa gave the agitated company commander an amused look, but didn't get out of the way.

"I heard you did good on Roanum. Let's talk when we get the chance."

"You're over in Second Battalion?" Mortas was

already sliding past him, not fully comprehending the brief discussion or why Dassa was on board the flagship.

"Until yesterday. I'm your new battalion supply guy, replacing Captain Follett." Dassa grinned fiendishly. "I haven't got the slightest idea how to do this, so don't eat your last ration."

Mortas squeezed past a squad from a different B Company platoon that was getting briefed in the corridor. The company was on the flagship because there wasn't room for them on the transport moving the rest of First Battalion, but that didn't mean they had a lot of space. B Company had been assigned to a large supply bay for the brief journey, but the metal cavern had quickly filled to capacity.

Mortas had just come from First Battalion's order briefing, given by a projected image of Colonel Alden. Force engineers were already preparing to clear the three mountain passes on Fractus, and First Battalion had been assigned to protect the southernmost lane. This would put them on the lowest elevation of the Orphan Brigade's sector, but it would also enable them to observe the open ground to the south where the enemy's growing mud field lay. The battalion commander had decided to leverage B Company's current lodgings, requesting the use of the flagship's shuttles to insert the infantry company before the rest of the battalion. The flagship's commander was more than eager to disembark the extra bodies and had agreed to the unusual request.

The other two companies of First Battalion would be inserted by cofferdam, enormous energy corridors reaching from their transport ships through the planet's atmosphere right to the ground. To maintain secrecy and avoid observation, the cofferdams would place the two companies several miles to the west. They would have to move on foot to the ridgelines shielding the pass they were to protect, carrying all their gear.

Second and Third Battalions would be delivered the same way, to the west of their assigned passes farther north. It was important to get actual troops on the ground in the brigade's sector faster than that, so it made sense to fly B Company almost directly into its positions.

The mud field continued to grow, baffling the humans as much as it presumably bewildered the Sims, and it was having a bad effect on the air around it. Reconnaissance robots flying over it had found their engines clogging with an ash-like dust of increasing concentration, and troops near the Sim-made bog had sent in emergency requests for filter masks.

As a result, Mortas was carrying a large bag filled with the black cups and elastic strapping of his platoon's masks. He passed into the supply bay and was surprised by the relative quiet. The ship's passageways had been brightly lit and alive with activity, but the large room where B Company was billeted was dark and almost silent.

He crossed the open space in the room's center, searching the gloom for his troops and finally finding them ranged against the far wall. Ground mats were spread out everywhere, and half of the men were trying to sleep while others sat in loose groups eating, talking, or cleaning weapons. They'd already received the ammunition and rations they would carry to the planet surface, and were trying to conserve their energy before the insertion just hours away.

He spotted Sergeant Berland, wrapped up in a light field blanket and obviously asleep, and was just looking around for one of the other NCOs when Sergeant Mecklinger's tall frame appeared next to him. Mecklinger was Dak's opposite in that his hair was light and so was his demeanor. He projected a calm confidence that Mortas respected, and his voice was a whisper from the shadows.

"Whatcha got there, Lieutenant?"

"The air in our sector's getting thick because of the mud munitions. Lots of grit and dust, so they gave me these to hand out. Three apiece, and they said they'd get us more after things had stabilized."

"I'll take care of that for you, sir." The NCO took the bag, but didn't move away. "Can you do me a favor? Private Jute's having some trouble with this mission for some reason, and I can't get anywhere with him."

Mortas knew the name but not much else. "He's one of the vets, right?"

"Yes, sir. Sometimes the seasoned men have more

trouble than the greenies. They know what it's like, so they have good reason."

"Is that what it is? He's been all right in the past?"

"Oh, very much so. But there's something about the way this one keeps changing that's got him thinking of his last unit, before he came to the Orphans." A thin smile. "I swear, the best recruiting tool this brigade has is all the lousy outfits in the rest of the Force. Could you talk to him?"

"Yes." What other answer was there, despite his own near-total lack of combat experience? "Where is he?"

"Right there." Pointing toward a silhouette against the darkened wall, a lean figure in fatigues. Sitting on the metal deck, knees bent, back against the wall, hands clasped in his lap. Not alone, but not right next to anyone either. Mortas nodded and walked over.

"How's it going there, Jute?" He didn't wait for the answer, lowering himself to a sitting position facing the man. Making out the features, the shaved head, ears that stuck out, but not much more. Good. Let him sit in the dark and get himself together.

"Uh, not so good, El-tee." The voice was grainy, a man's voice, uncertain but still willing to talk. Needing to talk. "Sergeant Mac send you over?"

"Just making the rounds, checking up on everybody." A bizarre memory, of himself inspecting the blisters on Gorman's feet back on the planet that now bore the dead mapmaker's name. "Anything you want to talk about?"

"Naw, I'll be fine."

"We got some time to kill."

"We do, don't we?" The bent knees disappeared, folding under him as he leaned forward and lowered his voice even more. "I been out here a long time, earned my spot as an Orphan. I'm no chicken. I'll go in when they say, and I'll do my best.

"But it's this mission. Every time I turn around they've got something new, like they don't really know what we're heading into. This mud field could dry up, or it could expand. The enemy's headed away from us, but they might come snoopin' around. We're opening up a counterattack lane, but it might just be for resupply. It's like Command is pulling this one right out of their butts."

"I bet you've been there before."

"Yeah." A brief, spasmodic laugh. Not much, but something. "After all this time, I really shouldn't be surprised the bigwigs have no idea what's going on down on the ground. But that's what got me thinking. My first unit, we took over part of a trench line one night, a defense that had been in place awhile, solid positions and good fields of fire and everything's quiet. And then, no warning, we got told to move.

"Going into battalion reserve, somebody said, but nobody was coming up to take over our holes. We were on key terrain, sir. It made no sense. But we formed up and marched off anyway, darker than three feet up a cat's ass even with the night vision, still quiet, walked for a couple miles, then we get the order to go back where we were.

"It had all been a mistake, and they knew it, so of course they rushed us back. Next thing you know we were practically running, carrying all our stuff, tripping over anything and everything, before long the column's all jammed together or spread out, I didn't recognize any of the guys around me. When we finally got there, nobody knew where they'd been because we'd only just taken it over a few hours before. It just got . . . crazy.

"The officers and the sergeants, they were trying to get things organized, but nobody wanted to just stand there, so the guys began occupying positions on their own. It turned into a real clusterfuck. Machine guns, boomers, chonks—none of the heavy weapons where they should have been. And right in the middle of all that, the enemy attacked us. Artillery, rockets, machine guns, and they just Sim-waved across the low ground straight at us. Everybody was firing from where they were, but before we could call for artillery they were almost on us.

"And that's when it happened. All of a sudden, guys are just jumping up out of their holes and running away. Me, I was on my stomach in the open, shooting, and the next thing I know I'm getting trampled. There's this huge number of Sims coming up the slope, our fire's slacking off to nothing, more and more people running off, so I jumped up and went with them."

The face was close now, the eyes wide. "We lost that whole position. They didn't even kill that many of us because we outran them. It took all day to get the company back together, they fired the CO, then we had to go attack the same spot to take it back. Our new commander was this absolute prick who said it was our punishment for running away, like he had any idea at all about what happened.

"You know what caused it? One stupid order. One guy on the radio, saying we had to move when there was no reason to move. That's what did it.

"And this mission right here? It's got that same fucked-up feel to it. I been an Orphan for a year now, this is one hell of a good unit, but it doesn't matter how good the outfit is if the guys calling the shots are jumping all over the place. And the way they keep changing this thing . . . I gotta wonder. I *wonder*, El-tee. And that's never good."

"You got me wondering, too." Mortas laughed just a bit, to hide the fact that he was speaking the truth. He'd heard tales like this one before, nightmare stories of units coming apart because of bad luck or stupidity. Officers and NCOs vainly trying to create order out of the running, screaming chaos of it all. Remembering the Sim assault on Roanum, utterly unexpected, the crush of the bodies in the tiny ravine, his own face jammed into the dirt until he was sure he'd suffocate. He actually shook his head to drive the memory away, and was glad for the darkness.

"And it doesn't help that we're so shorthanded, sir. We're missing a third of the brigade right now, even counting the new guys. I'm not sure Command understands that, assigning us such a big area."

Mortas was about to suggest that the reduced numbers might work in their favor in terms of avoiding enemy detection, but a better thought came along first.

"That's a good point. Shows you've got your eyes open and your brain engaged. And you're right that we've got some really new men, new to the war zone entirely. You know they're going to be looking to you and the other veterans, and they'll act just like you do."

There was a silence that he didn't interrupt. Finally Private Jute spoke, and Mortas believed his voice was just a bit firmer. "Don't worry about me, Lieutenant. I'm cool once it starts."

"I know you are." He patted a fatigue sleeve and stood up. "Orphans."

"Orphans, sir."

He turned toward the main door, and saw Lieutenant Kitrick silhouetted against the light. He seemed to be looking for someone, and somehow Mortas knew it was him. He walked over, and Kitrick gave him a conspiratorial smile.

"Come on, Mortas. A little fun before the big fun."

They passed into the corridor, and he was surprised to see Colonel Watt standing in the middle of a half dozen officers, including Captain Noonan and Emile Dassa. Most of them were from the brigade staff, so he didn't recognize them, but there was an air about the gathering that Mortas felt he should comprehend. Watt's eyes fell on him, and just before the brigade commander motioned him over he identified the sensation. It was the pregame edge he'd seen so many times among his lacrosse teammates, and Mortas wondered if it was related to the approaching mission. He didn't have to wonder long.

"Good. Come on, Jan, I'll tell you what we're doing while we walk." They moved down the corridor in a tight bunch, and Mortas immediately noticed the way the ship's crew moved out of the way. "This is one of your duties as an Orphan officer, and you'd be well advised to do this in any other unit too. You know about triage? The classification of the wounded when they get back aboard ship?"

"Yes, sir. On Roanum, Corporal Cranther said anyone deemed too hurt to survive got taken into something he called the Waiting Room, where they stayed until they died." The alien pretending to be Captain Trent had told him the same story, but Mortas decided to leave that part out.

"He told you right. And we don't tolerate it." Murmurs of aggressive agreement answered him, and Mortas stuck with Watt as they descended a wide ramp. "You see, the triage is handled by these brainless drones instead of the doctors. That's Force regulation, by the way, so in case you're wondering, what we're about to do is something Command considers a rather serious crime.

"Well fuck them. Handheld readouts deciding if a wounded man gets to see someone who can actually save him. God Almighty."

They arrived at a closed hatch in a wall that was covered with open insulation. The vibration of powerful machines came through the deck into Mortas's boots, and he knew they were deep inside the ship's innards. Kitrick stepped up and activated the hatch, and Watt stepped through before it was fully open.

It was a small room, full of exposed pipes and electrical boxes, and the paint on the walls was a dull, chipped red. Bedrolls lined the edges of the floor, some of them filled with sleeping forms, while a half dozen crewmen were seated around a table stacked with playing cards. Mortas was carried through the door by the press of bodies, and found himself right next to Colonel Watt.

"Hey, hey, there's no reason for this!" One of the cardplayers, wearing a tan full-body suit like most of the others, protested while standing up from the game. The rest of the room's occupants were already trying to get the table between them and the infantrymen, and Mortas could almost smell their fear. "We know the drill already—no Orphans go to the Waiting Room."

A bald-headed Orphan officer with broad shoulders and a barrel chest slipped past Watt, punching the man who'd spoken. It was a wide-swinging right that caught him high on the left cheek, and he would have gone down if the others hadn't caught him.

"You tellin' our colonel what's what, you slimy piece of shit?" The puncher shouted, his right hand flopping crazily as he shook off the pain from the blow. The sleeping men had struggled free of their bedding, but had crowded the other side of the table in a fearful knot after that. Noonan grabbed the table with one hand and flipped it out of the way, cards and betting chips flying. Glancing at his company commander, Mortas was surprised to see a malicious smile on the man's face. Remembering Noonan's excitement whenever the action in the training simulator had gotten particularly hot, Mortas decide he'd uncovered an important clue to his boss's distant behavior. Noonan clearly enjoyed action, and for reasons of his own went to great lengths to hide that part of his makeup.

The two groups of men stared at each other. There was the smallest fluttering instant when it could have cooked off, and Mortas felt as if he was no longer in control of his actions. He'd been in many a brawl at boarding school, but this was different. Without a conscious thought, he sought the eyes of one of the triage techs, a man his own size, and stared into them with overt malice. Knowing that if even one more punch was thrown he would sail forward with the other officers, intent on pummeling this total stranger.

"Apparently you *don't* know the drill." Watt's tone was arch, but he was otherwise completely calm. Mortas glanced down and saw that the colonel's hands were loose at his side, and only then did he see that his own were already balled into white-knuckled fists. He forced them to relax.

"So here it is: *no one* goes into the Waiting Room at all. I'm not going to trust a gang of imbeciles like you to know who's an Orphan and who's not. No one goes in the Waiting Room, no matter what your machines say. Got it?"

Completely cowed, the techs nodded and murmured their understanding. None of the infantrymen moved, but Mortas slowly let out a long, silent exhalation. Watt wasn't quite finished, though.

"Don't get stupid later on, gents. You know who told us where you were hiding, and they'll tell us if anybody gets mistreated. Even if there's only one Orphan left alive . . . you're all fucking dead. Remember that."

Watt turned and walked out, but the remaining officers stood their ground and Mortas did the same. The staring contest lasted for a minute, then the infantrymen closest to the hatch began passing through it. Mortas waited, feeling that as the most junior man he should be last. A hand pressed his shoulder, and he turned to see Dassa's face. They were the only ones left, and the captain motioned with his head for Mortas to leave.

The Orphan group was subdued as they went back up the ramp, clustered behind the brigade commander but leaving him to his thoughts. Drifting back, Mortas whispered in Dassa's ear.

"Who told us where those guys were hiding?"

"The surgeons. The docs don't like this shit any better than we do, so they tip us off. Oh, and this isn't all that uncommon in the rest of the Force. Sometimes the NCOs handle it, but here it's an officer thing."

"Anybody ever get in trouble for it?"

"Sure. But that's part of being in charge, Jan. Maybe the most important part. You can't let your people get fucked over. Not if you expect them to follow you."

"Well hello, Lee." Dev Harlec pushed his rolling chair back from one of the consoles in his office. A smile of indecent glee broadened his face while Selkirk crossed the open floor from the elevator. Bright sunshine illuminated the whole expanse, but the security man was in a dark mood.

"You know why I'm here."

"I do. And I must say you disappointed me. You took much longer to come by than I expected." Harlec shook his head. "It seems Ayliss has you better trained than I thought. But then again, over the years she's grown quite skilled at using people for her own ends. Obsession will do that for you."

"I didn't come to chat. Where is she?"

"Oh, I have no idea. My friends the linguists—"

"Drop it. Ayliss bought your story, not me."

"And yet you let her go. And then you waited. Just what tricks does she perform in the bedroom, to keep a man such as you in line like that?"

"Where is she?"

"You don't see it yet, do you? You're just another pawn in the great game of revenge she's playing with her father. You see, in her view of the universe there are only two kinds of people: the ones who hate her father and the ones who work for him. I doubt a Mortas family bodyguard would ever truly be one of the former, so she had to change you from being one of the latter."

"You don't know her at all."

"Nonsense. You think she relies on you, but Ayliss doesn't rely on anyone except herself. She has good reason: her mother died on her, Olech abandoned her, and even her own brother ultimately let her down. Jander Mortas had a whole universe of possible careers from which to choose, and what did he do? Bent over and got an HDF brand on his backside. No, our Ayliss learned long ago she can't trust anyone. But she needed you to cover for her, and so she seduced you, turned you, and when she gets what she's after, she'll discard you."

"But she's not going to get what she's after. Is she?"

"Most assuredly not. That's another problem with obsession: it makes one predictable. She played herself right into a trap that's going to ruin her father as she hoped, but it will finish her too. I'd go into detail, but you wouldn't understand half of it."

"Try me."

"No, I don't think so. You see, *your* obsession made you predictable as well. A bit tardy, but predictable. I knew you'd come by, that you'd leave the rest of your detail many floors below, and that you'd let my security people disarm you."

Movement from behind the tall data towers. Two very large men, each holding a pistol. They walked around and behind Selkirk, stopping when they were in position to shoot him without hitting each other or Harlec. Selkirk had little regard for most men that size, but he studied their movements and recognized that these two would be formidable even without the weapons.

"As you might have guessed, these gentlemen are not part of my security staff. They're not even Brodans, and once I've paid them they're going to leave this planet forever. But before any of that, they're going to break a significant number of your bones while I watch. And then they're going to take you out onto my shuttle pad and throw you off. An unfortunate accident, particularly after I warned you to be careful when you went out there."

Selkirk dropped his eyes to the polished floor. They came back up, defeated. "Why?"

"For a reason you'll understand. Once this little scheme has unfolded, dear Ayliss won't be welcome anywhere but here—even though the Brodan government will need convincing. I'll vouch for her myself, and give her shelter the way a true friend would. She'll be ostracized by the Brodans because of the particularly heinous nature of her crimes, and I will be her only friend. With you out of the way, it will be just a matter of time before she realizes that we have a lot in common and were meant to be together."

Selkirk allowed a tiny smirk to blossom. "Thank you. That's all I needed to hear."

The elevator doors opened with a loud burp, and the two hired guns looked toward the unexpected threat. Selkirk was already in motion, two stutter steps bringing him in range of the one to his left, his right fist swinging hard. The unmistakable sound of flesh striking flesh, and the gun clattering to the floor while the big man's hands grabbed at his windpipe. A diving forward roll brought Selkirk to the second gunman while also making him a difficult target to hit. Legs curled up for maximum power, he kicked both boots into the assassin's exposed kneecaps. A shriek of pain, then that one was down too.

"Don't move!" The voice was male, more annoyed than anything else. Selkirk popped to his feet easily as the speaker went by him, one of the men from Ayliss's security detail. He was pointing a boxlike pistol at Harlec, who had just started to roll away but stopped when he recognized the shock gun.

Another man and two women emerged from the elevator, the rest of the detail that Harlec had believed was waiting many floors below. Carrying several canvas bags and two more stunners, which they used on the gunman who was rolling on the floor clutching his knees. The shock guns rattled just long enough to knock him out, then one of the women knelt next to the other body.

"He's got a pulse. And he's breathing—sort of."

"The guards downstairs?"

"All trussed up. Second-raters, gave up the ghost the moment we got rough."

"Good." Selkirk turned to Harlec's seated figure while the others began opening the bags. "As you can see, we planned this out ahead of time. You lied to me about not knowing Ayliss's location. So why don't you use that great big intellect of yours to save yourself some real pain and tell me where she is?"

"You fools. This is Broda! You can't behave like this

and get away with it. You'll be hunted across the entire galaxy!"

"Save the lecture. We're Mortas family security, which means we know the laws of all the settled worlds from front to back. In case you didn't notice, we didn't kill anyone. And we're going to be gone in just a few minutes. Even sooner, if you smarten up."

"And why would I do that?" The smile returned to Harlec's face. "You just said you're not going to kill me."

"That's true." Selkirk turned to one of the women, who lifted another boxlike machine from inside one of the bags. It hummed when she turned it on, but Harlec knew what it was.

"Go ahead. Erase everything on the floor. Melt the machines down. Every bit of data is backed up."

"Really?" Selkirk leaned forward from the waist until his eyes were on a level with Harlec's. "If it's all backed up, that would mean somebody else could look at it. You know, Brodan transparency and all. And somehow I don't see you sharing much of anything with anybody—at least not the important stuff."

He straightened up and raised his right hand with the index finger pointed at the ceiling. The hand dropped, the digit pointed at the nearest data tower, and the woman started walking toward the repository of Harlec's work. The box vibrated with the energy that would wipe the tower clean, and she'd just turned it onto a higher setting when Harlec shouted.

"No! Stop! Tell her to stop!"

The box came back down, but the security woman didn't step away. Selkirk shook his head.

"Just like I figured. You don't belong on this planet any more than I do. Holding out on the very culture that embraced you." The box shut off, and was returned to the bag. The remaining bodyguards removed other items from the totes and moved to different consoles. Sitting down, they started to feed various devices into slots and connectors. "Must be some groundbreaking stuff, for you to try and keep from sharing it. We've been monitoring the emissions from this building, as well as its basic wiring, and my people tell me there's a lot of hours of work stored right here and nowhere else."

"What are they doing?"

"Installing a very special combination of electronic booby traps. Much too complex for a simple intellect like mine, but suffice it to say you're going to want to tell me exactly where Ayliss is, how to get there, and every detail of this little scheme of yours. Because right now a series of viruses is being fed into your system, viruses that nobody can fix without our help.

"You're going to tell me everything I want to know, then my friends and I are going to Ayliss. You send a warning, lie to us, try to remove the viruses, or basically do anything we don't like, and those bugs will eat everything you have stored. But if we get Ayliss back before this plot plays out, I guarantee you'll receive a visit from someone who will put everything back the way it was.

"Now. Do we have a deal?"

CHAPTER EIGHT

"Yeah, I was a shit-hot pilot, lots a kills, but I never learned to keep my mouth shut!" The man seated on the floor next to Mortas was practically shouting in his ear. The shuttle was loaded with half of First Platoon and all their equipment, and its interior had been gutted to accommodate them. The shuttle rocked violently, racing through the atmosphere of Fractus, and Mortas was having difficulty focusing. Berland was with the rest of the platoon in a different shuttle, and Mortas wished the platoon sergeant was there with him.

"So after getting my ass shot up by Sammy Sim's ground-to-air one time too many, I asked my squadron commander how come we were flying that ridiculous mission. Every single day, exactly the same course, and near as I could tell it was just to draw fire."

The shuttle lurched as if it had hit something, skittering to one side. The troops jammed into the compartment, clad in torso armor and helmets, all leaned hard in the direction of the skid and then flopped back into position. Every available space was occupied with rucksacks, water containers, and heavy bags filled with grenades. Although they would be inserted close to their assigned area within B Company's zone of operations, it would still be difficult to carry everything to their positions.

"So my squadron commander says, 'What, you don't like the scenery?' and I didn't know that was code for 'Shut up or I'll give you some scenery you're absolutely gonna hate!' and I said, no, I didn't like the scenery at all. And the next day I was out humpin' with this infantry unit as their ASSL."

"You really are an ASSL, Daederus," Sergeant Dak called over from under a pile of gear. "No matter how many times I hear that story, I still can't believe you messed up like that."

Although the former pilot was a captain, he'd been serving as an Aerial Support Systems Liaison with the Orphans for so long that he was on very informal terms with most of the veterans. Rumor had it that Daederus had turned down a shot at having his flight status reinstated. He was physically unremarkable, but in the short time he'd known the man Mortas had found him disarmingly jolly.

"You think he's fun now, just wait until he's got targets." Berland had advised him. "Daederus really loves killing Sims. Orbital rockets, drones, there's nobody better. He's one of the few ASSLs I've seen who's just as good at calling in artillery and mortars as he is with the aerial stuff. But you gotta watch out for him; he takes stupid chances, and he'll stay in one spot too long if he's correcting the fire."

The shuttle compartment brightened suddenly, as the blast shields over the side portholes opened. That meant they were through the atmosphere, driving hard for the ground. The long line of tiny transports carrying B Company would use the mountain chain to hide their approach, following a flight path that was well north of the fighting.

Mortas's mind raced with all the information it held. He'd studied the aerial footage of their zone of operation until he knew it by heart. First Battalion would be securing the southernmost lane to be cleared by the engineers, and B Company's zone was the southeastern end of that lane. Because of this, they would have an excellent view both south and east over the plain that was being consumed by the mud field. Extra ASSLs had been assigned to the company, to bring fire down on any Sim units approaching from either of those directions. Second and Third Battalion had the lanes to the north, and would be so buried in the mountains that only the units on the easternmost end of the passes would be able to see very far at all.

His battalion commander's words echoed in Mortas's head. "We can't have the usual aerial observation assets zooming around us because that might tip off the Sims. So everybody has to stay sharp. Orbital imagery will be sent directly to us as available, but cloud cover and the needs of the fleet may interrupt that.

"Additionally, the expanding mud field is fouling the atmosphere with particles of dirt. It's getting worse, not better, and is already affecting observation drones closer to the fighting. That may be a plus for us, because it will discourage the Sims from sending their own drones up to check our zone.

"They have their hands full far to the south, and if we maintain proper stealth there's an excellent chance the enemy will never know we were in place—until the counterattack launches from the passes cleared by the engineers."

Berland and most of the other veterans felt it was unlikely that the clearing operation would go unnoticed, and Colonel Alden seemed to suspect the same thing without saying it.

"Do not fire up the first enemy you see unless they attack you. We don't want to give away our positions and let them know that we're up to something, just because a lost vehicle rolls by out on the flat. I want good communications out there, with frequent radio checks. Call me with anything you see."

The shuttle banked hard, rocking the seated troops in that direction before leveling out. Mortas craned his neck to look out the porthole, just in time to observe the point where the vegetation began to change. The end of the mountain chain where they would be operating pointed south in a cone shape. The higher elevation where Second and Third Battalions would be located was covered by thick forest, but the greenery became sparser when the ground sloped downward toward the plain. The trees in First Battalion's zone thinned out well north of the pass they were supposed to protect, but the rocky ground still sported a variety of shrubs that would help conceal the Orphans.

The light from the portholes dimmed as they approached the landing zone, as if they'd flown through a cloud heavy with moisture. Mortas took one last look outside before sliding his goggles down, and was dismayed to see what looked like thousands of tiny insects hurtling past them. It had to be the dust from the mud field, but it wasn't supposed to have covered their zone yet. He lifted his filter mask over his mouth and nose, and changed the image on his goggles.

The camera under the shuttle showed him the approaching ground, a flat segment hidden by two low ridges of dark rock. The expanse rushed up toward him, and he flipped the goggles back to normal sight. All around him the bodies were shifting, straps going over shoulder armor, hands grasping the handles on the bags and the water, the tangle of legs resolving itself into separate bodies. Still wearing the tiger-striped camouflage and now covered from head to toe, the men around him looked like flat-eyed reptiles.

Captain Noonan's voice came through the earpieces in Mortas's helmet, calling the team from the battalion's scout platoon that was supposed to meet them on the ground. The scouts had been inserted several miles away the previous evening and had already checked B Company's zone for enemy and found none.

The scout team answered, informing Noonan that they had the shuttles in sight and that the landing site was safe.

The shuttle arrested its forward movement sharply, and the portholes showed a billowing dust cloud as they landed. Most of the back wall swung downward with a hiss, showing the other shuttles landing behind them with the rest of the company. The overloaded infantry waddled down the ramps and struggled off to either side as rehearsed. As soon as they were well clear of the shuttles, they dropped the water and the bags and ran to form a perimeter.

The low stone ridges to either side gave good protection, and Mortas now saw that the intermittent shrubbery was as tall as a man. In no time at all the camouflaged soldiers were facing out with their weapons ready, the high vegetation hiding them much more effectively than Mortas had expected.

The shuttles lifted off with much less dust, hovering close to the ground in order to stay concealed. The column of flying machines did a slow, lazy turn to the north in order to get higher elevations between them and the plain, then they were gone.

First Platoon's segment of the elongated defensive oval faced south, and the descending ground gave them their first view of the plain. It was enormous and almost flat, but a menacing cloud many miles wide rose above it, slowly turning like a fat, lazy tornado.

Peering over the berm, Mortas adjusted the settings of the goggles in an attempt to see into the dark mist. It didn't seem to help, but after a while he felt he was able to make out the damp shadow of the slowly expanding mud field. To Mortas, the lethargic motion within the gray cloud seemed to indicate a latent energy full of ominous power.

So far, the ash-like particles they'd seen while flying in were only present on the ground in small numbers, blowing about like tiny bits of dead leaves. Most of the troops had already removed their filter masks and stowed them away, knowing that the march to their sectors was going to be tough because of everything they were hauling.

"Get me a chonk over here." Mortas heard Berland's voice and looked over his shoulder to see the platoon sergeant adjusting the perimeter. One of the troops with a grenade launcher slid down the embankment and hustled over to the spot where Berland was pointing. "See that crack in the ground over there? Looks like a ravine? Sight in on it."

Pushing himself back from the edge, Mortas assumed a bent-over position and crouch-walked to the nearest machine gun team. Crawling up the incline, he came up next to the assistant gunner and looked out again. The veteran team had picked a good location, and so he said nothing. He'd spent the hours leading up to their departure circulating among the men, quietly asking them questions about the platoon's mission to ensure they understood the part they would play in it, until he'd sensed they were getting annoyed.

"Can't see into that cloud at all, El-tee." That came from the gunner, an older veteran named Catalano. "It's still outside my maximum range, but if it gets much closer Sam could use it to walk right up on us."

"Got it." Pleased by the consultation, Mortas chose his next words carefully. "I think I'm able to see the mud, not that far in under the cloud."

"Yes, sir. Same here." That came from the assistant gunner.

"Hopefully that means the mud's keeping up with the cloud. That way, even if we can't see into it, it's not likely the Sims can use it to get closer."

"Hope you're right." A distant rumble, like thunder. "You hear that?"

"Yeah. Is that what I think it is?"

"Yes, sir. Welcome to the war."

First Platoon's zone was farthest to the east in B Company's sector, so Captain Noonan traveled with them the entire way. The battalion's scout teams had marked out a route that used the undulations of the rocky terrain to hide the column as it moved, and they dropped off the other two platoons on the way. B Company's zone stretched for roughly seven miles on the southern side of the pass, with A Company covering eight more miles to the west and C Company occupying ten miles north of the pass. The other two Orphan battalions would be positioned along the length of both sides of their lanes, but because First Battalion faced the plain and was closest to the enemy, Colonel Alden had approved the placement of two full companies on the southernmost side of the pass.

Even with the two companies side by side, there was simply too much ground. The lane was roughly twenty miles in length, but the understrength Orphans couldn't cover that entire distance and so their zones left the westernmost five miles uncovered. The clearing operation would be responsible for securing the high ground on either side of them for those first five miles, and was projected to cover that distance in a matter of hours once the Orphans were all in place.

With First Platoon in the lead, Mortas was able to get a good feel for the terrain throughout the company's zone of responsibility. Much of it was solid rock, and there were so many folds and small ridges that the slowly diminishing company was able to stay concealed with only a few minor detours. In addition to the hidden route, the scouts had identified several stretches of ground that could be traversed using small multiwheeled vehicles known as Armadillos. The Armadillos were a mainstay for walking infantry units in rough territory, both for resupply and casualty evacuation.

Mortas added the scouts' markings to the map display inside his goggles, pointing out the places where the segments were separated by ground or obstacles the Armadillos couldn't traverse. In one case he was able to find a way around a small stone ridge that blocked the way, and in another he marked the dimensions of a rockslide that could probably be cleared without explosives. Unfortunately, there were three more locations that would have to be cut in some way for the Armadillos to drive the length of B Company's southern positions.

It was vital that they create that path, because without air support the Orphans would be hauling all their supplies and evacuating any injured soldiers manually. The Armadillos had low silhouettes and high clearance, and they could carry a surprisingly large amount of supplies or evacuate up to three men on stretchers. The assumption regarding actual combat casualties was that once any shooting broke out, all of the Force's air assets would immediately come into play.

"All right." Captain Noonan knelt, facing Mortas, Berland, and Captain Daederus. The platoon was in a loose circle around them in a large, bowl-shaped rock formation in the center of the platoon's zone. "Take your time doing this. There's no way to put bodies all the way across your sector, so the trick is to identify a few spots that will give you observation across your frontage.

"You've got the southeastern edge of this ridge, so you have to be able to see east as well as south. Captain Daederus, you know how to cover an area like this one, so I'm not going to tell you how to do your job. Lieutenant Mortas, Sergeant Berland, each of your observation points has to have enough people to pull all-around security at all times, and to defend itself if the Sims send infiltrators up here to see what's going on.

"We have to remain unseen, and we're shorthanded anyway, so I leave it to your discretion just how much defensive patrolling you do. While you're choosing the locations for these observation points, identify fallback positions that will still allow us to serve as the brigade's eyes and ears. If we get hit with artillery, mortars, or rockets, our only option is to move to a different spot.

"I'll be back in two hours to see how it's going. Do frequent radio checks with your observation points and report your status to me every hour. Any questions?"

The three men shook their heads, and Noonan stood. "Everybody above us seems to think the fight is going to continue far to the south and that Samuel's never gonna even know we were here. Let's hope that's not the case. See you in two hours."

Mortas was awakened by a low, insistent beeping in his ear. He knew, somewhere in the state between sleep and waking, that he'd set the alarm for an hour before dawn. His eyes opened to a dull grayness, but that was just the power-saving mode for the goggles. One of his hands absently reached up to scratch his nose, but the filter mask was in the way. Fumbling, Mortas came to full awareness of where he was.

The torso armor made sleeping on his side almost impossible, so he was stretched out on his back with his helmet resting on the base of his rucksack. His feet were cold inside his boots, but not from the outside temperature; the lack of movement had robbed them of their heat, and he chided himself for not having wrapped up in his field blanket.

The goggles came alive when he sat up, showing him the rising height of the ridge to the north and the depression in which he'd been sleeping. Hunt, the platoon medic, was rolled up in a field blanket just a few feet away, as was a junior member of one of the platoon's rocket teams. Mortas brought his Scorpion rifle up and across his knees before raising his arms and stretching. The stress and toil of his first day on a real operation had taken its toll, and his muscles responded with an uncustomary achiness.

Taking hold of the rifle, he rolled over on all fours and rose to a crouch, mindful of the low rock berm that shielded the observation post. Looking south, Mortas saw the boots of three men on their stomachs, heads peering over the hump of broken ground. The boots belonged to two members of the boomer team and Captain Daederus. After scouting out the ground in their assigned zone, he and Berland had decided that they would have to separate the platoon into five positions that roughly broke out into the three squads and two augmented rocket teams. The squads had received the platoon's machine gun crews with their powerful weapons in exchange for some of their riflemen and chonk gunners, and so each the five positions was manned by roughly the same number of soldiers.

Dak and Mecklinger had their reduced squads on the eastern and western edges of the platoon zone respectively, and the boomer team positions flanked Testo's squad in the very center. Captain Noonan had blessed the arrangement late in the day, and they'd begun their vigil on the cloud-covered plain to the south and east. The thick gray cloud had shown no signs of abating, and the mud field beneath it had continued to grow.

"Coming up," he muttered, the inside of his mouth covered with a gummy grit despite the filter mask. Two of the prone figures glanced backward, and then Mortas was down among them. Much of the rock in this area was covered with a coarse sand and tough surface weeds, and he felt them under his palm as he settled in.

"Haven't seen a thing, and nobody else has either," Daederus whispered, the voice eerie because it was uttered right next to him but came through the earpieces of his helmet. Mortas studied the revolving cloud and the open ground to the south for a long time, pleased that the grumbling of the distant battle had died out. On a whim he slid the goggles up inside his helmet, seeing the gray darkness and feeling a breeze on his cheeks. It smelled acrid, rotten, and before long bits of ash or dirt or dust got into his eyes and made him bring the goggles back down.

"How's the fight going?" He'd already switched the view to the schematic of the battlefield, but it seemed little changed.

"Looks like both sides are a little tired. Bringing up supplies and wondering just how far south that bog is gonna go."

The mention of logistics reminded him of the main reason he was up ahead of schedule. Mortas increased the resolution of the schematic, and once it had reduced the size of the area in his view the imagery changed over to an aerial photo marked out with unit positions and boundaries. The supply path picked out by the scouts was still there, annotated with his notes concerning the barriers, and at those points he now saw the military symbols for engineers. They were rigging explosive charges on the rock obstacles that couldn't be removed any other way, and a ruse had been set up to hide the sound when they detonated the charges.

"Here comes the noise." Daederus rolled over on his back, and Mortas did the same. Moments later he felt the ground trembling through his armor and switched the goggles over so he could see again. The vibrations got louder, then he heard the rumbling of a powerful engine approaching from the north. The nearest crest of the mountains to his rear stood out dark and menacing against a sky filled with stars, and just then the machine roared overhead. A massive, triangular shadow that seemed to be only a few yards above him, its engines shook the ground hard enough to actually move his body just a bit.

To the west, on cue, several explosions erupted as one when the engineers blew the charges. Although he'd been listening for them, Mortas was barely able to distinguish the sharp blast from the heavy grumbling that was now heading out, over the plain.

"Supply bird. The bad guys will think it's headed for the battle, maybe took a wrong turn."

Back to the photo in the goggles. Seeing that the rest of First Battalion was in place, A Company to the west and C Company to the north on the other side of the pass the battalion was guarding. Miles farther to the north, Second and Third Battalions were spreading out on either side of their lanes, but it was impossible to know if the mine clearing had begun anywhere.

Just then Mortas remembered the ASSL's more powerful radio, and Daederus's reputation for knowing what was going on everywhere.

"Hey, ASSL. Have the sappers started work yet?"

"Yep, but it's slow going. Finding the mines, exposing them, then disarming them by hand. It's a mixed bag of our stuff and Sammy's, some of it's pretty old with lots of antihandling devices. I still say they should send the disposal robots through, setting off every one of those things."

"Gotta figure the noise would attract attention."

"But it would be quicker, and for all we know there aren't any Sammies close enough to distinguish it from the rest of the fight. We're gonna be rooted to this spot *way* too long, doing it this way."

Looking at the rocky terrain that surrounded them, Mortas suppressed a shudder.

Later that day the first Armadillos drove the entire length of both A and B Companies' zones with supplies. The improved path was rough going for the squat vehicles, but their low profile allowed them to stay out of sight the whole way. Mortas noted that this development raised the spirits of both veterans and newbies alike when he visited his platoon's positions. He took it as a sign of a commonly held concern that they might be just a little too far away from help. There had been no enemy activity in the day they'd been in place, and as more Orphan units filled the tree-covered slopes to the north, the chance that they would get infiltrated from that direction lessened markedly.

Captain Pappas, the battalion intelligence officer, arrived at Mortas's position late in the day. He'd been ferried up by Armadillo, and walked the rest of the way with Captain Noonan. They'd signaled ahead, and so Mortas met them at the end of the trail where several large boulders allowed them to stand erect.

"We've been staring at that plain for a night and most of a day now, and haven't seen anything except that monster cloud." Mortas finished his report to the two captains. "Anybody figured out what it is?"

Pappas spoke from behind goggles and mask. "The mud field is still growing, but it's only expanding to the south. Obviously a munition that turns dry ground into mud messes with the composition of the soil on a fundamental level that may even be molecular. Honestly, our people still don't know how a thing like that could be possible, much less how it functions.

"The enemy's been forced to shift a lot of their units far to the south, where they're only just getting back into the fight. That means the Sims were as surprised as we were, which suggests that this new wonder weapon can work very differently on different planets.

"So to answer your question, we don't know what that cloud is. It's a dry dust, and so far the best we can speculate is that it was separated from the rest of the soil when the mud was created." He looked at the top of the nearest boulder, at the boiling cloud in the distance. "The field's getting bigger, the cloud's getting bigger, and if I had to guess, I'd say there's something going on under the ground that hasn't yet run its course."

"You think it's gotten away from them? A chain reaction of some kind?" Captain Noonan could have been sitting in a classroom, for all the concern he showed.

"Fits, doesn't it? The mud field was supposed to reverse itself within hours of deployment, and instead it's stayed wet and gotten much bigger. My personal suspicion is that it would have come this way as well except there's so much rock. But that cloud's not dissipating, and the bog itself is expanding, so I'm concerned about what's going on down below. For all we know, there's an ocean of mud under this plain . . . or maybe a rock shelf holding it up that's almost chewed through.

"I mean, what if this thing suddenly creates a sinkhole miles wide? Or simply shifts to our east? That could jam up our big counterattack—and don't think Command doesn't know that. I'm already hearing little things that say they're rethinking this whole pass-clearing operation. They've diverted an extraordinary number of air assets to the fight down south."

"You think if we got into trouble, the air support might not be there?"

"No, nothing like that. I'm more concerned with the orbital assets not paying enough attention to the ground just a few miles east of here, not giving us warning. I'm really surprised that we haven't seen any Sim infantry up here. Even with the passes cleared this isn't armored country at all, but when they pushed our line back that left this ground open, and it isn't like the Sims not to get some troops up here."

"What are you saying?"

"Make sure you keep your eyes open. It's not gonna stay quiet here forever."

Pappas was proven right just after the midpoint of nighttime on Fractus. Mortas was on watch with Hunt, the platoon's medic, and the leader of the boomer team, an NCO known as Sergeant Smashy. Smashy's skill with the rocket launcher was almost legendary, and the short, muscular man's real name was almost unpronounceable. Mortas had increased the security around their tight position based on Pappas's concerns about infiltrators, and he'd spent much of the night moving among the three tiny groups of men who made up the most complete perimeter he could form.

"Yeah, the earlier antipersonnel round for the boomer was tough to work with." Although they were shoulder to shoulder on their stomachs and communicating through their headsets, Smashy was whispering anyway. "It was basically a canister of nails, but if the range estimation was off even a little bit, it wouldn't burst close enough to hurt anybody. Sure scared 'em, and you never saw Sam run faster, but the new stuff has got sensors that know exactly when it's over a bunch of the Sammies. One time I blew down an entire squad . . ."

The words stopped, and Mortas immediately refocused his attention on the open terrain below them. The surviving shrubs on the final slope before the plain were sharply defined in his goggles, but the particles from the dust cloud began to break up the image soon after that. Despite the interference, far out in the gray-green world of his goggles he made out four white slivers. Tiny, like stars against a night sky back on Earth.

"Dismounts. Moving in this direction," Smashy observed. "What are they doing out there in the open like that? Sitting ducks."

The radio came alive with reports from First Platoon's other observation points, whispered words of warning.

"Okay, so everybody sees them. Cut the chatter." Berland spoke from his position on the other side of

Testo's squad. "Everybody hunker down and stay real quiet. Do not, I say again, do *not* engage."

Mortas bumped Hunt's arm. "Wake up Daederus."

The medic slid backward down the incline, toward the sleeping aerial support man. Mortas switched to the company radio frequency and reported the sighting to an NCO who answered in place of Captain Noonan. The company commander's voice came into his ear a minute later, probably just having been awakened.

"Dismounts? No vehicles?"

"They're all on foot. Counting six of them now, still a good—" Mortas was about to check the range when Smashy held up two fingers in front of his goggles. "Two thousand yards, coming toward us."

"Make sure no one fires unless they start climbing." Noonan's voice took on an edge of excitement. "Tell me everything they do."

Daederus crawled up on his other side, maskless, a tight grin on his lips. He began a whispered conversation with the other ASSLs, and Mortas was sure he felt the man's arm vibrating through the barrel of his Scorpion. The white slivers in his goggled vision had grown in size, taller and slightly wider because they were wearing the bulky Sim battle smocks, still too far out to distinguish weapons.

"Everybody take a good look around you; don't get stuck on these guys," Berland warned. "Rear security, stay awake."

Mortas felt a tiny pain in his right hand, and realized he'd been clutching the stock of his rifle as if it were the last handhold over a thousand-foot drop. He pressed his dirty palm against the dirt, feeling the muscles beginning to relax but grateful for the pain. He was wide-awake, fully aware of his surroundings, and because they'd planned ahead he knew exactly what to do. An unfamiliar thrill passed through him as the approaching enemy resolved into six Sim infantrymen with long Sim rifles.

Mortas opened his mouth and let out a long, silent exhale inside his mask. He wondered if this was the same sensation hunters felt when they spotted their prey. His eyes began to smart from staring so long through the goggle night vision, but he had difficulty closing them, even for the few seconds it would take to tear up and moisten the tissues. He did it finally, but only after reminding himself he would have to be able to shoot at them if they kept coming, up the slope.

The lead soldier raised his arm, a hand signal that halted the others, and they sank to a knee as one. The Sims in the rear turned their backs to the rocks, protecting the others, and Mortas was thankful for the low whistle of the breeze. Most Sim infantry didn't have devices enabling them to see at night, but that was reputed to be the reason they were such excellent infiltrators. Not relying on technology to warn them of danger, they were supposed to have developed hypersensitivity to both sound and smell.

This bunch was not infiltrating, though. Their suicidal decision to walk out in the open made little sense, but its purpose became somewhat clearer when the lead man rose and the others imitated him. Still five hundred yards out from the beginning of the incline, they turned and began to walk parallel to the rocks. The Sim in the center, the one who appeared to be in charge, made some more hand signals. The troops farthest out sidestepped even more, but he had to perform the same silent command a second time before they attained the spacing he desired.

Mortas grabbed Daederus's forearm through his fatigue shirt, feeling dried dirt crumbling from the sleeve. The ASSL looked at him, and Mortas cupped a hand over his mask before speaking as softly as possible. The enemy was already well away, but he didn't want to take any chances.

"They're checking the ground to see if it can support vehicles. They just spread out to compute the distance between the rocks and the bog."

"Oh, baby." Daederus sounded like a teenaged boy seeing a naked woman for the first time. He began a hushed message, telling the other ASSLs and fire controllers on both the ground and in the air that he suspected the enemy was scouting out a route for a larger force. One with wheels or tracks and, in either case, armor.

The message was relayed through the company to battalion, then to brigade. Noonan came up on the radio just once, to ask if they could estimate the width of the route the enemy was establishing, the distance between the rocks and the impassable mud. Again Sergeant Smashy came to Mortas's rescue, this time with one raised finger in the gloom.

"Maybe a thousand yards."

Berland, to the west, spoke in a mutter. "Just passed us, pushed out even more. They're definitely checking the ground. Agree with thousand yard estimate."

Daederus had been in a steady conversation with the fire control people, but his voice began to rise in anger and Mortas grabbed his arm again to quiet him. The ASSL gave him an exasperated look.

"As usual, somebody in orbit thinks he's smarter than we are."

"What, about the distance? How could they tell from there?"

"Naw, they're saying this is just routine patrolling. They haven't seen any buildup anywhere near us, so they won't divert the assets."

"You mean we're not covered?"

"Oh, we'll have help if we need it, but they think this is just gonna be a scouting party. A few armored cars at most." He went back to the argument, and Mortas went back to scanning the emptiness to their front. He searched his memory of the classes at Officer Basic, when they'd been taught the enemy's most common practices. Diagrams flew through his mind, different echelons depending on the size and type of an attack, and the distances between them. Scouts of some kind always came first, but this was such an unusual situation that he couldn't imagine what would come next or how long it would take for them to get there.

The tense minutes passed, then turned into a dull hour where nothing new appeared. In the meantime, the enemy dismounts had passed in front of First and Second Platoons' zones and were about to leave B Company's surveillance entirely. By prearranged command, any enemy reconnaissance that didn't move up on the high ground was supposed to be ignored unless they got so far west that they left the area covered by the infantry. In that case, they would be destroyed by a drone gunship because that had been adjudged the least likely weapon to indicate human presence near the passes.

"No, I'm saying don't take them out at *all!*" Daederus hissed to someone. "They're walking that route for a reason. *Something* is coming behind them, and we want to see what it is."

A similar discussion was taking place on the battalion command net. The commander of A Company, to the west, was insisting on killing the Sims while Captain Noonan was arguing to leave the enemy dismounts unmolested.

"If they were worried about the passes, they'd be checking them out. This is something different. They don't know we're up here, or they wouldn't be acting like this. Let's see what comes next, once they call back the go-ahead." Noonan's voice was tight, and Mortas noted the same timbre of anticipation he'd heard from Daederus.

"There is *nobody* to our west! What are you suggesting we do?" A Company's commander objected. "Just let them walk all the way through and disappear?"

"Hold on." Colonel Alden's voice. "Where are they now, and what are they doing?"

"Still walking, just about to leave B Company's zone."

"All right. A Company, keep watching them, but do not engage unless approached. I want to hear if they stop, if they move away from the high ground, or if they do anything except keep walking west."

"What do we do when they reach the end of our zone?"

"If they get that far, we'll have to kill them. But not until then. I want to know what they're up to."

An hour passed in relative silence. Although he was in constant communication with the four soldiers covering the rear of the observation post, Mortas slid down the embankment to check up on them personally. He moved in the hunched-over posture that was becoming second nature for the Orphans in that part of the brigade sector, calling ahead as he approached each two-man team.

The first security position was manned by Ladaglia and a veteran member of Smashy's rocket team, a corporal named Arrow. They'd found a clear space in the middle of a clump of tall bushes, and thinned out the weeds at its edges in order to observe the area around them without being seen. Like so much of the rest of the platoon sector, the ground they faced rose in front of them and was crisscrossed with stony wrinkles and depressions. Dak's squad was to their northeast, farther uphill and closer to the pass.

Mortas had checked the spot several times before, rotating men in and out of it, so he got down and crawled under low-hanging branches to enter the position. The two soldiers inside were on their stomachs facing in two different directions, their boots touching so they could silently alert each other to danger. Mortas crept over the human V, feeling the bushes scrape the top of his helmet. He opened the front section of his camouflage cover so he wouldn't be lying on the magazines for his Scorpion, and lowered himself to the dirt between the two men.

"Everything's quiet, Lieutenant," Arrow whispered. "If anything's headed our way, it's gonna come from the plain where you saw those Sammies."

"That seems to be the consensus. So far nothing's followed them."

Mortas rested his chin on his hands, staying back from the edge of the team's hiding spot. Weeds stood up dark and tall in front of his goggles, and it took him some time to focus beyond them on the slope ahead. Too much ground for so few men, in terrain that badly restricted their fields of vision. And fields of fire.

"How far are they with the clearing operation, sir?" Ladaglia spoke without moving, and Mortas experienced a sensation of unreality at not knowing which of the two men in goggles and masks was which.

"It's picking up speed. They're almost to A Company's area." Remembering Ladaglia's standard joke. "Think we might win the war right here?"

"God I hope not. They might make us garrison the place, or even colonize it. What a shithole."

The three men enjoyed a brief, quiet chuckle before Mortas slid back out and went to check on the other security team.

At the second position Private Jute, the veteran from Mecklinger's squad, was paired with one of the new men whose name Mortas couldn't recall. The older man nodded at him from behind helmet, goggles, and mask when Mortas lowered himself onto his stomach between the two soldiers.

They'd picked a spot in the middle of three round boulders that rose five feet from the broken ground. Facing uphill, they were covering the rear approach to the observation point that was closest to Testo's squad.

"Any idea what those Sim dismounts were doing, sir?"

"They looked like they were checking the ground to see if the mud had gotten this far. It hasn't, so we're expecting more guests, maybe scout cars."

"Is it true Command's thinking about not coming up here at all?" Mortas couldn't tell if Jute was hopeful, or still focused on the uncertainty surrounding the operation.

"I heard that rumor too. We'll have to wait and see. But the lane clearing is starting to cover some ground, so every moment that passes without trouble gets us closer to the finish line."

"Think they'll pull us out of here once the lanes are open?"

A piece of dust worked its way into his right eye, forcing Mortas to slide the goggles up to dig it out. He rubbed his eye hard, longer than it took to dislodge the particle, for the simple reason that he hadn't thought that far into the future. As far as he knew, no one had.

"Maybe. Not sure. Even with the mines removed, somebody's got to secure the high ground around those passes."

"You might want to ask about that, sir." Jute's voice was neutral, but he suspected the veteran was working hard to keep it that way. "Sam likes his artillery, and as soon as the first tank comes out of those passes he's gonna rain it down all over this ridge. Can't dig in, and if we're still here when that happens, it ain't gonna be fun."

Mortas stared ahead, noticing the gravel and cracked stone all around, the remains of the shelling this area had suffered sometime in the not-too-distant past. Imagining the huge explosions blasting the rock into lethal chips, throwing the fragments in all directions.

"Thanks, Jute. I mean that." He looked over at the new man, who had said nothing yet. "When are you supposed to rotate to the center, get some shut-eye?"

"Another hour. Doesn't matter; I wouldn't sleep anyway."

"All right. I gotta get back out there."

They both mumbled some kind of goodbye, and he slithered backward before rising to a crouch and shuffling away. Down to the depression where the men who'd come off watch would sleep, quite suddenly feeling the tug of his own fatigue. No one was there right then because of the enemy movement, and Mortas was considering reducing the position's security status to get the sleep rotation going again when Daederus spoke on the radio.

"Two thousand yards southeast. Looks like three vehicles, coming this way."

His mind sharpened by the alert, Mortas carefully moved up the slope until he saw the prone figures peering over the lip. Crawling on his belly, slipping into place as naturally as a lizard. The familiar scene of the plain, drenched in gray and green inside the goggles, the towering cloud to his right and three olive blobs to his left.

Hearing the muttered words, the more clearly enunciated answers from farther back or farther up, as the message and description were passed. Unable to keep from staring, the pulsating cones of heat growing larger as they rolled toward him. A triangular formation, one vehicle in front and two others back on either side.

"Scout cars," Daederus observed.

"How do you know?"

"Uniform heat signature. Light armor, all around.

If they were tanks, the frontal armor would block a lot of it; looks like a floating green doughnut." Mortas remembered Major Hatton's story about something the troops had labeled the "doughnut resupply" somewhere else, sometime in the past. Now hearing the engines, a low humming, and unable to believe that there had ever been a time or a place other than where he was right now.

Berland's voice in his ear. "You know the drill. Fingers off the triggers. Let 'em go by."

The blobs resolved into something Mortas had seen firsthand on Roanum, the image of a Sim armored car. Big wheels, a nose like the prow of a boat, and a revolving turret with a gun barrel. Mortas expected to see heads and even upper torsos protruding from the hatches, but just before the lead vehicle began the turn he registered that all the hatches were closed.

The dust. They'd come from the south, where the ash storm was no doubt more severe, and so they were completely buttoned up. Individual Sim infantry didn't have night-vision devices, but Sim vehicles did, and so the occupants of the scout cars were driving on instruments. As if thinking the same thing, Daederus and Smashy both began sliding backward. Mortas followed suit.

Imagining the human troops all along the high ground, watching the vehicles, pressing themselves down into the rock to avoid showing up on the enemy's scopes. The humming was loud now, mixed with the crunching as the huge tires rolled across the hard, flat terrain. Only his helmet and the very top of his goggles above the level of the grass and the dirt and the stone, the nonarmored parts of his body feeling a part of the very soil.

The three armored cars rolled by quickly, aware that they were offering their profiles to high ground that had not been scouted. As soon as they passed, all three men wriggled back up to the edge and looked out. The heat from the rear engines showed up almost white in the goggles, and when Mortas turned to look back out on the plain it took a moment for his eyes to adjust. There was nothing there.

Again, the question of how long it would take for whatever was following the scout cars to get there. It was largely academic, given the situation, because the Sims inside the vehicles could be reporting that the ground was fit for foot soldiers and scout cars but not armor. They might also be sensibly advising against sending a major force until the forbidding high ground had been cleared.

Or they might be radioing back that they were traveling with no opposition at all and that significant forces should follow as soon as possible.

Daederus, once again speaking to his partners and bosses on the fire control net, stopped talking with a sudden turning of his head. His goggles stared into Mortas's, and he seemed to be listening to something the lieutenant could not yet hear. In the gray-green world, he raised a hand and wiggled all five fingers before pressing it into the dirt. Mortas followed suit, his eyes widening in amazement at the sensation in his palm.

The ground was trembling, a vibration he remembered from Roanum when gigantic Sim earthmovers had approached the ravine where he and the others had been hidden. He looked back out over the plain, expecting to see the lumbering silhouettes of many Sim tanks, but at the same time wondering how they could be rattling the dirt beneath him from so far away.

"Oh boy." Sergeant Smashy sounded worried, and Mortas soon understood why. There was no longer a need to touch the ground to feel the tremors, which now passed through his armor. Voices came up on the net, tumbling over each other, asking if anyone else was feeling that and did anyone know what it was.

"It's a fucking *earthquake!*" Daederus shouted, but his words were barely audible above a series of booming crashes from the distant mud field. Mortas was reminded of thunder, the instantaneous explosion of a bolt that was practically on top of the hearer, then of the waves from a tropical storm he'd once witnessed, slamming into the rocks of an oceanside cliff.

The vibration beneath him was interrupted by what felt like a kick to his armor, a subterranean burp that was followed by a long, ripping sound far out on the plain. The dust cloud was the first indication of what had happened, as it lost its serene spinning and suddenly flattened as if struck by a typhoon wind from above. Its outer edges bulged and the whole cloud shrank, covering the plain in an instant. One moment the open ground was visible for hundreds of yards and the next it was hidden inside the fog.

Mortas felt the breeze on the edges of his mask and goggles, the sting of tiny dirt specks moving at great speed, then the breeze was a wind and the wind was a storm and the flecks were pebbles and he got his head down just in time. Pulling his hands down under his throat, the pebbles rattling against the top of his helmet and his shoulder armor like hail on a metal roof.

Though astounded by the event, he still remembered his platoon and how many of them weren't facing the low ground.

"Get your heads down, there's all sorts of junk flying around!"

A chorus of voices acknowledged his message with variations of "No shit!" and, despite the stone rain, Mortas found himself laughing. He lifted his head just enough to look at Daederus, and saw that the ASSL was convulsed with giggles as well. Shielding his goggles with one hand, Mortas turned to look outward and saw that the fog was almost on them, billowing, driven by unseen forces, laden with dust and dirt and rock that flew past him.

The rock rain ceased without warning, and the others looked up in time to see the fog recede, rushing back like the tide, then even farther, as if being sucked down into a mighty hole.

They were exchanging looks of wonder when the plain erupted, thunderclap after thunderclap, blowing a dirty gray mushroom miles into the atmosphere.

"Yeah, it kinda sucks to be right about something like this." Captain Pappas spoke to Colonel Alden, Captain Noonan, and Lieutenant Mortas in a rocky depression inside the First Platoon sector. The battalion commander had come down to see the devastation for himself, but to little avail; the dust cloud had engulfed much of the brigade's zone and was particularly dense in A and B Companies' area.

Colonel Alden, inspecting Third Platoon's positions, had been appalled to discover that Lieutenant Kitrick's unhealed wound had rendered him unable to walk. Kitrick had suffered through the march to his platoon zone, but was barely able to stand when the battalion commander arrived. Over Kitrick's express objection, the seasoned platoon leader had been evacuated. This left First Platoon as the only platoon with an officer, and so Captain Noonan had announced he would be shifting his small command group between Second and Third Platoons.

The air was eerily still, and the ashen fog drifted like smoke all around them. The observation points had gone from being able to see thousands of yards out to only a hundred, and sometimes less. The goggles allowed the humans to see into the cloud, and the ships in orbit were allegedly scanning for Sim movement as well, but the cloak that had descended on them had put most of the Orphans in a jittery mood.

Intermittent breaks in the vapor told the story that Pappas had predicted: the mud field had collapsed into an enormous sinkhole that was getting deeper and wider. It had spewed forth such a volume of dirt and cinders that the battle to its south had simply ended. Both sides had withdrawn to defensive positions because the noisome air had begun to choke any engine that was exposed to it for too long.

"Command sees this as a big opportunity." Colonel Alden spoke from behind goggles that were already covered in dust and a face mask that looked like it had been used to strain muddy water. "They were starting to come away from the northern counterattack idea, because they figured the Sims would be able to shut the passes back down by simple bombardment. But with this cloud all over us, there's no way to conduct aerobot reconnaissance—theirs or ours. The dust up here's not as thick as it is in the south, so they figure we can push a lot of armor through here before the Sammies get wise."

"How far along is the clearance effort, sir?" Noonan asked.

"Just under halfway on our corridor, one-third of the way on Corridors Two and Three. They've encountered reactive mines in all three lanes, some of which still have enough power to detect a human electrical field. The sappers have been forced to wear the dampening suits, and it's really slowed them down."

"I only asked because we're spread awfully thin out here. And with the visibility as it is, if Sam wants to come up here and have a look around, he's not gonna have a lot of trouble doing it."

"I understand. Captain Pappas?"

"Our air reconnaissance has been affected the same way Sam's has, and of course we weren't flying much of it in this area anyway. Orbital recon hasn't detected any enemy movement in this direction. The Sims' earlier attack, combined with the long fight down south, seems to have exhausted them. They're digging in on the ground they took from us."

"If that's true, what was that bunch we killed last night?" The six enemy foot soldiers who'd crossed First Platoon's area had been gunned down by A Company while running for the apparent safety of the rocks when the ground had started to give way. The three fleeing scout cars had been destroyed by rocket teams from B Company's Second and Third Platoons, and the Sims who had bailed out had been cut down by rifle and grenade fire.

"The dismounts were obviously checking the ground to see if it was safe for vehicles, but it might just have been for the scout cars that came later. Command believes it was a long-range patrol of some kind. So far, orbital recon hasn't seen anything that would suggest Sam had anything waiting to follow them."

"These orbital eyes and ears you keep mentioning. They didn't see those armored cars coming at us."

"They should have. Our area is their priority because we've got nothing else watching over us. I asked what happened, and they basically said we should be able to handle three scout cars on our own."

"So they missed it."

"Yes."

Colonel Alden broke in. "I discussed that with the brigade commander, and he forcefully took it up with higher. We've been assured it won't happen again, but Colonel Watt is skeptical and so am I. It is vital that we keep our own eyes and ears open, so even though we're shorthanded, every platoon has to continue patrolling in its sector. As an added set of eyes, the brigade's scouts have been inserted in the mountains across from us."

Alden let that sink in. The long-range reconnaissance teams at brigade level were extremely good, but the distance between them and the rest of the Orphans was excessive. Separated from their fellows by miles of open plain, they would have to rely on aerial support fire and shuttle evacuation if they ran into trouble.

A straining motor sounded from down the rocky path, and the four men looked into the grayness to see what it was. The eddying fog seemed to slip away as a four-wheeled motorcart rolled up. Its driver was caked in gray dirt, wearing a bulbous set of driving goggles over his electronic eyes. He shut the engine down and dismounted, and when the driver began scrubbing away at the outer goggles with a filthy rag Mortas recognized him as Captain Dassa.

"Good timing, Emile." Colonel Alden walked

toward the cart, and the others followed. The back of the low vehicle was filled with canvas sacks. "Hand grenades and dragonflies, gentlemen. We're going to keep pushing these forward, along with lots of boomer rounds, extra water, and replacement masks until this operation is completed."

He hefted one of the cylindrical explosives.

"Let's hope we'll all get hernias carrying every bit of this back out again when this is all over."

Colonel Alden departed with Noonan and Pappas, and Mortas stayed with Dassa to wait for the men from his platoon who would carry the supplies to the different positions. Mortas examined the smaller version of the Armadillos that had been running up and down the company sector.

"Never seen one of these before. Or even heard of them."

"Yeah, Sergeant Major got four of them from the engineers clearing the lane. Not enough 'dillos to get the job done." Dassa looked around. "I don't know what Sam's doing down south, but that patrol last night tells me he's at least thinking about coming back up here. And if he does that, he'll use this cloud to get infantry up onto this ground."

"We've got the plain under observation, and even with this shit in the air, we'll be able to pick up the heat signatures."

"Sam won't come across the open like that. He'll

infiltrate from the north, where there's all those trees. Even at full strength we wouldn't be able to stop him from sneaking through the brigade's sector, not with all the folds in the ground, and we're nowhere near full strength."

A stab of doubt passed through Mortas, and he felt the need to get Berland in the conversation. He was just about to call the platoon sergeant when Dassa spoke again.

"You already walked your whole sector?"

"Yes."

"Marked the spots where infiltrators could hole up, like this depression here? Got chonks sighted in on them?"

"Yeah, my guys did that without being told."

"That's what I figured. Let me show you something that might be helpful." Dassa took out his handheld, and Mortas switched his goggles over to the map of First Battalion's area. A and B Companies' observation points on the ground south of Lane One formed a line that resembled an archer's bow, with Lane One representing the bowstring. B Company formed the eastern half of the bow, and First Platoon's positions curved up almost to the pass itself.

Depressions in the platoon sector were marked with target designations for the grenade launchers, so that anyone receiving fire from the rear would be able to call in the location for the chonks. This technique grew less effective farther north, where the trees were thicker. Dassa continued giving advice.

"I see you've got your machine guns covering the plain. Pretty useless, really." Mortas felt his cheeks burning inside his mask. "So much open ground that's beyond their range, and whatever might come at us from that direction would be armored. Here's something I've done in the past." Dassa drew a line on the handheld that appeared on the map in front of Mortas's eyes. "It's unconventional, and most units can't handle it, but it fits here because we haven't got a lot of guys and the ground's mostly covered in bushes."

Mortas's eyes widened as Dassa sketched a narrow, fan-shaped field of fire for the machine gun team at Dak's position. Instead of firing out over the plain, it would be shooting to the rear, into the platoon's zone. One side of the fan followed the edge of Lane One, and the other side of the acute angle came up behind Mecklinger's position on the western edge of the platoon's area.

"I know it looks like you'll be shooting into Second Platoon, but the rising ground is going to block that."

"It's going to do that well short of Second Platoon. My machine guns won't be able to fire more than a couple of hundred yards facing this direction, and the ricochets will be flying all over the place," Mortas replied.

"Sure, except they won't be shooting straight ahead. If you raise the barrels, you can send plunging fire up and over any intervening high ground." Dassa jabbed his handheld, making several enemy personnel symbols appear around one of the depressions behind

Dak's position. "If you throw up some dragonflies, they'll show you the heat signatures of any Sammies who have gotten behind you. Your people are all hugging the edge here, so if you take fire from the rear, you can work the machine gun rounds right onto the target without too big a chance of hitting friendlies. The dragonflies will show you the heat from the slugs, and you can adjust right onto the enemy."

"That's brilliant."

"Yeah, but you've got to establish sectors of fire for every gun and set those in stone. Gunner gets excited, Sam jumping all over the place, it's just too easy to overshoot into a friendly unit. Talk to your platoon sergeant and see what he thinks."

A dark thought. "How come Captain Noonan didn't come up with this?"

"Oh, I don't think too many other guys have actually had to do this. I had to make it up on the spot because Sam got in some low ground behind us, and we were almost out of chonk ammunition." Dassa paused, then went ahead. "Noonan's all right, but I heard he comes from an outfit that went by the book too much. Some guys, if they're not allowed to show initiative in their first assignment, they never learn how." His attention returned to the handheld. "Now I'll show you how to set up those sectors of fire."

CHAPTER NINE

It was late afternoon, and Ayliss had found Dr. Kletterman alone in his office. Concerned about appearing to be merely waiting out the two days until she could leave, Ayliss had immersed herself in the outpost's work. The entire day had been spent moving from console to console and from lab to lab, asking questions, hearing the answers, asking more questions, and the whole time maintaining a veneer of friendly interest.

Not that the topics, or the people studying them, were dull. She'd found the researchers highly engaged in their work and refreshingly open about it. Many of them were close to her in age, and Ayliss couldn't help but compare their sincerity and eagerness to the machinations and shallowness of so many of her contemporaries back home. Python had explained this as a function of the isolation and secrecy the small group of scientists had been enduring, but she'd felt that was only half the answer.

Much of the staff found the Sim subjects deeply intriguing, and the remainder considered their involvement with the Ant Farm as a patriotic duty to the human race. Even those people expressed little hostility toward the Sims, and their naïveté caused Ayliss no small amount of guilt. If her plan succeeded, most of the researchers would be ruined professionally by what would no doubt be an intentionally prolonged exposure to the public, the courts, and perhaps even the prisons.

"Doctor. I was hoping to sit with you for a few minutes if you're not too busy." Ayliss wore a bright face as she stood in the doorway.

"Oh, by all means come in!" Kletterman stood up and lifted a stack of readouts from the only other chair. "I'm just catching up on some internal correspondence. You wouldn't think we were all living together in essentially one building, the way some of these people send me messages."

"I've found that was a good way to create a record as I went along, so perhaps that's what they had in mind."

"A politician who wants to create a record of what they've done? You jest." The bushy eyebrows rose and fell, once.

They shared a laugh, even though Ayliss felt slightly ruffled by the comment.

"Politician? You've got me confused with my father."

"I doubt it would be the first time that has happened. I've never met the chairman, but a man in my field can tell a lot from footage on the Bounce broadcasts. Your physical resemblance is striking, even for father and daughter, but I couldn't help noticing the shared mannerisms. In the terms of my field, you and your father are practically identical."

"I wasn't aware I had similar mannerisms with my father." The incessant hunt for intelligent questions kicked in, saving her. "And his duties kept him away from me for much of my childhood, so I doubt I picked them up in imitation."

"I doubt it as well." Kletterman leaned back, his bulk making the high-backed chair squeal. "Someday we will fully understand how gestures, facial expressions, and other idiosyncrasies are sometimes passed down across generations. Sadly, that is one of the many areas of my work where we are certain the behavior arises from genetic coding, but still have practically no idea how that can be."

"This would seem to be an area of study that would be of value regarding your subjects, I would think." A day's interaction with Kletterman's people had almost removed the word "Sim" from her vocabulary.

"Certainly." Kletterman straightened in his chair. "I'm pleased you brought that up. While I'm thoroughly enjoying the observation of our guests, and honestly could happily devote a lifetime to that alone, I have been wondering when the second phase of this project would begin."

Her mind searched for a response that would not reveal her complete ignorance, but Ayliss soon gave up on that.

"I'm sorry to have to admit this, Doctor, but it appears this 'second phase' was left out of my briefing. Perhaps my father believed it might bias my observations."

"Marvelous!" Kletterman leaned back, smiling. "Encountering the scientific method in the political world. I wonder if it has always been there, or if perhaps the collaboration between our spheres caused by the war could be credited. A cross-pollination, so to speak."

"God knows we could use it."

"Indeed. But at the risk of biasing you, the original intent of this facility was more directly linked to my specialty. Specifically, it was to continue the research into the genetic material of our opponents. Searching for the coding that makes them so formidable in battle, if such a thing exists, or what facilitates their forming into groups with such ease."

"Are you planning to take samples from your subjects?"

"No. As I mentioned earlier, I was not consulted on the manner in which they were procured and delivered, and as a result that opportunity was missed. However, the Force has been collecting samples for almost the entire duration of the war, and so the procurement of more recent material won't be a major problem."

"What are you hoping to learn, Doctor?"

"Obviously our opponents were manufactured for this conflict, a designer enemy if you will. Ongoing Force research has already revealed that the latest versions of our opponents are larger, stronger, and faster than the originals. It is undeniable that some entity is creating—and modifying—them."

"Go on."

"If such an entity went to that much trouble to oppose our progress across the stars, or does in fact intend to eradicate us, it stands to reason that this entity would not want to replace us with a larger, stronger, and more formidable version of our race."

Kletterman stopped, an amused expression creeping onto his face. Ayliss recognized it from school, the teacher who wanted the student to find the answer with the available information. It didn't take long.

"You're looking for something in the Sims' makeup that would allow this entity to get rid of them once the war was over."

"Exactly. What that scoundrel Python refers to as the 'on-off' switch."

"That's the last of them."

Berland sat with his back to a large rock, tapping information into his handheld. Mortas sat next to him, tired from having physically visited every geographic rise and dip in the platoon's sector. Three Orphans in the nearby brush were guarding them while they finished plotting out Dassa's plan for the machine guns.

Mortas switched the view in his goggles so he could see the map of the platoon's area. The five observation posts curved southwest from Dak's squad near Lane One, through Mortas's position farther downhill, then to Testo's squad before heading west through Berland's position and Mecklinger's squad and ending at the start of Second Platoon's zone. Every piece of low or shielded ground was now identified, and they were waiting for Noonan's blessing of Dassa's plan.

Despite the dust in the air, Mortas slid his lenses up on their frames so he could look at Berland. Instantaneous communication and the size of their sector had kept them separated since the start of the mission, and the lieutenant found it comforting to actually be in the seasoned NCO's presence.

"Enjoying yourself, Lieutenant?" Berland's smile creased his grimy face.

"I honestly didn't understand Captain Dassa's idea until we actually walked the ground. It's incredible."

"Yeah, I gotta hand it to him. I would never have thought of this."

Noonan came up on the radio, having studied the novel use of dragonflies to direct machine gun rounds fired up and over obstacles inside the platoon's sector in order to hit enemy soldiers seeking shelter in the low ground. He added several control features to the map, restricting the fire well short of friendly positions, but the plan was left intact.

"That is fantastic. We are going to kill anybody who comes at us from behind. Well done, First Platoon." Noonan's voice almost dripped with anticipation, as if the company commander was hoping the enemy found a way to infiltrate that far south. Noonan switched over to Second and Third Platoons, directing them to begin working up similar fire plans.

Mortas made sure his radio wasn't transmitting, and whispered to Berland, "I think the CO likes killing Sims almost as much as Daederus does."

"Oh, I could have told you that, sir. That last mission, hunting the Sims in that mountain chain, Captain Noonan was practically losing his mind because he wasn't in on the action. We had patrols and ambushes all over the place, and he had to manage all of that instead of actually being out there.

"After a few days, he started moving the command group a lot. Kept saying he was having trouble communicating with everybody. The company ASSL told me that Noonan basically turned the command group into a tiny patrol, hoping to run into Sam.

"I think the CO spent his platoon leader time in one of those outfits where the whole company was always together in one place. Probably had a boss who didn't let him do too much, so when the shooting started he got to join in. From what I saw on that last mission, I think he developed a taste for it."

Mortas's earpieces pressed down just a bit, and an unfamiliar voice spoke to him.

"Engineer survey team to your west, heading toward you. Don't shoot us up."

He flipped his radio back to transmission mode. "Come on."

Berland was already facing outward, the handheld stowed and his Scorpion in his hands. Recognition signals were exchanged with the incoming patrol, first using the goggles and then the radio once the engineers were in sight. It was a three-man team led by a tall lieutenant who was mapping out the next phase of the lane clearance.

The newcomers joined them in the concealed hollow, and Mortas greeted his fellow officer.

"I'm Jander Mortas. Can't tell you how happy I am to see you."

"Lar Tottleman, good to meet you too." The engineer shook hands with Mortas and Berland. "Try not to be too happy. I'm only this far up because I got tired of sitting around back there. We are *way* behind on the timetable, and it's getting worse."

"What's the holdup?"

"Most of the mines we're encountering are really old, both ours and theirs. Command wants us to disarm every one of them without making any noise, but some of these devices are really unstable. Even when we're familiar with them, there's a good chance they'll go off while we're working. It's crazy."

"But you're making progress, right?"

"Sure. And there are some open stretches, too, so we're not exactly crawling back there." Tottleman slid his goggles up and wiped sweat from around his eyes with a rag. "This junk in the air doesn't help, either, but at least it's keeping any aerobots from finding us."

Berland spoke up. "How many people you got back there? Shouldn't be enough to get Sam interested, especially if it's going so slow."

"It isn't us. We've got only as many engineers in the lane as necessary, which may be part of the problem. Somebody on high is just raring to go, and we have to keep shooing the cavalry scouts away."

"You're kidding me."

"I wish I was. We'd been on the job for just a few hours when a whole platoon of them rattled up behind us. We chased them off, but that armored division is pretty lathered up to run the pass as soon as it's clear. They're spread out pretty well now, but for a while there they were stacked up like we were going to give them the go-ahead at any second."

Tottleman's head moved in a jerky fashion just then, as if he hadn't been aware Mortas and Berland were in front of him. Squinting, he leaned over to inspect the dust-covered tiger striping on Mortas's fatigues.

"Now I *know* we're fucked. What jungle did they pull you guys out of?"

It was night, but the thickening cloud of dust had kept the platoon's positions in the dark for many hours before the sun set. Mortas was on his third filter mask and already beginning to calculate how long the platoon's supply would last. He was back on his stomach again, between Daederus and Smashy, and wondering if the pain in his chest was from lying prone for so many hours or a lung infection from the tainted air.

"Ah, that's no good." The ASSL spoke to himself, but both Mortas and Smashy looked in his direction, knowing his radio gave him information that was denied to them. The fire support man finally whispered in explanation. "Orbital Command has lost contact with the southernmost brigade scout team."

Mortas placed both palms on the dust-covered stone and pushed himself onto his knees. He squinted inside the goggles, as if that would allow him to see through the darkness or the drifting soot that he couldn't keep off of his lenses no matter how many times he wiped them.

The plain in front of him got murky and then vanished long before the high ground miles across from them, where the brigade's scouts were on lookout. Only one team was out of contact according to that report, so it could be something as simple as malfunctioning equipment, but it was a bad sign that it was the scout team farthest to the south. If the Sims were trying to swing north around the giant hole that they'd created, the first scout team they would have encountered would be the one that was out of contact.

Mortas had personally taken a three-man patrol through the platoon zone only a few hours earlier, and had come back convinced that the only presence on their part of the ridge was human. So far there had been no reports of infiltrators anywhere in the brigade sector, but the opportunity created by the reduced visibility could not be dismissed.

Sliding back down onto his chest between Daederus and Smashy, Mortas fought the odd combination of fatigue and apprehension. The entire platoon had been going on less and less sleep because of the heightened patrolling, and it was beginning to take its toll. At one point his mind felt sluggish and dull, and the next it was racing through all of the unpleasant possibilities suggested by their position and recent developments. No aerial support beyond orbital rockets. Natural depressions and a few old shell holes their only protection if they got hit with artillery or rockets. If they had to abandon their positions, their path to safety went uphill and then over ground that still hadn't been cleared of mines.

Mortas blinked hard, cursing the grit that had slipped past the goggles, and in his mind he saw the enemy foot patrol that had passed directly in front of them the previous night. The armored cars that had followed them. The solid ground that still existed along the ridges to the east and to the south.

"Hey, ASSL."

"Yeah?"

"If they send armor at us, who's going to shoot that minefield onto the plain?"

"Right now we're covered by the artillery of the armored division that's waiting for the lane to be cleared. Don't worry; I gave them detailed coordinates for a mixed obstacle belt right after we got here. They could shoot it blindfolded."

"When are you authorized to put that in place?"

"Only if we see Sim armor."

"Right. That's what's got me worried. An engineer lieutenant told me our tankers are all fired up to run the pass when the lanes are cleared, but it's taking longer than planned. What do you think they'll do, that armored division with the artillery that's supposed to deliver our minefield, if they hear enemy tanks are out on this plain while the pass is still blocked?"

Daederus didn't reply for almost a minute, and Mortas began to wonder if the ASSL's brain was getting as foggy as his own. To his right, Smashy began to fidget as if the conversation were giving him a rash. Finally Daederus responded.

"You got a good point. Our tankers will want to get out onto this ground right here, to fight Sam's tankers. Even if their artillery wanted to shoot that minefield, their commander might countermand them."

"They're stacked up waiting to run the passes, so it would take them a while to get down here. We could get overrun before that happened if they didn't shoot that obstacle belt into position."

Daederus began muttering over the radio again, a hurried conversation that quickly got heated. "Don't tell me they'll lay the field before they move out! As soon as they know there are tanks out here, we lose them as our priority support! And you wouldn't know this because you're not down here, but the dust is so thick that nothing is going to fly in to help us."

A pause.

"Thanks bunches. You're all heart." Daederus turned grime-covered goggles in his direction. "Command says we've still got orbital rocket priority if things get rough."

"What do you think of that?"

"Not much. When it's there it's the best thing to have, but I usually have the drones and artillery as backup. I don't like relying on one system, not in a spot like this. And we still don't know what happened to that scout team." His chin dropped, then came back up. "Fuck it. I'm gonna seed those mines right now."

"Really?" Mortas almost laughed out loud, as if the ASSL were performing some kind of harmless prank.

"Yes. What are they gonna do? Take away my wings and make me walk with the infantry?" He focused his attention on the dark plain, and began calling in the code that would start the heavy guns miles behind them firing antiarmor and antipersonnel mines across the company front. Mortas flipped to the fire control net, certain that the request would be denied, and he wasn't disappointed.

"Wait wait wait wait wait." A bored voice broke in. "What are you seeing? Why are you calling this mission?"

Daederus reached up and pulled his grimy filter mask aside just long enough to show Mortas a huge smile. The lieutenant was about to ask the reason for his mirth when the fire control net jumped with communications from the rest of the battalion's ASSLs. The same code message was repeated over and over, some voices speaking softly while others were shouting. He had just noticed that no one had claimed to have seen the enemy when the bored voice came back with urgency.

"Understood! Mission cleared!"

Mortas flipped back to the platoon frequency. "Get ready! The artillery is going to shoot the minefield in front of us!"

He heard Berland and Dak respond in the affirmative just as several burps sounded from behind him. Far back, on the other side of the high ground that held the passes, the massive tubes of the field artillery were already firing the mission.

Mortas turned his attention to the dark expanse, remembering the original dimensions of the planned obstacle belt and wondering just how many of the munitions would land in the newly collapsed mud field. It wouldn't matter because the crater was its own obstacle, but in his mind he saw the heavy projectiles arching through the dust cloud, passing overhead before nosing over and hurtling toward the deck.

More burps from behind him, then the first impacts. The projectiles carrying the different mines were hot from the launch, and he could pick them out even in the dust cloud. They started seeding the ground a thousand yards out, then moved so close to the opposing ridgeline that he actually saw one of the falling canisters bounce off the far cliffs. Dirt and dust swirling as more and more of the rounds plummeted from the sky, the ASSL sending words of encouragement, and the guns finding a rhythm.

The first row of glowing canisters reached across the solid ground and found the muddy bog, the shining orbs dropping and disappearing. The ASSL let the mission continue, marking the estimated dimensions of the mud field and discussing the adjustment with the artillery's fire control personnel. More and more burps, heated metal falling like meteors through the grayness, and the belt started anew to the west, in front of A Company.

Watching the light fade as the first projectiles cooled, Mortas began to feel a lightness entering his body. In no time at all they would have an extensive obstacle belt in place, shielding them from enemy armor approaching from the plain. The Sims were adept at breaching minefields, but the belt would slow them down, and orbital rockets would take over from there. Drowsiness began tugging at his brain, and he was drifting pleasantly when it all came to an end.

Directly behind them, close to the pass, a massive explosion leapt out of the darkness. The shock wave went right through his chest armor where it rested on the ground, and the floating dust jumped as if startled.

"Short round! Short round!" An unidentified voice screamed over the radio. Another concussion, farther out, slapping the air over their heads where the three men pressed themselves into the dirt.

"Those aren't ours! That's enemy!" Daederus's voice sounded incredibly distant even though he was so close to Mortas that their sleeves were touching.

The sound dampers in his helmet kept the next explosions from deafening him, but Mortas was forced to endure the rest. High-explosive rounds landed only yards behind them, heart-stopping in their suddenness, the blast traveling through the rock like an electrical charge, stone splinters flying over them, dirt and stones landing on their legs and helmets and chest armor, one explosion after another until they were being yanked back and forth by the concussions.

Pressing into the stone for all he was worth, his hands up under his jaw, his rifle forgotten next to him, every flying pebble the hard finger of the Reaper, tapping on his armor. The shock waves fluttering his fatigue pants, imagining a chunk of steel shooting straight for his unprotected groin, sensing the slope ahead of him and wanting to madly crawl down it, down and away, below the lethal, flailing, unseen claws, but too afraid to move.

Voices in his ears, remarkably clear because of the dampers.

"Hold your positions! Hunker down!"

"Watch the plain! Anybody seeing anything?"

"Shit goddamn motherfucking son of a bitch will somebody *make it stop*!"

The last words scaring him past the terror of the shelling because for a moment he thought the voice might be his own. His hands coming up over his mask, but it wasn't him because the screaming continued and then was muffled as if someone had landed on the screamer. Someone or something.

"Lieutenant? You there?" Berland's voice, shouting but calm. He pulled his hands away, desperate to answer.

"Yes! Yes! Still here! What's going on?"

A pause that seemed to last for days.

"I think they're shelling us. I could be wrong."

Another blast, not so close this time, but more dirt and stones bouncing over his helmet. Unable to process his platoon sergeant's words, frightened for a moment that Berland had lost his mind, then understanding. His own words were the ones that didn't make sense. Mortas let out a shaky laugh, then forced his head up just enough to see out over the plain.

"I'm not seeing anything to my front. How about you?"

"Nothing so far. But they're coming. Too much artillery for it to be anything else."

The explosions mercifully shifted back, toward the pass, and he tried not to think about how easily they could return. Looking at the ASSL, who was now peering out from under his helmet, studying the open ground.

A voice Mortas knew but couldn't place, calm, confident. It was a moment before he recognized it as the brigade commander, talking to every Orphan facing the plain.

"They're going to follow this up with armor. ASSLs, kill the tanks. Orphans, protect the ASSLs."

The glowing orbs reappeared, dropping through the mist and continuing to lay the minefield. Behind them, a pulsating succession of blasts made the stone shake, and continued.

Dak's voice, vibrating, from the platoon's position closest to the mouth of the pass. "They're throwing concussion rounds at the lane! Airbursts! They're trying to open the pass from this end!"

Similar reports came in then, confirmation from Second and Third Battalion that the same kind of ordnance was landing on lanes Two and Three. The concussion rounds were meant to set off the mines that choked the passes without creating the debris that would have been generated by high explosives.

Mortas felt his sphincter clench, and a coldness invaded his entrails. It all fell into place perfectly, and for an instant he was miles over the battlefield, seeing it all for the first time. Command wasn't the only entity that had seen an advantage in the mud field's continued growth to the south. Although the Sims had initially tried to slip past the steadily enlarging obstacle on ground that would give them room to run, they had also taken note of the passes through the southernmost tip of the mountain chain to the north. They'd shifted forces in a way that had avoided detection, one of their specialties, and now they were going to force the passes.

Somewhere across the flat, massed inside the dust cloud, would be thousands of Sim soldiers in tanks and armored personnel carriers. They'd managed to kill one of the brigade's scout teams on their side of the open ground, but when the humans had started to seed the minefield they'd been forced to move.

Daederus grabbed his arm. His words rattled with the continued vibration of the ground. "Tell your people to be ready with the dragonflies, and to take over for me if anything happens."

Mortas almost asked why the ASSL hadn't told him, an officer, to take over directing the aerial fire. But then he realized that anything that happened to Daederus would probably happen to the men right around him. He relayed the instructions and received terse acknowledgment from Berland and the squad leaders, who as veterans were no doubt ready to assume the role without being reminded.

The blasts behind them took on a hollow sound, and the rock beneath them shook even more. The Sim concussion rounds were landing directly in the pass, and Mortas pulled his eyes away from the plain to look back up the slope. No air assets were able to fly in the dust, and the Sims had no ships in orbit, so how could be their fire be so accurate?

Sergeant Dak answered the question. "Everybody watch out! Sammy's got somebody adjusting his fire!"

Infiltrators. Somehow, perhaps coming all the way through the brigade's undermanned sector from the north as Dassa had predicted, Sim soldiers had gotten into position where they could observe the lanes. They wouldn't be alone, and the priority of the infantry with them would be the removal of ASSLs and any human outposts in a position to direct fires onto the plain. It was time to put Dassa's plan into action, but he needed to pull his security teams in to do that.

"Jute! Jute! Do you hear me?"

Nothing. He called the second pair of Orphans manning the tiny perimeter around his observation point, and Ladaglia answered. Mortas ordered him and Corporal Arrow to move to the depression, then scrambled backward, down the incline, coming to a crouch, slapping the dirt off his Scorpion, and moving quickly to the depression that had been their sleeping area. Hunt was there, waiting for the security men to join him, prone behind a large rock and covering the rear with his Scorpion.

"I'm going to go see what happened to Jute's position."

"You're not going alone, Lieutenant." Hunt was on his feet, bent over and clutching a grenade in the hand that wasn't holding his rifle. A sack of the deadly missiles hung over his shoulder, and Mortas simply nodded before heading out through the rocks. Unable to see more than a few yards because of the broken terrain and the eddying cloud. Fearing the worst for Jute and the other man with him, dreading the artillery that could start landing on them at any moment. Hearing the other observation points adjusting, pulling their security teams back. Hunt's voice, terse words.

"Slow down, sir."

Forcing himself to pause, dropping to a knee in the now-familiar cut that would take them to the silent security position. Dirty goggles sweeping the looming hillside and the nearest boulders, all of it so close, so confining.

"Jute. Jute. Do you hear me?" Waiting, then glancing momentarily in Hunt's direction. "You know the name of the troop who was with him?"

"One of the new guys, didn't talk much. I dunno."

"Okay. They're not much farther." Just beginning to rise when Hunt's hand seized him by the shoulder armor and pulled him backward, falling to a sitting position, the Scorpion banging against the rock with a loud crack.

"Grenade!" Seeing Hunt's small bomb flipping through the air, up, over the next turn, then scrambling across the ground on his buttocks to get behind the cover of the rocks. Fighting his way back up into a crouch, waiting, counting the seconds, then the grenade detonated. The dampers in his helmet snugging down, the gray cloud blossoming with the shock wave from the other side of the obstacle.

Eyes unbelieving, seeing a gray figure rushing toward him. Amazed by the detail. Bald head, formfitting shirt, every inch covered in gray soot, the blackened blade of a fighting knife appearing and then disappearing as the figure hurtled toward them.

And then the wraith was gone, thrown backward, its chest erupting and the Scorpion was at Mortas's shoulder, jumping as he fired. The Sim smashed into the rocks, going limp, collapsing. Mortas feeling his mouth starting to open, shock and surprise at what he'd done, what he'd managed to do, then Hunt's strangled scream from behind him and turning to see another one of them, all gray, a phantom, the knife already punching downward into the base of Hunt's neck.

Too close to swing the rifle around, the Sim pushing Hunt's convulsing body toward him, Mortas's hands letting go of the weapon and his bent legs throwing him forward. Gray skin, blue eyes, a roar of angry chirping, but then his hands were on the face, fingers spread, feeling the knife scoring his armor, legs pumping, then the weight shifted and he was driving the Sim backward.

Slamming the head against the rock, the knife stinging his left arm just once, then gone, the body collapsing, but still he kept pounding, the sickening crack of the skull hitting the stone, and it was only the thought that there might be more of them that made him stop.

Kneeling. Eyes flashing in all directions because he was alone, but always coming back to the ground in front of him. The three rocks that had sheltered Jute and the other Orphan so new to the unit that Mortas hadn't learned his name. The artillery landing in the pass, so close its concussions slapped the air around him.

Weapons, goggles, and ammunition all gone. Spirited away by the infiltrators, hidden so the humans couldn't use them. Both men on their backs, throats torn out, trousers pulled down and groins a mass of red. The gray mist flowing all around, as if he had already followed the two dead men into the next world.

Knowing he should get out of there, already having passed the warning about the infiltrators and the death of the platoon's medic. Coming back up into the hunched-over locomotion, bouncing forward with his eyes searching the fog. Squatting next to Jute, looking into the blank eyes, remembering the man's all-too-accurate prediction.

Excited voices on the radio. Third Battalion, farthest north, under sudden close attack by hordes of enemy infantry. Sharp, short explosions far on the other side of the pass. Grunted reports that the enemy was going right through Third's thinly defended zone.

Daederus, the ASSL, spoke to the platoon. "Okay, here it comes! Get the dragonflies up and keep on spittin' 'em!"

A rush surging through Mortas, a giant hand clenching inside his chest. They were coming. Lots of them.

The brigade commander's voice, loud but not shouting. "Latch onto 'em, Orphans! Bite down hard and do *not* let go!"

The brigade-wide message briefly left the channel open for a response, and Mortas heard dozens of male voices, young and old, from all over the ridge. Punctuated with explosions and rifle fire, the rattle of machine guns and the roar of the boomers.

"Orphans! Orphans! Orphans!"

Bent over on one knee, Jander Mortas gritted his teeth inside his filthy mask. He gently slapped Jute's chest. "You were right, buddy. It's a clusterfuck. But I'm gonna get 'em back for you."

He half stood, then hustled back the way he had come.

The artillery was hitting Second and Third Battalions when Mortas got back to the edge. Ladaglia and Arrow had already reached the depression and were facing uphill, sacks of grenades at the ready. A glance toward the plain showed Daederus and Smashy, the ASSL on his chest at the edge while the boomer man waited just below, the big-bored weapon loaded to fight the armor.

Mortas switched the goggles to see the image presented by scores of dragonflies circling over the brigade. It was jumpy, flashing out of focus even inside the fog, and Mortas decided the small recon robots' engines were being clogged by the dirt. As one fell out of the sky the others adjusted the imagery, quilting the picture together until they too plummeted to the ground.

They presented an appalling sight. Long, thin clusters of glowing dots, all headed south. Briefly bunching up when they hit the northernmost passes, looking like ants that had encountered a stream, spreading out east and west to find a spot to cross. Explosions rippling the cloud, dashed lines appearing as the sensors picked up the heat from the machine gun rounds fired by the Orphans to the north. The Sim infantry was bypassing the positions in Second and Third Battalions' areas, obviously bent on seizing the ground that faced the plain. First Battalion's ground.

Mortas spoke while moving. "Okay, you see 'em! Pull everybody back to the south and keep launching the 'flies! As soon as Sam crosses our lane, hit him with everything we have!"

Berland's voice took over, coordinating the machine guns, chonks, and boomers. His directions then shifted to a sequential launching of the dragonflies, which were being knocked out of the air in alarming numbers by the choking particles.

Skidding to the ground in the depression, Mortas flipped open the top of his rucksack and reached all the way to the bottom. First he pulled out a small roll of dark cord, then he took out Cranther's fighting knife. Drawing it from its sheath, he remembered the Banshee's note that had been concealed inside the scabbard.

Paranoia is healthy, Lieutenant. Nurture yours.

Cutting two lengths of cord, he stuffed the roll back into the rucksack and quickly tied the sheath to his calf. He was sliding the long blade back into its home when he saw Arrow regarding him curiously.

"You nailed the infiltrators, sir?"

"Yeah." A brief, involuntary shake of his head. "But I was too late. For Jute, for Hunt, for the new guy."

"Forget that shit, sir. Now we get to kill 'em."

They exchanged tight nods, then he was back on his stomach, between Daederus and Smashy. The artillery blasts to their north were getting closer, the Sim guns trying to sweep the human observers off the high ground before the armor came out into the open. The darkness out on the flat was somehow thicker, and so he flipped the goggles to see what the ASSL was seeing. The ground beneath them began to shake as the enemy high explosives came their way again.

Dragonflies circled across the platoon's front, stitching together a seamless picture of the plain. At first it was nothing but a gray smudge, but then he shifted the view as far out as he could and saw everything he didn't want to see.

Tiny red bugs were beetling forward, far down under the fog, coming in staggered rows. Two armored groups, debauching from the high ground to the south and to the east, beginning to spread out and move into assault formation. The dragonflies got a fix on the heat signatures, and began designating each dot with tiny crosshairs that also identified the target as a tank or an armored personnel carrier.

The picture began to flicker, then to hiccup, and finally to fragment as enough of the circling aerobots choked to death and fell from the sky. He and Smashy both pulled fresh dragonflies from the sack at their feet, and across the front other Orphans spit the vital insects into life.

The image was reduced to a small portion of the ground before the new eyes got into position, but then the picture expanded and came back into focus. Mortas noted the proximity of the lead vehicles to the mine belt, then switched the goggles back to standard vision.

"And . . . *found* 'em!" Daederus shouted. Mortas, confused, flipped back to the aerial view but only saw the vehicles that he'd seen before. He switched to the fire-control frequency and heard a voice from orbit.

"—tracked the flight of the rounds to point of origin. Rockets on the way."

Just behind them, an artillery round impacted. Stone chips flew through the air, one hitting him in the buttock. It felt like someone had just kicked him, hard, but when he reached back there was no blood. Another blast, then another, feeding his anger even as the concussion fluttered his uniform and the rock splinters rained down on him.

"Here it comes! Check it out!" Daederus was beside himself, whooping and pointing at something invisible in the gloom. It didn't stay invisible, however, as a tunnel of light suddenly raced down through the dust and dark to disappear behind the high ground to the west. A rock smacked the back of Mortas's helmet, jolting him, but then he saw it for just a second. The outline of the ridge across from them, impossible to make out until the rockets from the orbiting ships exploded behind it. A volcanic spray of fire, a horizontal flash of light that silhouetted the distant promontory, then echoing booms. More tunnels boring down, then a succession of flashes, and the explosions grew to a syncopated rumbling.

"Oh yes, baby! Yes!" Daederus was pounding his arm, sending a burning sensation from where the Sim knife had cut him, but Mortas was beyond caring. Another salvo of rockets from above, and he finally noticed that the Sim artillery had stopped landing.

"That is fucking *beautiful!*" he hollered, unrestrained joy and utter gratitude blending together in a tidal wave of relief. Other voices joined his, curses, taunts, and thanks, then Berland came up.

"Calm down! Calm down! Three-sixty defense! Sam's infantry has gotten through Second Battalion! Dragonflies and grenades! Dragonflies and grenades!"

Mortas changed the view to see that most of the aerobots had died while the Orphans had been hugging the ground under the shelling. Reaching out, blind, grabbing several of the thin tubes and jamming them into the spaces behind his ammo pouches. Spitting one up into the air, now seeing the aerial view again, the enormous number of red bugs scuttling across the flat. Small, subdued bursts of light in front of the beetles, imagining the heavy cannon firing as the tanks charged, then realizing it was the mines detonating.

Behind him, the platoon's machine guns sputtered into life, then chattered a sustained roar. Chonks lofted grenades high over the brush, exploding among the dots of light that were the Sim infantrymen who had finally reached the platoon's area. For the briefest of moments the wave of heat signatures hurtled forward, unstoppable and uncountable, then intersecting dashes of light found them. Dassa's plan working almost perfectly, the dragonflies guiding the machine gunners as the deadly streams of heated slugs ate into the dots of light. Many of the dots seemed to freeze where they were and moved no more.

The Sim infantry, their charge broken by the concentrated fire, split up into smaller groups and hunkered down in low ground or behind fingers of rock. It did them little good, because chonk grenades and machine gun rounds arched up and over the obstacles, the gunners adjusting the fire right onto them using the imagery from the dragonflies. The chattering of the automatic weapons and the blasts from the grenades joined in a thunderous roar, and Mortas turned back to the plain.

He now remembered a class in Officer Basic where they'd discussed different Sim techniques for breaching minefields. Tanks pushing heavy rollers in front of them, vehicles blasting the ground with compressed air cannons, and machine guns raking the dirt to set off the deadly obstacles. What had the instructor said? They had to slow down for any of that to be effective, which meant they were easy prey for antiarmor rocketry.

Daederus was calling in the mission, and Smashy was sighting in his boomer when the first Sim grenade went off several yards away. The dirt around them began to jump with incoming rifle fire, then all three of them were rolling in different directions, frantically trying to get off the incline that made them perfect targets.

"They're behind us! They're behind us!"

"Grenades! Throw grenades!"

"Shoot the bastards!"

"Orphan! Orphan! Orphan!"

The cries came from all around the platoon's zone, then the heavy banging of the machine guns started again. Explosions from grenades, and the chattering of rifles. Mortas had scrambled downward with the first shots, and came to a knee behind a boulder that almost completely covered him. Arming a grenade, peeking out, seeing motion uphill, Sim combat smocks and flanged helmets, what was left of their infantry, rushing from rock to rock in the dust cloud.

Throwing the grenade at the movement, reaching down and getting another. Feeling a light slap on his right and realizing it was an enemy grenade that had gone off just out of range, the idiotic thought crossing his mind that the beating from the artillery was much worse than this. Throwing the grenade, then raising the Scorpion, his goggles telling him exactly where his shots would strike, sweeping the weapon back and forth to find a target.

Flanged helmets popping up, just for a moment, sometimes to see and other times to heave a grenade. Using the rocks to their advantage, especially the covered route that Mortas had used only minutes before.

The long row of boulders, coupled with the folds of the ground, offered protection to what might have been an entire Sim squad. Too close for the platoon's machine guns and the chonks.

He lowered the Scorpion as more grenades went off, human and Sim, and was arming one of his own when a heart-stopping boom exploded directly behind him. Pushed off balance, scraping his cheek against the boulder, the goggles knocked out of place for a moment, but not before he saw what had happened.

The rocket sailed past him, trailing smoke and blowing the dust aside in the mere seconds it took to go uphill. It slammed into the rock wall shielding the enemy, blasting an enormous hole and sending lethal fragments flying in all directions. He was already on the ground, frantically clawing at his goggles to get them back in position, looking back to see Smashy ducking behind more rocks, the wide barrel of the boomer still on his shoulder.

Corporal Arrow appeared next to Smashy's rock, another round in his hands, when Sim gunfire found him. Sparks flicked at his torso armor, then struck his exposed neck, blood and shocked surprise appearing on his face as he went down. Not deciding to do it and surprised to be in motion, Mortas rushed toward the body, snatching up the fallen round and diving behind cover next to Smashy.

More grenade blasts, the tattoo of a human machine gun at one of the squad positions, voices shouting on the radio for a medic, Smashy yanking the round out of his hands and loading the launcher. Now coming into a squatting position with the boomer on his shoulder, duckwalking toward the opposite side of the rock, hopping out and firing almost at the same moment, veteran instincts, killer instincts, the launcher's roar punching Mortas in the chest through his armor, then Smashy was propelled toward him, the boomer falling to the ground.

Hands grabbing at his armor, Smashy's filter mask gone, his mouth in a rictus of pain, then he was sagging away, exposing the torn uniform and the ripped flesh and the red that was everywhere from the enemy grenade that had killed him.

Mortas lowered the body to the ground, suddenly aware that he might be the only one from their position still alive. Looking down, surprised to see he'd brought the Scorpion with him. Snatching it up and running back out, toward the enemy.

CHAPTER TEN

"**W**hy didn't you tell me about this sooner?" Olech Mortas hissed even as the elevator descended into the very bowels of Unity Plaza.

Leeger, the only other occupant of the circular car, answered calmly. "Because somebody ordered me not to bring him a status report every time Jan went to the latrine."

"How did we not know the Orphans had been put in such an exposed position?"

"The battle was far south of them and moving away until just a few hours ago."

"And so an entire Sim army just appeared out of nowhere?"

"There seems to have been a mix-up involving reconnaissance responsibilities. And the dust storm created by the mud munitions isn't helping."

The door slid open, and they were presented with

the secure room deep underground where Olech Mortas tracked the war. Circular in shape, its walls were black where they weren't taken up with large screens depicting everything from planetary positions to unit locations in actual battles. The room was a hive of activity, with uniformed personnel chattering into headsets, punching away at consoles, or rushing about on a gantry that ran all around the room several feet over their heads.

The activity came to an abrupt halt as more than a dozen heads turned and went silent. The meaning couldn't have been more obvious, but Olech ignored it. Reminding himself to maintain the charade he'd been playing for almost two decades.

Leeger conferred with one technician, and the largest display screen changed to show a cone-like piece of mountain terrain, pointed south where it descended to level ground. Three passes cut the cone from west to east, and military symbols were massed all around them.

"Where's this dust storm you were telling me about?"

"This is an earlier photograph. From the reports we're receiving, that whole screen would be gray if we used the latest feed."

Olech stepped forward, intimately familiar with the martial symbology. Enemy armor was converging on the cone from the south and east, while Sim infantry was simply all over it. The three battalions of the Orphan Brigade were defending sectors on either side of each pass, with Jander's B Company from First Battalion holding a large piece of terrain on the southeast edge of the cone.

Human engineers were clearing extensive obstacles in the three lanes, but it was hard to tell how far they'd gotten.

"What's going on with the passes here?"

"Our sappers were clearing them of mines when the attack began. The Sims have been hitting all three lanes with concussion rounds, probably to set off the mines so they can force the passes."

"I assume we have assets that can reblock those lanes if necessary?"

"We're being told that the overall commander is planning to do just that."

"Why are so many of the Orphans in the red?" When a unit dropped below fifty percent strength, its symbol turned red. If it went below forty percent its marker would start to flicker, and a flickering unit that went below thirty percent simply vanished. Over the years Olech Mortas had seen many unit symbols disappear in that fashion.

"They're taking casualties, but there's a question about what strength they were at when they were committed. They hadn't been brought back up to one hundred percent following their most recent mission."

The questions screamed inside his head. How could a brigade that was supposed to be a quick-reaction force be left understrength? And who would commit such a unit to hold so large a piece of ground?

Harsh, cold suspicion answered both questions for him, and Olech became aware of the glances, the fearful looks. They knew his son was out there and that it was going badly. He set his private accusations aside, hiding inside the role he'd assumed so long ago.

"Stay here and monitor the situation," he ordered Leeger before turning toward the elevator. The entire room had heard the next line before, many times. "Don't update me until the battle is over."

Olech forced a pleasant expression on his face, but moved through Unity's teeming corridors in such a way that most of the people he encountered knew not to speak to him. Nodding infrequently, unable to focus enough to see smiles or even hear greetings. So sick of the toadies and the climbers and the people who plotted against him while swearing loyalty to his face.

So sick, so sick of it all. The ugly façade maintained over the last seventeen years, the mask that so many found so attractive, the one that had driven away his two children in the name of saving them. And to what end? Ayliss scouring the databases for his downfall and Jan fighting for his life under the command of idiots. Perhaps even dead. Dead already.

Olech reached the throne room and passed inside. The door hissed shut behind him, leaving him temporarily in darkness, and he reached out for the wall. His palm flattened against the cold surface, and his other hand came up in front of his eyes. Fighting back the grief that wanted so badly to surge over the dams of his self-control.

The shock of the news accessed memories that Olech Mortas sometimes believed had never happened. Bursts of light and sound, explosions and screams, adrenaline surging through him and his breath coming in short gasps. The shattered bodies of the teenagers and preteens, the Unwavering, who had fought beside him during those awful weeks before he'd been wounded. The chaos, the terror, the frantic fighting when the Sims appeared, seemingly out of nowhere because nobody seemed to know what was going on.

The room's lights hummed into life, blinking, calling up a mental picture he'd trained himself to forget. A teenaged Olech Mortas, grubby, hungry, footsore, shambling up a muddy hill as fast as he could move in the flickering darkness. A disordered clutch of boys behind him, following him simply because he'd told them to, passing the ruined fighting positions that had been blasted into splinters by Sim artillery. Flares floating in the night sky on parachutes, swung by the wind so that their light threw crazy moving shadows all around.

Reaching the summit, directing the others to form some kind of defensive perimeter because no one was there. Olech had left the position only hours earlier as part of a detail sent to get more ammunition, and a Sim bombardment had commenced while he was gone. The few boys he still knew, from an infantry company shrunk to the size of a platoon, the teens he'd trained with and fought with, had been trapped up there while the merciless explosives rained down on them.

Picking through the debris, finding the bodies, many of them unrecognizable, and finally admitting to himself that every last one of them was dead.

Olech tottered across the throne room to the dark chair on its cylindrical post. Activating the system alone, specifying that he wanted the most recent feeds even though he'd never requested them before.

The room going dark as the chair ascended, the Earth spinning into existence in front of him, the utter hubris of it punching him in the stomach over and over. He was barely able to give the command.

"Take me to Fractus."

No astral voyage this time, no feeling of riding the nose of a rocket. The room going pitch-black again, then the new planet rotating into life. Unfamiliar stars, lots of them, their pinpoints of light helping him to see the planet where his son was fighting. A bizarre world, most of it water, and the largest continent alternating between lush vegetation and an ugly gray slate.

"Take me to the battle."

The planet enlarging, as if rushing up to hit him, then he could see the ugly cloud stretching for miles. Rectangles popping up all around its southern edge, human units confronting Sim units. So familiar, in-grained after all those years, able to read the terrain and see how the commanders were using it. Tanks in the open, maximizing their speed, armor, and firepower while avoiding closed-in areas such as mountains, woods, and swamps. Armored infantry with the tanks, artillery behind them throwing shells and rockets in front of them, logistical units running supplies from massive dumps up to where the battle raged.

The fight in the south had started up again, the symbols overlapping where the humans and the Sims were contesting the same piece of ground. The display stuttered as new data came in, and one of the Force armored brigades went red. Under fifty percent. Another rectangle began flickering, a supply outfit somehow caught far away from the others and surrounded by enemy. Under forty percent.

"Shift north."

The depiction rotated downward, taking him over the enormous cloud, but not before the data refreshed and the endangered supply unit disappeared. Under thirty percent. Destroyed. Annihilated.

The globe stopped moving, showing nothing more than an ominous gray smudge that spread its cottony plumes far up into the mountains that had made the southern approach more attractive. Somewhere down there, under the dust cloud, Jan's unit was caught between armor and infantry.

Remembering that a unit that had been destroyed would no longer appear on the display, knuckles digging into the arms of the chair, the Chairman of the Emergency Senate croaked a command with a dry throat.

"Take me to the First Independent Brigade."
The resolution didn't change, but the cloud became
opaque. Now he could see the incredible sinkhole created by the Sims, the jutting end of the mountains, and
the three passes. His hand came up and clamped on
his mouth, but not before he begged, "Please show me
the Orphans."

Tripping over hunks of blasted stone and torn bushes,
Mortas rushed forward. Half-falling, he pushed himself back up with the butt of his rifle, keeping his eyes
uphill the whole time, boring through the fog. Straight
for the spot Smashy had hit, where the rock wall was
gone, sure that a Sim helmet or Sim grenade would
appear at any moment and that would be that. Choking, not from the fumes but from the blocked mem-
branes of his filter mask, knocking it aside and feeling
it fall away. Smelling smoke and cinders and the stench
of devastation.

And then he was barreling through, sent sprawling, tripped by a dead body that must have been in the
direct path of the boomer round's explosion. Hitting
the dirt hard, rolling, and seeing.

Pressed up against the remaining rock, combat
smocks and skeletal Sim rifles. Three of them standing, more of them sitting, the seated ones dazed and
wounded and bodies all around. The three who were
on their feet turning looks of surprise in his direction,

but then the tall rocks were chipping and sparking because he was firing without aiming, and so of course he was missing.

Suddenly aware that he had no idea how many rounds were left in the Scorpion's magazine. Pressing the butt into his shoulder armor, the steps he'd been taught on so many rifle ranges coming into his mind even as the goggles told him where he was pointing the rifle.

Adjusting, forcing himself to slow down, the dot slipping up high onto one Sim's torso. Squeezing the trigger, trying not to pull it off target, the enemy soldier looking right at him when he stiffened as if shocked with electricity, then began to crumple. Shifting the dot to the next one, who dived out of the way but came to a stop on the ground where the dot and the bullet found him a second later.

Sweeping the weapon back up, past the wounded who were feverishly casting about for some means of defending themselves, in time to see the last standing Sim pointing his rifle right at him. Mortas knew in that instant that the slug was on its way, and that he was as dead as the enemy soldier he'd just killed, because like that dead Sim he too was motionless on the ground.

The Sim's head jerked sideways as if he'd been slapped, and Mortas saw his shoulders sag and didn't need to see the wound where he'd been shot. Running forward from his left, where he'd come around the barrier, Ladaglia recognizable because he'd lost helmet, goggles, and mask. He skidded to a halt and fired a single long burst at the seated enemy, stone chips flying, bodies contorting, and a grenade falling from the lifeless hands of one of them.

Before Mortas could shout a warning, Ladaglia jumped forward with his arm sweeping down. Snatching up the deadly explosive, lobbing it over the wall before throwing himself down among the bodies. Mortas rolled to his side, elbows in, knees up, and heard the dull boom on the other side of the rocks.

And then the real booms, the orbital rockets raining down. Curled up on the ground, facing downhill, Mortas saw the dust storm brighten like lightning inside a storm cloud, narrow lines of light slamming into targets on the plain. Enormous explosions, missiles fired from outside the planet's atmosphere crashing on top of the tanks and personnel carriers and Daederus's voice back again, hooting and laughing and calling for more, more, more.

Desperate fire from the machines dying on the flat, trying to kill the observers who were killing them. A round from a tank's main gun detonated just up the hill, throwing rocks and dirt down on him. More blasts, and a tugging at his sleeve. Looking down, astounded by a single dart-like object that was sticking out of his arm. Puzzled, and then recognizing the shrapnel from an antipersonnel round fired by the tanks down on the plain. Casting his eyes about and seeing more of them, thin hard nails with feathery flights, blunted when they'd hit the stone and bounced off.

"Lieutenant."

Raising his helmet and seeing Ladaglia, sitting with his back against the rock as if imitating the wounded Sims. A dozen flights sticking out of his armor, blood coursing down both arms.

Mortas was up and running again, sure that another of the horrible antipersonnel rounds would burst behind him, lurching side to side as more rockets impacted on the enemy far to his front. Grabbing the stricken man by the armor and dragging him, unprotesting, down into an ancient shell hole. Propping him up as best he could, fingers through the holes in the sleeves, ripping, seeing the flesh covered in pulsing scarlet. Reaching into his side trouser pocket for the tourniquets, looking where he should have looked before, seeing the hole in Ladaglia's throat and the lethal rush of blood that ran down under his armor. Leaving the tourniquets where they were.

Eyes losing their focus, the head sagging back against the smashed dirt. The lips moving, Ladaglia seeming to smile. Mortas leaned forward, straining to hear the words over the explosions.

"I lied, El-tee. I was kinda hoping we'd win the war right here."

In a dark room on Earth, the most powerful human in the universe sat on a chair that was mockingly referred to as his throne. An entire world shone before him, marked with the different units of his army that were even then locked in a vicious fight for survival.

So many of them red, so many of them flickering, so many of them gone forever.

One unit symbol, a rectangle with the markings of infantry on a piece of high ground guarding three mountain passes, had been red when it finally appeared under the dust cloud. Large enemy forces were converging on it, infantry chopping through from the north, armor charging from east and south. No doubt such an attack was accompanied by a ferocious amount of artillery fire.

The lone infantry symbol began to flicker, and the man let out an anguished moan. He finally released the arms of the chair, leaning forward so that he was in danger of falling out and plunging down through the darkness. His hand reached out, trembling, passing through a light display meant to indicate nearby stars, fingers straining to reach the blinking rectangle.

Abruptly, the symbol representing the First Independent Brigade of the Human Defense Force vanished. One moment it was blinking, and the next it was gone. The man's hand dropped to his lap, and when he spoke his voice was choked with tears.

"Jan. Jan. Don't leave me, Jan."

Back down the slope, tottering on exhausted legs, inhaling the noisome vapor, headed back because no one farther up the hill was alive. Hearing the voices on the radio, now that the desperate fighting had abated and the rockets had stopped falling. For the moment.

"—musta been a dozen rounds landed right on the command party. Colonel Alden's dead, Ops is dead, XO is wounded—"

"Knock that off right now." Mortas knew he should recognize the voice, but with the battalion's three most senior men gone, he couldn't imagine who would be taking charge. "A Company, B Company, get your wounded to the supply line. Armadillos are on the way with Captain Dassa."

Zacker. It was the wiry battalion sergeant major he'd met on his first day. Taking charge because the rest of the battalion command element was gone. Mortas tripped over a smashed tree trunk, falling to the rock surface and simply lying there, too weak to move.

"Company commanders, give me your status. Re-form your lines, but be prepared to fall back over Lane One and establish new positions to the west of C Company."

A Company's executive officer came up, telling a horrifying story in a halting voice. Company commander wounded, first sergeant killed, three platoons that had been at half strength before the battle now reduced to a handful of men still able to fight.

As if to confirm this assessment, Mortas's eyes finally focused on the bodies scattered nearby. Sim and human, broken, bloody, dismembered, lifeless. Hearing Daederus somewhere out there, calling in long-range fire on the retreating tanks, but the voice was dull, as if his radio was dying. Pushing himself up onto all fours, Mortas coughed loudly and then called Berland.

"This is Mortas. I think the ASSL and I are all that's left of my position. What's our status?"

Mecklinger came up in response. Dry, croaking voice. "Sorry, sir. Berland's had it. Most of the guys with him got nailed in the barrage; the survivors brought him to my position. My squad's down to five guys, and I can't raise Testo or Dak."

Mortas tried to imagine the platoon layout before the assault. Dak's squad had been to his northeast, and Testo's had been to his southwest. If they were all gone, that meant his observation point would have to cover that entire area. He stumbled forward, but stopped when a familiar voice spoke to him.

"I ain't dead yet." Berland's words came across the radio, weak and slow. "Lieutenant, you should get everybody headed for the supply line. It'll take every man to move the wounded anyway. Can't hold this spot."

"You got it. That's what we'll do." Mortas didn't know how to ask the next question. "How are you?"

"On my way out, El-tee." Coughing, then a loud hawking and spitting sound. "Hey, Lieutenant?"

"Yeah."

"You get out of here, how about doing me a favor? Get what's left of the platoon a nice job guarding your dad."

"Only if you come with us."

"Now that ain't fair. Fuckin' officers, always asking the impossible."

Mortas reached the spot where he'd left Daederus, but didn't see him. He dropped to a knee and peered around the biggest rock available, not believing his eyes.

The rocket fire had blown the cloud back thousands of yards. What had been an open expanse of flat ground right next to the sinkhole was now a junkyard. Tanks and personnel carriers covered the narrow lane between the high ground and the mud field, in every variation of destruction. Turrets thrown to the side, long guns twisted backward, some hulls looking crushed straight into the ground. Smoke billowing, fire licking, more crumpled bodies.

Far in the distance he saw a mob of men walking, disorganized, reeling away from the carnage as if drunk. He stood to get a better look, exposing himself and not caring, and that was when he saw Daederus. Seated with his back against the stone, lifeless eyes on the masterpiece of malice he'd constructed, blood covering his trousers, empty dragonfly tubes all around him, and his stilled lips twisted in a smile of pure enjoyment.

An engine revved not far away, and Mortas looked around in confusion. One of the tanks, its treads damaged on one side, turning slowly in place as if nailed to the spot. Whoever was trying to drive it away finally gave up when the straining engine reached a heated pitch, but then the turret began to revolve in his direction. Mortas shook his head weakly, remembering a different tank on a different planet, his own hands

directing the main gun so that it could fire one round.
He lowered himself to the dirt, sitting next to Daederus, imagining a lone figure inside the armored mast-
odon loading the gun.

A sharp blast barked from his left, out on the flat,
and the tank burst into flame. A human machine gun
began rattling, and was then joined by a couple of Scor-
pions. Filthy figures surged around the tank, using the
other wrecks for cover, then they were coming his
way, falling back in twos.

Mortas stood with effort because it seemed to be
the right thing to do. The figures hustled past him,
hands grabbing his armor and pulling him back under
cover. Dak's voice on the radio.

"Hey, we got the lieutenant. Looks like everybody
else here is gone. We're headed to the supply line."

"**A**yliss, can I have a word?"

She looked up from the latest data display on the
latest screen, grateful for Python's interruption. It was
afternoon of the second day on Echo, and Ayliss wasn't
sure she was going to be able to feign interest much
longer. She promised the researcher she'd be right
back, and followed the large man through the buzz of
activity on the site's main floor.

They went up the stairs and emerged on the launch
platform, where the sun was shining and the birds
were singing in the nearby trees.

"Python, is there any chance we could just get out

of here now? I'm sure you and your girlfriends are enjoying the visit, but I'm not sure how much longer I can keep this up."

"Actually, that's what I wanted to talk about." He took her elbow and steered her off to the side, close to the railing where the blast doors would keep them from view. In the sunlight she noticed that he'd cut his beard close and that his hair was freshly washed.

"Cleaned up for the trip home?"

"In a way." A smile crept onto his lips, and she found it unsettling. Python reached behind him, under his untucked work shirt. His hand came back into view holding a small black box that she recognized as an emergency transmitter. A chill passed through her.

"You had that the whole time."

"Of course. I needed to be able to send progress reports. And things are progressing *so* nicely."

Ayliss became aware that her heartbeat had quickened and that her muscles were tensing. Suddenly she felt quite exposed, standing out there on the platform. Being at the site at all.

"I can't say I'm much for riddles."

"Neither am I. Or, really, I didn't used to be. Not when they drafted me and made me a lieutenant, but after the experience on that island with the Sims, I learned fast."

"You never said you were an officer."

"Oh, I still am. Captain Python, at your service."

"What kind of game are you playing?"

"The same one you're playing, only I'm much better

at it. I told you the truth about that island, about how we got stuck there with the Sims and ended up with our own little truce. Command sure didn't like that when they found us, so they killed the Sims and locked us up. You can imagine what they wanted to do to me, having been the lone officer there."

"You rat-fuck bastard."

"That's accurate. I was headed for the chopping block, so I just told the bosses that I tried my best to keep the war going, and the troops disobeyed me. So they went to the block, and I stayed in jail.

"You see, they would have killed me too— Command is like that—but I had this one story that the interrogators liked a lot. Every morning when we were done using the island's water source, I hung back and watched the Sims coming up. I was far enough away that they weren't terribly worried about catching whatever we humans carry that kills them, and one of them decided to try and communicate with me. Hell, there wasn't anything else to do on that lousy little patch of sand.

"He'd stick around after they were done, and try to talk to me from a distance. He'd bring something we both recognized, like a rock or a stick, and he'd hold it up and tell me its name in bird-speak. Cawing and trilling away, smiling the whole time, looked like an escapee from a lunatic asylum.

"But I did it right back, mostly because I was bored, and started telling him our names for the same items. He couldn't make any of the sounds I made, but after a while he could alter the chirping enough that you could understand the word he was trying to say. I never got very far with the bird talk, but it did hurt just a little when Command came in and killed that guy along with his buddies."

"Where are you going with this?"

"Oh, I'm getting to the point. You see, one of the interrogators was part of this informal group inside the Force. A bunch of guys and gals who didn't particularly enjoy the Purge. People with long memories, dead relatives, and a taste for revenge. They saw something in me, the way I saved my skin, and so they took me out of that lockup and said they wanted to set up a covert site—this site—and bring some captured Sims there. *Much* too close to the settled worlds, staffed by people who were convinced they were there at the request of your father."

He stopped, the smile broadening as the truth sunk in. Olech wasn't behind this installation at all. In fact, he didn't know anything about it. Renegades within the Force had set it up, and they'd needed some way to connect it to the Chairman of the Emergency Senate.

His daughter.

"That's right. I brought you here because we needed somebody better than the Doc to prove this was all your daddy's idea. And you were so hot to ruin him that you never considered this might be a trap. Not that hard a trap to construct, either, in an outfit like the Force. They kill people for stepping out of line, and they ship anyone who asks too many questions straight to the war zone. You'd be surprised how many different patrol routes go right by this place, how many planetary supervisors know something's up, but not one of them ever asked what was going on here.

"Which makes the next step really easy. Right now there's a Force raid party headed here, mostly made up of people sympathetic to our little project, but just enough of them completely in the dark. They're going to hit this place and arrest everyone here. And then Doc and the others are going to start yapping about how they were doing this for your dad. Of course, no one's going to waste any time talking to him or any of the others, if you're still here."

The adrenaline was coursing straight through Ayliss, her entire body seeming to throb with it. Mouth dry, feet cold, her mind racing to find the way out. Knowing that Lee was out there somewhere, looking for her, but how far away? Python's last words finally made it through the tangle of thought.

"*If* I'm still here?"

"That's right. You don't actually have to be captured. We've got an entire station's worth of people who will swear you were here, and lots of tape from the last two days of you getting briefed on how things are going. You really are a great actress, by the way. That tape is going to prove you were very interested in what was happening here and that you were going to take it all back to Daddy."

"So why wouldn't I be captured too?"

"Because your new best friend Python has this

radio. I can call the orb down here, and you and I can head up to my ship. I'm going to be leaving anyway; my work's done, and nobody wants me in front of a microphone. You know, it's going to be so funny, hearing the testimony from Doc and the girls and the rest, swearing there was this mysterious guy who they only knew as Python. Anyway, I'll run you back to Broda. You're going to need some friends once your father and his entire apparatus are in jail, and they'll give you asylum if I ask them. You see, I'm about to take a big step up in the universe. They're going to start by making me a major, and after that it's the fast track for old Python."

"I assume there's a price."

"Spoken like poor doomed Olech himself. Yes, there is. First, you agree to confess. It's a lot smoother that way, and you'll still get what you were after. Spoiled little bitch, never missed a meal, never wanted for a damned thing, and yet your whole life was one long temper tantrum because Daddy didn't pay attention to you."

"The confession is only the first thing?"

"Oh, you're going to earn your ticket out of here. Many times over." The radio disappeared behind him, and the smile widened even more. Large hands reached down and lifted the shirt, slowly unfastening the belt buckle. The fatigue pants dropped to the deck, showing him rigid and ready. "Now you know why they call me the Python."

She'd never felt so rooted to a spot in her life. The

cold concrete reality of the deck beneath her feet, the looming structure behind her, the woods and the water and the island loaded with Sims. She could practically feel the approach of the faux raid force, sent by the losers in the Purge, and yet her racing mind couldn't find a solution. Not a good one, anyway.

Courses of action swirled through her brain, evaluated and then discarded until only two were left. Neither of them desirable, but the plain fact was she'd been outsmarted. She'd forgotten that there were many people who hated her father as much as she did. She could see the report on the Bounce, the footage of Olech Mortas's daughter being dragged out of the building in handcuffs, then paraded before the reporters and her face flashed all over the galaxy.

Presented with two bad options, she automatically knew what to do. Pick the least objectionable, even if it was an act pressed on her right there on the platform. Try to salvage something, make the best of a bad situation. Ayliss forced a smile onto her lips.

"Why didn't you let me in on this sooner?" She walked toward him slowly, appraising eyes on his midsection. "I don't care who gets him, as long as I have a part in it."

"This is your part." The voice hard, dominant, cruel. The real Python at last. "Now get over here."

Ayliss stopped, still smiling. She squatted where she was, two yards away. Telling herself it would be all right, that it wasn't her fault this was happening. "No. You come over here."

"It doesn't work that way, bitch. I *own* you. You're going to do everything I say, for a very long—"

Ayliss leaned forward, just a bit, feeling her weight shifting toward the big man, the tall man with his back to the short railing. Just as her balance passed the tipping point she pushed off with every muscle in her legs, the fibers singing with frenzied energy, terrified he'd get hold of her hair as she lunged, arms out in front, and her hands were against his shirt and her legs were driving and his eyes were enormous and then his feet, tangled in his trousers, kicked her in the chin as he went over backward.

She still came on, fingers scrabbling for the tube of the railing, moving so fast and so hard that her momentum almost carried her over. Her torso hanging out in the absolute nothingness, her feet leaving the deck for a gut-clenching second, then she was suspended, looking down, seeing the flailing arms and the ridiculous shackles, then Python slammed into the grass below so hard that he didn't even bounce.

She stared down at him, vibrating with rage, unable to stop looking and not knowing why. Urgent commands bounced through her consciousness, but she kept staring until the true sensation revealed itself. A cold, competent joy radiated through her, and Ayliss Mortas smiled at the crushed body below. Her enemy. Her conquest. Her kill.

An escape ladder ran the length of the building, not far from where Python lay, and finally one of the orders screaming in her brain got her attention. The radio. She took the few steps necessary, looking all around to make sure the event had gone unnoticed, then she was over the railing, feeling the deadly pull of gravity, rushing down the rungs to the grass. The populated floors of the station were far overhead, and there were no windows anywhere nearby.

Walking slowly then, thrilled beyond belief, then becoming ecstatic when she saw Python twitch. Standing over him, taking in the blood that ran from both nostrils and his mouth, not sure but imagining his head was swelling, finally sure he was conscious and aware of her presence. Kneeling now, reaching under him, yanking the small radio off his belt.

"Lucky for me these things are designed to survive all sorts of accidents." She turned it on, then switched it to an emergency frequency taught to her as a child. Her mind was performing perfectly now, and so she didn't risk having her voice caught on tape somewhere. Standing over the dying Python, Ayliss Mortas began whistling into the radio, a love song popular just a few years earlier. She stopped after the first stanza.

"Oh, but I'm being rude. This is our song, Lee's and mine. No matter where he is, he'll have some kind of device listening for it on this frequency."

The radio began whistling back, the next stanza of the same song, and she smiled. "See? He's close."

The radio's thin screen blinked, and a message appeared saying Selkirk would be there in minutes.

"I'm sorry, but I have to go now. Apparently Lee's *very* close." She glanced around, found what she sought, and walked over to get it. When she returned, Ayliss was holding a skull-sized rock. She raised it, testing the weight, seeing the fear in the dying eyes.

"I want to thank you for this experience, Python. It really is quite exciting, isn't it?"

Later, standing on the bridge of the Force cruiser responsible for patrolling that sector, Ayliss watched the erasure of the thing to which she was undoubtedly connected by surveillance footage and audiotape. None of that would be of any value at all, if the site itself was gone and the island's unusual tenants were eliminated. The calculation was exact, cold, and logical.

Selkirk had been in touch with Hugh Leeger since hearing of the plot from Harlec, and so every clearance necessary had been put in his hands long before he'd brought Ayliss up from the planet. The cruiser's commander was a living, breathing example of the Force officers Python had mentioned, the ones who knew that asking questions got people sent to the war zone. He couldn't have been more complimentary, already accepting the story that Chairman Mortas's daughter had uncovered a nest of unspecified treason that had to be eradicated posthaste.

A single rocket was sufficient for the station, where she'd last seen Kletterman running across the launch platform, waving frantically as she and Selkirk had ridden the transit sphere back up to the station. Perhaps they'd been baffled by her sudden departure and thought Python was with her, or maybe they'd found his body and had been pondering what it meant, but the ship's sensors said no one had left the station. The tall building disappeared in a circle of light on the cruiser's main viewing screen, the shock waves flattening many of the trees when they rebounded off the hill.

And then the gunships had gone in, providing much closer footage, the bizarre traitors on the island appearing to welcome them at first. Running from their huts, arms waving, jumping up and down, some embracing, all of them looking so human that no one ever thought for a moment that they were anything else.

The miniguns tore them to pieces, even the ones who tried to swim away, and when the sensors finally indicated nothing was left alive, a thermal bomb flew in and made sure.

Standing next to Ayliss, stone-faced because of the proximity of the ship's bridge crew and its commander, Lee Selkirk couldn't ask the question that he later decided to simply forget. Watching out of the corner of his eye, sure in the knowledge that Ayliss had never witnessed real violence, he couldn't help but wonder just why the carnage seemed to have no effect on his paramour at all.

CHAPTER ELEVEN

"They gave him a sedative, so he'll be asleep for hours." Reena stood outside the door to the suite she shared with Olech. Leeger stood before her, pain and remorse evident on his face.

"I shouldn't have let him go off alone like that, not with Jan's unit in that kind of a spot. He's had the same reaction so many times in other battles that I honestly thought he was just going back to work."

"He should never have been allowed to use that room by himself. But that can wait. What is the status of the Orphans?"

"Badly chewed up, but not wiped out. They were already at half strength when they went to Fractus, so when they started taking major casualties, it looked like they'd been destroyed."

"Do we know if Jan is alive?" Reena asked, afraid of the answer.

"Not yet, but I personally wrote the flash order telling the sector commander to find out immediately. We'll know soon."

"All right." Reena pondered something for a moment. "Olech was babbling away at me when I found him. Saying it was all for nothing, that Jan was dead and all he had left was a daughter who hates him. I've told him so many times that he should have taken them into his confidence long ago."

"So did I."

"Just before he drifted off he told me to find Ayliss and bring her here. Maybe he's going to finally listen to us. Do we know where she is?"

"Yes." Leeger looked even more uncomfortable. "Actually, that was why I was so busy. Selkirk contacted me with a minor problem Ayliss encountered out near Broda, but it's been handled and they're both on their way back here."

"A minor problem?"

"I wasn't going to mention it until we got a definite status on Jan."

"It's been handled?"

"Yes. A little messy, but nothing to compare with the day we've had here."

"All right. Get an answer on Jan, then get back to me."

"Yes, Minister."

Leeger was almost out the door when Reena spoke again.

"Hugh."

"Yes, Minister?"

"Did you say the Orphans were at half strength when they went into this thing?"

Back aboard ship, Jander Mortas walked as if in a dream. The huge receiving bay rang with the calls of the different medical personnel and the moans of the wounded. They seemed to be everywhere, but this last load consisted of the nonpriority cases, the ones who weren't likely to die waiting for treatment. Bloody bandages underfoot, used tubing and injectors strewn about, and everywhere the filthy figures from the battle for the passes.

After what was left of Dak's squad found him, Mortas had taken charge and moved them to link up with the remainder of the platoon. Berland and Testo were both dead, and he'd quickly realized he didn't have enough healthy bodies to move the wounded, much less the deceased. Struggling to come up with an answer, he'd been saved by the arrival of Emile Dassa and Sergeant Major Zacker, leading an entire company of volunteers from the armored division that was now stuck on the western side of the passes. Both sides had fired new obstacles into the lanes, rendering the entire contest moot.

The tremendous barrage had blown the dust cloud away just far enough for the shuttles to get in, so they'd been evacuated after the wounded and the dead.

Counting Mortas himself, First Platoon now consisted of fifteen relatively healthy bodies.

The battalion had taken a ferocious beating, losing Colonel Alden and the operations officer as well as the commanders of both A and B Companies. Captain Noonan and his tiny command group had been found dead inside a natural trench from which they'd ambushed one of the Sim columns as it rushed southward. Enemy bodies were strewn all around the position, and Noonan's party had used all its grenades and much of its ammunition before being overwhelmed. All three of the Orphan Brigade's battalions had been designated combat ineffective because of their losses, and would not be recommitted to the fight.

Mortas stared about him mutely, not recognizing the men on the stretchers. All of them were covered with many days' worth of dirt and dust, so it was impossible to tell if they wore the gray camouflage or the tiger stripes of B Company. Though mixed in with the wounded from other specialties, the infantrymen were easily identifiable by the ruts across their noses and under their eyes where the frames for the goggles had dug in from prolonged wear.

On the shuttle ride up from the surface, Mortas had tried to get comfortable by leaning back against a bulkhead, but kept tilting from left to right until Dak had told him to lean forward. He'd obeyed, uncomprehending, while the NCO tried unsuccessfully to adjust something on the back half of his torso armor. He'd finally asked for Cranther's knife, and dug away for more than a minute. When he was finally done, Dak had presented him with a handful of antipersonnel darts that had been buried in his armor.

A face appeared in front of him, clean, earnest. The man was wearing the full-body flight suit of the ship's crew, and for some reason Mortas felt he should know who he was.

"Sir? I'm one of the triage techs."

"I'm fine." His throat was clogged with the ash from the planet, and Mortas had to clear it loudly. "Go help somebody else."

"No, I mean I'm one of the triage techs from the night before your brigade went down there." The face was doubtful, and a cold anger rose up within Mortas's chest. He slowly reached out, taking a handful of the tan fabric in a hand that was black with dirt and cross-hatched with thin red lines.

"You didn't do what we said?"

"No, no!" The earnest expression returned, and the man made no effort to free himself. "Every casualty went right to surgery. Even the ones that . . . every one of them went to surgery."

Mortas let go, his mind too fogged to go further.

"We were following the battle from up here, especially the Orphans."

"You liked the show?"

"No. That's not what I'm saying. I'm saying I know you need new men." The tech looked around him, as if fearing he'd be overheard, but then the man straightened up and looked right into Mortas's eyes. "You're the only Orphan officer I've seen, so I figured you're the man to talk to."

"So talk."

"I didn't ask for this shitty job, sir. I hate it. I fucking hate it. I hate my supervisors, I hate this ship, and I hate"—he came up with a handheld that Mortas didn't recognize—"I hate this goddamned machine, telling me who gets to the docs and who doesn't."

The tech flung the device away from the wounded, against a dark bulkhead where it made a loud crack before falling to the deck.

"I been out here a year, and I've never seen any of my bosses stand up for anybody. And when your colonel came in with you and the others, threatening us, telling us not to send anybody to the Waiting Room, Orphan or not . . . I only wish I'd had the guts to say what I'm going to say now."

"And what is that?"

"Take me with you."

"I thought you'd look a little different." Reena Corlipso greeted Ayliss in an empty hallway at Unity. Olech's daughter had been escorted to one of the lowermost floors, which meant they were far below the surface of the Earth.

"What's that supposed to mean?'

"I dunno. Me, when I make a whopper of a mistake, it shows. But you don't think you make mistakes, do you, Ayliss?"

"I was about to say the same thing to you."

"Walk with me." Reena didn't wait to see if her command was being obeyed. The walls of this particular corridor were a mottled gray, a composite material loaded with sensors that reported the slightest movement, vibration, or change in the electrical field.

"So what's that you're wearing? Is this the official 'reprimand' outfit?" Ayliss asked as she came up beside her.

Reena smiled tolerantly, glancing down at the severe black suit. "As a matter of fact it is. But you're not the recipient of today's reprimand. Not from me, anyway."

"So you're taking me to Father."

"I am. But I wanted to talk to you first."

"Not surprising. We've always been so close."

Reena stopped short. "How about thinking about somebody other than yourself for a few minutes? When the fight went against us on Fractus, Olech thought Jan's unit had been wiped out. He thought Jan had been killed."

"But he wasn't. And he's still out there in the zone, so forgive me if I don't believe Father was all that broken up about it."

"What are you saying?"

"That Father doesn't care about Jan or me. If he was so worried about Jan getting killed out there, he'd have brought *him* back here, not me. He never cared about us, or Mother." The blue eyes took on an appraising glint. "I would have expected you to have figured that out by now. Unless, of course, you're not willing to consider what that might mean about you and him."

"You really are amazing. You're so much like him—"

"Don't ever say that again."

"You're so much like him, and yet you can't see that it's all an act. An act he's kept up for seventeen years."

"Tough role, especially the part where he had to screw all those young women."

"No wonder you got fooled so easily out there. You've got his mind for strategy, but you don't use it. You don't ask any of the right questions. You let your anger propel you through life, and you were surprised when somebody used that against you."

"I'm here, aren't I? And they're all . . . found out, aren't they? Not sure I fell for anything."

"Lie to yourself all you want, but Hugh already debriefed your idiot boyfriend. You got lucky, both of you."

"So what were those questions I was supposed to ask, Reena? Those 'right' questions?"

"You could start by wondering if you're simply wrong. If your assumptions aren't as good as you think they are."

"And what assumptions were those?"

"That your mother died of natural causes."

Ayliss stepped in close, anger twisting her features,

raising lines that Reena had never seen on her face before.

"Bullshit. You weren't there."

"You were six years old, so you weren't there either. It was poison, slow-acting and painful, and not hard to identify."

"You're making this up."

"Why would I? Why would I bother even talking to you? You have no idea how many times I've told Olech to take away your credentials, put you someplace where you can't hurt him, and *forget all about you.*"

"He already did that last part."

"Here it is: your father was rising quickly in the Interplanetary Senate back then. One of the Unwavering, smart, loaded with charisma, but hard to control. So somebody murdered his wife to let him know that he was going to get in line or suffer more of the same. Get it?"

"Is that what he told you? He's a born liar. He's lied to me so many times I lost count."

"I doubt that. Keeping score is one of the few things you do well. But you don't have to believe me. When Hugh's done chewing out your boyfriend, he'll be happy to confirm this. Your father distanced himself from you and Jan to save your lives. The only way to protect you was to act like he didn't care about what happened to you . . . or what happened to your mother."

"So who's supposed to have committed this murder? I bet there's a great big nasty part of this story where a whole bunch of bad guys got chopped into little pieces.

Oh wait, I got confused. That was the Purge. And it had nothing to do with my mother."

"To this day Olech hasn't learned who murdered Lydia, and you'd be surprised by how little he had to do with the Purge."

"That's not what Python said. According to him, that whole setup on Echo was arranged by people seeking revenge for what Father did to their relatives. You know, the way a normal person would react if somebody murdered someone they loved."

"You poisonous little bitch. I'm done talking with you." Reena pointed to the end of the dark corridor. "Your father's waiting in there. Maybe he can convince you there's something bigger than your hate."

The room was dark, but Ayliss could tell it was large. The door slid shut behind her, as silently as it had opened. Her father stood twenty yards away, near the space's only light source. A single spotlight shone down from the shadows far overhead, on a piece of equipment with many reflective parts.

She walked forward slowly, not the least bit afraid. As she got closer, Ayliss saw that the piece of equipment was the size of a large desk and that it was apparently an outdated space probe. The main segment was a metallic cylinder that sprouted a couple of large antennae and an array of solar cells. Two small hatches stood open atop the cylinder, the doors made from the container's curved walls. The entire rig was perched on a display stand, but there was nothing to explain its purpose or why it was kept in so secure an area.

"You like it?" Olech wore one of his military-style suits, the red ribbon of the Unwavering standing out against the dark fabric. Her father was standing slightly in shadow, and she noted that his hand gripped the display stand as if to steady him.

"Looks like a heap of old space junk."

"It is, in a way. But it's also an important artifact. The only fitting piece to display next to this one would probably be the first wheel."

"Bit of an overstatement, if you ask me." She leaned over, peering inside the empty container. "Looks like one of those old 'alien contact' probes, the ones they used to send out to see if we were alone in the universe."

"That's exactly what it is. Sort of a cross between a time capsule and a message in a bottle. They launched thousands of the things over the decades, hoping to make contact with other life-forms. They loaded them with tapes and video and printed pictures because they didn't know how a different life-form might communicate. They even included star charts showing where Earth is—pretty stupid, given what we know now.

"They lost track of most of them, and believed that they'd been destroyed in space. So many things to run into, or that can run into you." He flashed her a smile. "But you know all about that now, don't you?"

"Is this some kind of silly metaphor?"

"Sadly, no. You see, this heap of space junk was the only one that ever came back."

"But they weren't designed to come back."

"Exactly. So just imagine the shock, all those decades ago, when this thing's locator suddenly started beeping inside our solar system. Not that far from Earth. There had been some unusual readings just prior to this probe's reappearance, and for a while nobody knew what that was. So of course they went out and got it."

Olech released the stand and walked over next to her, looking down at the machine. "Honestly, I think we would have been a lot better off if they'd just destroyed it. But there was no explanation for the thing being where it was, as if it appeared out of nowhere, and so they brought it back.

"The contents were missing, but they'd been replaced. With this."

He pressed a button on the stand, and lights all over the cavern slowly came on. The walls turned a golden hue, then came into definition as hundreds of small panels encased in glass, rows of them reaching high on three of the four walls. Ayliss walked over silently, choosing a panel at random. It showed a heavily detailed electrical circuit, in script that appeared to be painted on a piece of parchment. The one next to it consisted of humanoid stick figures that appeared to be coiling thread onto a spool the size of a man. She reached back to her education and decided the spool was some form of electromagnet and that whoever painted that picture wasn't sure if its intended audience knew exactly how to construct such a thing.

Olech spoke while she was still looking at the panel. "The unusual readings that preceded the probe's return have since been identified as the first human observation of the Step."

In spite of herself, Ayliss looked at her father in surprise.

"That's right. We didn't invent the Step. Or the Transgression, as it was first known. Personally I think we should have stayed with the original name. Some entity, or entities, used the Step to send us this set of illustrations showing us how to do it. They had to provide much of the instruction in the form of pictographs, but luckily there were a few electrical schematics on the body of the probe that they deciphered."

Olech waved an arm, encompassing the entire room. "That saved them a lot of work, but as you can see it was an intricate thing, teaching the humans of that day how to reproduce the technology.

"And of course, being human, the people interpreting these instructions decided not to tell the world about them. I suspect they were hesitant to reveal the existence of an entity far more advanced than we are, that knows where we are, and might even have visited us. It's one thing to tell humanity we're not alone; it's quite another to tell them we're completely outclassed.

"And of course there was a lot of money to be made, so it was a lot easier to keep quiet about the contact, play around with the miracle technology, and finally announce that mankind had invented the Step. Over time I imagine it was like any other big lie; tell it enough times and you'll begin to believe it yourself."

"Have they contacted us again?" Ayliss asked, her mind a blur.

"Not to our knowledge. Which doesn't make a lot of sense, does it? Give us the means to travel faster than light, then ignore us. Unless, of course, they're so advanced that we aren't capable of understanding why they do the things they do."

"This sounds a lot like a different puzzle we've been wrestling with."

"Precisely." Olech smiled with approval. "Some of the people who know about this probe suspect it was sent to us by the same entity that's making the Sims. That it's all a great big gladiatorial contest, and that we were given the Step because we were taking too long to meet up with the enemy they'd designed for us.

"Others think it might be a bit more involved, that whatever gave us the Step isn't the thing that made the Sims. That they're enemies, or merely competitors playing a game. Makes you wonder about all those ancient Greek myths, doesn't it? The ones where the gods set different nations at war, as surrogates for their own little pissing contests."

"What do *you* think?"

Olech cocked his head at her. "I don't believe I've ever heard you say those words to me before."

"You never said them to me."

"Well I will be saying them, and much more often. I can't go on like this, Ayliss. When I thought Jan was dead, it was like losing your mother all over again—"

"Really? This isn't how you behaved when Mother died. You pushed me and Jan away. And if you think I bought that ridiculous lie Reena just told me, or that I don't know you put her up to it, you better think again."

"I can't remake the past. And if I could, this is one thing I wouldn't change because it kept you and Jan safe. What Reena told you is the truth. Believe it, don't believe it, it doesn't matter to me. But I can't go on like this, knowing that you and Jan could be snatched away at any second, and I would never get the chance to tell you that I acted the way I did in order to keep you safe."

"You've lied to me my whole life. Why would I believe you now?"

"Why would I be lying? Why would I pretend to care after all this time?"

"I'm sure there's something in it for you."

"There is. Jan's just a lieutenant, turned me down when I tried to make him something with power, real authority—"

"And you want to make me the ambassador to the Holy Whisper?"

"Of course not. You have no connection to them, and I've already filled the position. But I do have a job for you, a big one, and if you still want to dig up dirt on your old man you'll get tons of it. Without falling into any more traps."

"I'm finding out everything I need to know, just from the Auxiliary's files. Why would I want a job you're so eager to push on me?"

"Because it's Veterans Auxiliary, for one. I just took several colonies of supposedly quarantined veterans and put them under the Auxiliary's control. I need someone to run that for me, someone who's sharp enough not to let the rest of the coalition turn those colonies—all of which are on resource-rich planets— into their own private mining concerns."

"Why should I help you?"

"It's simple. A moment ago you asked for my opinion about what sent us this probe. What gave us the Step. I have no idea, but I do know one thing: twelve years ago, somebody sent out a fresh wave of very special probes, containing a message meant for whoever gave us the Step. He didn't ask anybody's permission, and that got him murdered."

"Larkin? President Larkin did that?"

"Yes. You see, he understood that whatever is making the Sims is so far ahead of us that even if we win the war, we're still doomed. So he just decided on his own that whatever sent us the Step is separate from whatever is making the Sims. He sent out a new wave of probes containing messages for those entities—a lot like the images on these walls—saying that we're losing a war of survival. He announced it on the floor of the Interplanetary Senate, and when he told us that he'd already launched them the place went crazy.

"It was pandemonium, senators rushing the

podium, everybody yelling, Senate staffers trying to shove back the crowd, and finally the fists started flying. I didn't know the president well, but I liked him and was trying to reach the dais to protect him when it got out of hand.

"Different security details pushed their way into the chamber, and before you knew it they were fighting each other. Then the shooting started, bodies falling everywhere, and I was only saved because Faldonado stopped a bullet throwing himself on top of me."

The name stirred up distant memories of a beefy man even taller than her father. Stern, distant, always *Mister* Faldonado when Ayliss addressed him. She'd learned of Larkin's assassination at boarding school and hadn't seen her father until more than a year later, after the Purge had run its course. Hugh Leeger, who had been Jan's bodyguard, was the head of Olech's security detail by then. Ayliss's rejection of her father had almost kept her from asking about the change in personnel, and the only answer she'd received was that Faldonado had died.

"That's really how it happened? The assassination?"

"I've always had a hard time calling it that. There were people in that chamber who already wanted Larkin dead, and many of them were furious that he'd launched those probes without consulting them, but as I said it was chaos. Larkin was killed in the cross fire, along with many others, and when it was over the only way to explain what had happened was a complete takeover. All the lies about Larkin's plan to radiate a hundred Habs to head off the Sims, the purging of the officer corps, the creation of the Emergency Senate, all of it was set in motion by Larkin's decision to try to find humanity an ally as powerful as our enemy."

"That's insane. From what you're telling me, it's just as likely that whatever gave us the Step is making the Sims."

"That's what I thought, until Jan's little adventure on Roanum."

"You mean the rumors are true?"

"Yes. He encountered something we've never seen before, a shape-shifting entity that imitated a human being. We know almost nothing about it, so we're left with some very basic suppositions. Either it was one of the things that are making the Sims, or it wasn't. If it was, then it's a creature of amazing capabilities that is already our enemy. If it wasn't, then it's a creature of amazing capabilities allied with our opponents. We only saw the one, and we still don't know what it was trying to do. But it is conclusive proof that there are entities more powerful than we are."

He turned and looked at the probe. "Larkin's message in a bottle was sent out using the Step twelve years ago. There is something out there, and I can no longer assume that Larkin's message won't ever receive a response. That's why I need as much help as I can get from everyone around me, including you. We have to make this coalition start functioning again, so we can stop holding the Sims off and start actually defeating them."

Olech stared at her with an expression of fierce determination. "Because if something does answer Larkin's call, it's going to make its own decision about this conflict. If we want any chance at gaining an ally here, we better not be losing this war when it shows up."

The two of them stood in silence for several moments, Olech half-expecting a rejection similar to the one he'd received from Jander over the ambassadorship. For her part, Ayliss was mentally reviewing what Harlec and Python had said about linguists seeking to communicate with the Sims. The revelation about the alien Jan had encountered slipped into place like the missing piece of a puzzle she hadn't been trying to solve. Her face suddenly lost its pensive expression.

"The thing Jan encountered. It was working with the Sims?"

"Yes. Jan and the others had been captured by the Sims in transit, and the shape-shifter was slipped in with them in the guise of a human. It was all a setup."

"So that alien was able to communicate with humans *and* Sims?"

Olech's eyes widened, then sought the floor. When he looked up again, it was with a look of astonishment. He spoke slowly.

"No one noticed that. Not me, the Force in the war zone, or the SCOTS. No one until now."

"The alien was destroyed?"

"Yes. And so far we haven't encountered another one."

"Well if there is another one in existence, it could serve as something we've never had." Father and daughter exchanged cold smiles. "An interpreter."

CHAPTER TWELVE

Mortas was sitting at his desk in the platoon's empty command post when Sergeant Major Zacker poked his head in.

"Hey there, Lieutenant. Doesn't seem to be much of First Platoon around."

Mortas glanced at the clock on the wall, the one behind Berland's empty chair. He looked around uncertainly, realizing he'd been sitting there motionless for an entire hour.

"Yeah, yeah, Sergeant Dak and Sergeant Mecklinger are trying to round everybody up. I mean, one or two days of cutting loose is one thing, but a few of the guys disappeared when we got back."

"You'd think the military police would have scooped 'em up by now, but around here they know better than to mess with the Orphans. Boys are just out having a little fun, deserve it after what they went through. I'm a little surprised you didn't go out yourself."

"I'd just finished in-processing when we were alerted for that jungle mission. I honestly don't know where the fun is around here."

"Well you might want to find out, and reel the boys back in. Colonel Watt is going to address the brigade tonight, one battalion at a time, so we need the troops out on the athletic field at sundown."

"All right, Sergeant Major." He looked down at the empty desktop, his mind refusing to come up with a place to start.

Zacker watched him from the door. "Major Hatton's back."

He remembered the bearlike battalion executive officer from his first day. "I heard he got nailed in the same barrage that hit the field command post."

"He did, in a way. He says he was standing right next to Colonel Alden when it happened. The concussion put him in a coma for two days." Zacker smiled, as if contemplating the antics of a wayward child. "Looks like nothing can kill that guy."

"**M**erkit. Come on in and have a seat." Reena spoke from behind her desk without rising. She still wore the black dress from her discussion with Ayliss.

"That's 'General' Merkit, Minister." The heavyset man's face was already set in a scowl as he crossed the office's gold carpet. Although they were deep inside Unity's main tower, a lifelike display on one wall let in bright sunlight from fake windows. The opposite wall was decorated with a large wooden carving of the Corlipso family crest and numerous photographs of their home planet of Celestia.

"Oh, that's right," she replied evenly, lifting a stiff sheet of paper from the desktop. "Yes, it does say you're a general here."

She put the document down and picked up another one. The seal of the Emergency Senate had shone through both papers. "But here's another one that says you're a private. You can understand my confusion."

"I don't find that funny, Minister."

"You know what wasn't funny? When I found out the Orphan Brigade was at half strength when it was committed to Fractus."

"I have nothing to do with tactical decisions in the war zone."

"That could be truer than you think. You see, both of these sheets of paper have orders written on them, over the chairman's signature block. One says you're the general in charge of Force Personnel, and that you're headed to MC-1932 in order to help the Orphan Brigade's commander rebuild the unit."

"That's not my job, Minister."

"And the other paper says you're a private, headed to MC-1932 as the newest replacement in the rebuilding of the Orphan Brigade. So you might be right after all."

Merkit's face lost some of its usual color. "Why?"

"You already know why. In the past months the Orphans' commander, this Colonel Watt, sent you several communiqués informing you of the brigade's status and asking why he wasn't receiving the replacements he needed."

"I don't handle assignments at that level, Minister. By regulation, the Orphans are supposed to receive the files of any volunteer who is physically fit enough to serve in that unit, and anyone they select from those files is supposed to be reassigned immediately."

"So you are familiar with how it's supposed to work. But according to Colonel Watt's messages, going back several months, he hadn't been receiving those files. So what happened? Volunteers dried up?"

Merkit slid forward in his chair. "Minister, you might not know this, but there is a good deal of hostility toward the regulations governing this unit. Many senior commanders object to losing some of their best men to the Orphans, to the extent that some of those officers have sometimes misreported the qualifications of the volunteers."

"That's a shame, but it's good that you were aware of it. This Colonel Watt seemed to be aware of it as well. In fact, his adjutant and his sergeant major took a little survey of nearby units and found no shortage of qualified men who claimed to have submitted their request for transfer but were told they'd been turned down." Reena gave Merkit a bland smile. "Were you aware of that?"

"Of course not, Minister. And I promise that I'll get to the bottom of this—"

"I know you will. And that your deputy will ably execute the duties of your office in your absence while you work diligently with Colonel Watt on MC-1932 to bring his unit back up to full strength with soldiers he approves."

"I really don't think it's necessary for me to actually go out there, Minister."

Reena dropped the smile, and the paper. "I'm not concerned with what you think. You don't seem to understand that Chairman Mortas is going to sign one of these documents. You're going out there, and it's up to you to decide how you do it—as a general or a private. Of course, the general will be coming back here once everything's fixed, while the private will be staying."

Merkit's lips disappeared for a moment, then returned. "I'll be happy to go and supervise the rebuilding of the Independent Brigade, Minister."

"Your offer of service is deeply appreciated, General. And when you return, I imagine you'll be much easier to work with."

"Yes, Minister."

"Have a safe trip, General. I'll be monitoring the situation, so please let me know if you need any help." She reached for the next piece of paper in the stack, and her visitor rose to leave. "Oh, and General?"

"Yes, Minister?"

"You might want to tell those senior commanders out there, the ones who weren't following the regulations, to use the Orphans properly from now on. Because if that unit gets chopped up under questionable circumstances ever again, I'll reconstitute it myself, starting with the most senior people in the war zone."

"**H**ave a look."

Hugh Leeger punched a button on his desk, and a display screen on the office wall came alive. Seated in front of the desk, Lee Selkirk turned to see what it was.

He quickly recognized the landing pad outside a penthouse apartment in Buenos Aires, the home of Ayliss's college classmate Marco. During his extensive debriefing, Selkirk had postulated a suspicion that Marco had been involved in the plot that had so nearly ensnared Ayliss and even the chairman.

The sky over the penthouse was a vivid blue, marred by billowing gray smoke that plumed out from an ugly tear in the transparent wall facing the landing pad. Fire was eating everything inside the penthouse, and so he stopped watching.

"I guess that glass wasn't rocket-proof after all."

"Oh, but it was. That was a bomb, planted by a certain redheaded woman in our employ. Poor Marco was stupid enough to let his lady friends come and go without being scanned. The cover story says the bomb was planted by someone who doesn't like fat cats."

"He was certainly that, and annoying as hell. I never liked him."

"Of course not. He wanted to do to Ayliss what

you've been doing to Ayliss. Most normal people would recognize that emotion as jealousy, but not you."

"So you're firing me."

"I have good reason. You completely compromised yourself, and because you couldn't keep a professional distance from your charge, you let her wander off with what turned out to be a hostile party."

"I don't need the lecture, Hugh. I know what I did wrong, and what I did right, and that we came out ahead in the end." Selkirk tossed a finger at the screen behind him. "How much of that ring have you rolled up?"

"Quite a bit. We finally identified that Python character—what a piece of work *he* was—and that put us on a bunch of different trails. Mostly disaffected elements, people who lost someone in the Purge, nothing we haven't seen before."

"So I suppose there are a few more bombs exploding on different planets?"

"Bombs, rockets, even a few up-close-and-personals where we decided a clear message was in order."

"Harlec?"

"No, not Harlec. You're to be commended for the way you handled him. If you'd killed him it would have come back on the Chairman, and the Brodans are already trouble enough. That was well done."

"All right. So are you firing me or not?"

"Oh, you're already fired. That's straight from the Chairman. You're no longer part of Ayliss's security detail, and because of your poor judgment I can't reassign you. Just so we're clear, if the Chairman hadn't ordered your removal, I would have done it myself."

"So why are we talking?"

"I've known Ayliss all her life, and I've never been able to predict what she was going to do or understand very much of what she does. I don't know if she was using you, or if you were just part of her sick obsession with hurting her father. We'll find out soon enough, now that you're an outsider. But my money says she really does have feelings for you and that she'll keep you with her. At least for a while."

"Since you're no longer my boss, I couldn't care less what you think is going to happen between me and Ayliss."

"Oh, but you should. You see, there's an excellent chance that she's about to head out to a new job in the war zone. It's quite dangerous, and I'm not talking about the Sims. The Chairman stuck his thumb in several powerful eyes a few days ago, and this new job is part of that."

"He really doesn't care what happens to her, does he?"

"If that were true, we wouldn't be having this discussion. He's hoping Ayliss will take you with her. You'll have no authority over her security detail, which will be completely restaffed, but he's more than happy to have you with her."

Leeger smiled. "You see, the Chairman is quite a pragmatist. Most fathers wouldn't realize that it's not a bad thing to have a trained fighter sleeping next to their daughters. You can't be one of her bodyguards anymore, but as the boyfriend of a woman who's probably headed to a dangerous place, you've got a lot to recommend you."

The sun wasn't quite down when Mortas noticed the activity outside his office window. B Company's first sergeant was directing a work party of some kind, and they were erecting tall poles at intervals along the edge of the parade field. He walked over to the window to see what they were doing, and slowly became aware of the sounds inside the barracks. The building had been practically empty for the last two days, but now it echoed with young male voices.

The work party finished setting up the poles on the barracks side of the field, then broke up into teams that moved out onto the grass. Separated by many yards, they began setting up even more of the unidentified rods, this time in large circles. Intrigued, Mortas looked around the office for his hat.

The filthy rags he and the others had been wearing when they were evacuated from Fractus had been destroyed aboard ship, and every man had been scrubbed within an inch of his life before undergoing chemical decontamination. They'd been issued the one-piece flight suits worn by Fleet personnel over the loud objections of the surviving Orphans, and he'd made a point of getting out of the suit as soon as he'd returned to the battalion area. He now wore the woodland camouflage that had been issued to him on his first day.

Going out into the hallway, Mortas was surprised to see shadows all along the corridor from inside the soldiers' rooms. Dak and Mecklinger had been successful in rounding up the remaining members of First Platoon, it seemed.

Heading down the stairs, Mortas encountered one of the new men leaning heavily on the side rail. The soldier gingerly took a step down, then used his free hand to move what was an obviously wounded leg. Mortas remembered him as a baby-faced blond who looked a little pudgy, but when he got alongside him the face that suddenly snapped in his direction was worn and thin. The eyes were startled and angry, but they softened immediately.

"Sorry, Lieutenant. You surprised me."

"I know the feeling. Here." Taking the man's arm, he looped it over his shoulder. They slowly worked their way down the steps.

"The other guys said we're gonna do some kind of memorial. That true, sir?"

"I hadn't heard that, but the sergeant major told me Colonel Watt's going to speak to us."

"You hear the rumor, sir?"

"Which one would that be? The one where the war is over?"

"I like that one. No, I heard that we're so understrength that they're gonna bust up the outfit."

They'd reached the bottom of the stairs, and Mortas

managed to keep the shock off his face. He released the man's arm and opened the outside door, holding it ajar with his boot while helping him to limp forward.

"No. I hadn't heard that one. You suppose that's what Colonel Watt's gonna tell us?"

"God I hope not." They went down the three outside steps and onto the grass. The sky was darkening, and soldiers in woodland camouflage were gathering on the field in twos and threes. "I'll tell you the truth, sir. When they told me I was going to the Orphans they said this brigade was made up of kill-crazy suicide machines. I thought I was a goner for sure."

Two First Platoon soldiers appeared out of the shadows, taking the new man's arms over their shoulders after greeting Mortas. The new man stopped them when they started leading him toward a spot where the rest of the platoon was gathering.

"But ya know, right in the middle of that whole thing, all the explosions and the shooting and Sam showing up out of nowhere, I suddenly realized that everybody around me knew what he was doing. And I was scared to death, but I joined in, and I kept doing what the others were doing, then all of a sudden it was over."

"You did fine, Ithaca." One of the veterans holding him up muttered. "We all did."

"Ithaca? That's your name?"

"Yes, sir."

"I'm sorry I didn't know that, Ithaca. I promise I'll remember."

"Aw fuck that, sir." Ithaca grinned, and the baby face was back for a moment. "If you got any say in this, how about you keep us with you? They break us up, try to keep the platoon together."

"I'll see what I can do. Maybe they're gonna leave us alone."

A light burst into life behind him, and Mortas turned to see what it was. One after the other, the poles bordering the field caught fire. Torches. He looked out into the darkness and saw figures among the circles of the tall rods, lighting tapers, then setting the circles alight. He finally understood what had been going on. The brigade commander would address the remnants of the battalion, then they would separate into smaller units and move into the different circles to eulogize the fallen. It was a warm night, but he shivered at the prospect of memorializing so many dead.

Aided by the fire, he spotted Dak and a clutch of First Platoon troops. More and more soldiers from the battalion were arriving on the field, and there seemed little organization to any of it. He passed several men from other companies as he walked, mostly faces he recognized, and was touched to be greeted with warmth. With inclusion.

Getting closer, it was impossible not to choke up. The platoon had never counted more than thirty members, but now they were under twenty, many of them clearly just returned from the hospital. All around him were leg braces and slings, and he noted that Ithaca was now sitting on the grass with two other First Platoon men who were too injured to stand for long. He decided that was why they weren't falling in for the standard battalion formation as he walked up. Quiet voices greeted him, hands squeezing his shoulder or brushing his sleeves, and he returned the gestures.

"Hey, sir."

"Good to see you, Lieutenant."

"They bustin' us up, El-tee?"

Mortas managed a smile. "I'm just a new lieutenant. What makes you think they tell me shit?"

They shared a subdued laugh, then First Sergeant Ettleman's voice came from the direction of the battalion headquarters, gentle, respectful.

"B Company, on your feet."

The same commands sounded from the other companies, and Mortas looked up to see a group of men coming down the walkway from the hilltop command building. They were helping a tall, stocky man whose left leg was in a brace, and he found a smile—a real one—blossoming on his face.

"Hey, it's Major Hatton!"

"I thought he was dead."

"I heard he lost both his legs."

"Ya think they'll give him the battalion?"

"Why not? They're gonna break us up anyway."

"Fuck you. We ain't goin' nowhere. Who'd do all the dirty work if they got rid of the Orphans?"

The chatter ended with a chorus of startled commands, from the troops closest to the approaching group.

"Battalion, atten-shun!"

"It's Colonel Watt! It's the brigade commander!"

Mortas had already come to attention, automatically, an ingrained response, but he now saw that one of the men helping Major Hatton was Colonel Watt himself. Emile Dassa was one of the others, as was the intelligence officer, Captain Pappas. They carefully lowered Hatton to the grass, slightly uphill and facing the semicircle of troops, before Colonel Watt spoke.

"At ease, men. Please have a seat. Everybody sit down." The throng in the shadows made a long, sighing sound as the wounded were helped back to the grass and the others, mostly sporting aching muscles and minor injuries, joined them with effort.

Watt's broad shoulders were outlined by the lights from the battalion headquarters behind him, and he raised his hands with the fingers spread, as if holding something in front of him that no one else could see.

"It's hard to know how to feel, isn't it? I can't tell you how sorry I am about the way things went. But I also can't tell you how proud I am of the way things went. I'm heartbroken to see how many Orphans we're missing, and yet I'm grateful to every one of them.

"So if you're having a hard time—as I am—figuring out how you feel, that's all right. I won't pretend to tell you how to handle this, but I will suggest that if our dead comrades were given the chance to switch places with any of us here, they would turn that chance down. Just as I know that every man here would gladly, *instantly*, take the place of our lost Orphans if he could."

Watt's hands came together, and his arms trembled slightly.

"Tonight you will be memorializing your fallen brothers. You'll speak of their strength, their humanity, their humor, and their flaws. I'll leave that in your capable hands."

The stocky man stopped for a moment, and for that instant Mortas heard only the hissing of the nearby torches. Even before the brigade commander began to speak again, Mortas knew what was coming. Tears welled up in his eyes, making him glad of the darkness.

"I won't talk much longer. I just wanted to say that I've been in ten different units during this war, and that I've never seen one that came even close to the Orphan Brigade. This unit was a special unit, a different unit, made up mostly of people who volunteered to be a part of it. We did things the right way, the smart way, and when that word got around it attracted soldiers who wanted to fight alongside the very best."

Watt's face broke into an involuntary grin, and he didn't try to hide it.

"I'll never forget this one time . . ."

Hours later, Mortas emerged from the silent barracks onto the bare parade field. The torches had been extinguished and removed, but the scent of smoke still lingered. The night air was cool, made more so by his attire. Shorts and running shoes, a T-shirt and his scarred torso armor. The bandage on his left arm was now visible from the wound where the Sim infiltrator had cut him, and he scratched it idly as he walked out onto the grass. Spreading his legs, he bent over and began to stretch.

The platoon had gathered inside one of the torch rings after Colonel Watt was finished eulogizing the brigade, and they'd taken turns memorializing the fallen. Dak had taken the lead, but he'd asked Mortas to say something about Berland. Mortas had been surprised by the number of things he'd been able to mention, wisdom Berland had passed to him in the short time he'd been his platoon sergeant.

An ASSL who'd known Daederus had joined them and spoken about his friend, and Mortas had been able to contribute a few words about the grounded flyer's last actions. Ladaglia had so many friends in the platoon that he'd seen no reason to recount the man's passing, but no one had seemed to have known Jute very well. Mortas had told them about the man's prescient assessment of the fix they'd been in, and his dedication to stand with the Orphans no matter what it ultimately cost him.

All around them, warmed by different torch circles, the battalion's survivors had praised, mocked, and bid farewell to the men who had marched and slept and eaten and laughed and died next to them. Mortas had been surprised by the amount of laughter, but as each group had finished and then walked off, they'd done so in silence. Many had gone to their bunks, but many more had gone back out to continue the unauthorized celebration of the fact that they were still alive. Dassa had appeared out of the gloom as Mortas had walked toward B Company's barracks.

"Hey, Jan."

"Sir."

"It's Emile. Don't make me beat that into you."

"Somehow I knew we were gonna have to finish that fight, one of these days."

They'd shared a laugh, and Dassa had stopped walking. Mortas had done the same, and the younger man had waited until they were alone. Shadows moved around on the field, dousing the lights, but they were out of earshot and might as well have been ghosts.

"You did really well out there, Jan. For a first-timer, under circumstances like those, you did just fine."

"Thanks, Emile. That means a lot, coming from you."

"I don't know how they're gonna work this, but if we both got shipped to the same unit, I wouldn't complain."

A breeze had washed across Mortas's face just then, and he'd felt some of the weight lifting off and floating away with the wind.

"I'd like that too."

They'd shaken hands, and Dassa had disappeared. Standing there, watching the wraiths taking down the smoking torches, he'd remembered Berland's request that he get the platoon reassigned to a safe, cushy job somewhere. The words of the memorial had come back to him, the stories and the names and the sad truth that he hadn't known so many of those men. He hadn't even known Ithaca's name until the new man told it to him.

"I didn't know them. They were my platoon, and I didn't know them." The words had come out unbidden, whispered, then gone. Carried away like the smoke and the eulogies and the Orphan Brigade itself. The truth remained, however, and he didn't like it. So he decided to do something about it.

While changing into his athletic clothing, Mortas had studied the platoon roster on the office wall. It hadn't been updated since the battle, and the names of the deceased had bitten into him. He'd only read the entire list once, and spent the rest of the time memorizing the names of the living.

He finished stretching and began to jog slowly in place, the words whispered under his breath.

"Sergeant Dak, platoon sergeant."

He shuffled forward, his sore legs fighting the weight of the armor as he crossed the dark expanse.

"Sergeant Mecklinger, squad leader."

The grass ended, and he was out on the road, jogging now, feeling the machine coming alive. Telling him that he was alive. That the uncertain future was a thing for the next day, the next hour, maybe even the next minute, but at that moment, right there, he was alive and in control.

The names came out evenly now, and Mortas repeated them as he ran down the dark road and disappeared.

ACKNOWLEDGMENTS

No book comes into existence by itself. I want to thank my editor at HarperVoyager, Kelly O'Connor, for her invaluable advice in the writing of *Orphan Brigade*. Additionally, I'd like to acknowledge HarperVoyager publicists Pamela Spengler-Jaffee and Lauren Jackson, for all their hard work in promoting this series. Special thanks goes out to publicity expert Beverly Bambury, for her marketing expertise and her tireless efforts.

I would also like to thank my West Point classmates who have provided feedback on the series so far, especially Michael McGurk, Meg Roosma, Chris Franchek, Keith Landry, and Ginni Guiton. Many of them took the time to read different drafts of *Orphan Brigade* as it was being written, providing helpful insights along the way.

ABOUT THE AUTHOR

HENRY V. O'NEIL is the pen name used by award-winning mystery novelist Vincent H. O'Neil for his science-fiction work. A graduate of West Point, he served in the U.S. Army Infantry with the Tenth Mountain Division at Fort Drum, New York, and the 1st Battalion (Airborne) of the 508th Infantry in Panama. He has also worked as a risk manager, a marketing copywriter, and an apprentice librarian.

In 2005 he won the St. Martin's Press Malice Domestic Award with his debut mystery novel *Murder in Exile*. That was followed by three more books in the Exile series: *Reduced Circumstances*, *Exile Trust*, and *Contest of Wills*. He has also written a theater-themed mystery novel entitled *Death Troupe* and a horror novel featuring his first female protagonist, a tale of the supernatural called *Interlands*.

www.vincenthoneil.com

Discover great authors, exclusive offers, and more at hc.com.

ABOUT THE AUTHOR